Rainbows

URI RASKIN

Rainbows

A Story of Love and Intifada

A Novel

URI RASKIN

GREEN TEA BOOKS
ATLANTA

LIBRARY OF CONGRESS CATALOGUE–IN–PUBLICATION–DATA

Raskin, Uri
Rainbows
A Story of Love and Intifada

ISBN 978-0-9797585-1-5

Cover Design by JSR All Productions
Cover Photo Creative Commons
Printed in the United States

To The Peoples

Of All Faiths

Who Have Prayed For Peace

In The Middle East

And Are Still Waiting

An Answer!

OUR MIND IS CAPABLE
OF PASSING BEYOND THE DIVIDING LINE
WE HAVE DRAWN FOR IT.
BEYOND THE PAIRS OF OPPOSITES
OF WHICH THE WORLD CONSISTS,
OTHER NEW INSIGHTS BEGIN.

HERMANN HESSE (1877-1962)

Chronology

United Press International (UPI) Archives

Dec. 7, 1987: Four Palestinians die in car wreck involving Israeli truck driver in the Gaza Strip. Local residents believe the incident was deliberate.

Dec. 8, 1987: Widespread rioting erupts after funerals for the men.

Dec. 9, 1987: Hatem Al Sisi, 17, becomes first 'martyr' of uprising when Israeli soldiers open fire on rioters in Jabalia refugee camp.

Dec. 12, 1987: Arab merchants stage commercial strike.

Dec. 19, 1987: Youths smash bank windows, set up burning barricades on the main commercial street in Arab East Jerusalem.

Dec. 22, 1987: Prime Minister Yitzhak Shamir's spokesman predicts violence will soon end.

Jan. 19, 1988: Defense Minister Yitzhak Rabin announces policy of 'force, might and beatings' to crush protests. Hospitals filled with protesters with broken bones.

February, 1988: Military closes all West Bank schools for four months, affecting more than 300,000 students, charging schools are centers for violence.

March 14, 1988: Gaza Strip police resign en masse in response to call by uprising's underground leadership.

March 20, 1988: Soldier killed in Bethlehem, the first Israeli killed in the uprising. At least 98 Palestinians killed so far in uprising.

April 6, 1988: Hike of young Israeli settlers with armed guards sparks clash near West Bank village of Beita. Two Palestinians, one Jewish teenager killed by guard's shots.

May 5, 1988: Israeli kills Palestinian shepherd, seven months later the first Jewish settler convicted for slaying an Arab during uprising. More than 12 Palestinians are believed killed by Israeli settlers in past year.

ONE

Day was slowly beginning to break above the hills. Down in the valley as we drove through still lingered a strangely refreshing coolness. Last night was unseasonably hot on my moshav, the West Bank collective farming settlement where I live. May weather in Israel is as unpredictable as the political situation.

"Things got hot while you were in Gaza?" Chaim's voice thundered as it broke the silence in the valley. Hot, I recently learned, was a relative concept used by the army not only exclusively for weather.

"You can't imagine, Chaim," I said. "Those Palestinians tried every trick they knew."

My recent reserve duty was the worst of my life. They were thirty days I was glad to get over and to be home again. Instead of my normal stationing, I was ordered to spend April in Gaza. Funny, December 7th is a very famous day. The Japanese attacked Pearl Harbor in 1941 on that day. President Franklin Roosevelt in his declaration of war declared it would be "a date which will live in infamy." The Japanese attack stunned virtually everyone in the United States military.

A week earlier before December 7, 1987, an Israeli salesman was killed in Gaza by local terrorists. Several days later a semi trailer truck accidentally swerved across a line of oncoming traffic. Doing so, he entered a service station at the Erez border checkpoint and collided with two vans taking workers back to Gaza from Israel.

Four Palestinians were killed and seven injured some critically. The next day our military were also stunned by the explosive uprising that followed the funerals. As long as I live, I hope never to go back to Gaza. Khan Yunis, Rafiah, Jabaliya and Deir El-Balah, places that seem now so distant yet, were so very real only yesterday.

"I guess you had a lot of Intifada down there," Chaim joked.

"Intifada you call it?" defensively I said. "Hell was what we called it day in and day out. Hell was Gaza, Chaim, you just wouldn't believe."

"Ari, don't drive so fast," Chaim shouted. "They have been up to some tricks around here too while you were away."

"What do you mean by tricks?"

"Almost every day during the past two weeks, I've found rocks and nails scattered on the road between the moshav and Beit El-Safa . . ." Chaim kept filling me in on what I had missed while I tried to gazed at the beauty of the rising sun now topping the hills. ". . . not to mention the rock throwing and tire burning."

"Tire burning! You don't even know what that is, Chaim. In Gaza, since the Intifada began, thousands of tires have been burned. Gaza always had a perpetual black cloud hovering over."

Chaim, somewhat amazed by the scope of what I was saying, looked at me with a disbelief I too shared only a month ago when my reserve duty began. Remembering my first impression of that black cloud, ironically it reminded me of a Charles Dickens's novel, thick black smoke everywhere. Dickens's smoke, however, was the beginning of the Industrial Revolution. Could Gaza's black smoke also be the beginnings of a revolution? I wondered.

"Ari! Stop!"

Not quite fast enough were my thoughts as I got out of the truck looking at the rear tire melting into the pavement. "Radio it to the army, Chaim, and I'll get the jack."

"Before you do, see if there are any more ninja's on the road."

Ninja's were evidence that the Intifada had become more sophisticated. When it began, Palestinians scattered nails freely on the road, some causing a puncture, some not. Ninja's, on the other hand, were large nails bent in a vice at right angles perpendicular to each other. Lying on the road they struck each tire like a snake.

Flat tires were our way of life in Gaza. Once, after our second puncture of the day, we stopped the first Palestinian we saw and made him change it, our way of fighting back. It didn't make us feel good to do it, but we did it anyway. Gaza had a way of clouding how we viewed right and wrong.

"Look at this, Ari!" Now the sun was well above the hills and the coolness of the valley had all but disappeared. Chaim approached with two hands outstretched. "Can you believe it, Ari? Twenty-one ninja's!" Really twenty-two I thought looking at the tire settling in the back of the truck.

Only yesterday I was in the middle of the Gaza strip dreaming of getting home, away from that hell. A month ago I left for Gaza. Was a month really long enough for the Intifada to reach the Ayalon Valley? Forty-eight hours ago in Gaza I had my sixteenth flat tire and now number seventeen was only four kilometers from my home. As a warm breeze entered the truck window blowing my hair, we passed the sign directing people to our moshav.

"What was that you said, Ari?"

"Mevo Ayalon—six kilometers, Chaim, just reading the sign." *Six kilometers.* Yesterday it seemed six thousand kilometers away.

"Chaim, remember when we first moved to the moshav?"

"I try to forget those times. Why all of a sudden are you getting nostalgic, Ari?"

"Gaza gave me a chance to think . . ."

"Think, Ari? That could be dangerous for you!"

"Very funny," I replied not the least bit amused. "Seriously, remember those days?"

"Yeah, I remember no electricity for two weeks, working day and night putting up a security fence because our wives were scared to sleep, water available only four hours a day, having just a two-way radio for contact with the outside world and you forgetting to recharge the batteries, no roads, the heat and . . ."

". . . and that very first night when people from the religious kibbutz nearby brought a Torah scroll. Remember we danced and sang by the light of bonfires all night?"

"Are you trying to make a point?" reluctantly Chaim asked.

"Looking back those were really the best years of our lives. All we cared about was establishing our moshav at the approaches to the Ayalon Valley. Vickie and I had just gotten married; you and Aviva were expecting your first boy. We were we forever young and idealistic."

As we reminisced about those times, I almost lost sight of where we were.

"Stop the truck, Chaim!"

"Ari, there are no ninja's here, I promise," Chaim laughed. Here was the border police station on the hill overlooking the Ayalon Valley.

"Chaim, come with me."

"Ari, we're late enough after the puncture!"

"Just a minute," I begged.

Getting out of the truck, I was struck with the awe of what I saw. From my vantage point was the heart land of Israel—the Ayalon Valley. Day was just beginning all around. Behind us the silence was broken by sounds of the border police doing their morning exercises. From the road were the screeching sounds of a truck loaded with Portland cement winding down the hill to the valley. Our truck's radio chattered as each settlement began its life anew for another day. But amidst it all, the chirping of a lone bird on the power line above seemed to drown out the morning noises.

"Come on, Chaim," I whispered.

"Ari, can't it wait till later?" Chaim begged as he lowered the radio. "We have workers remember? It is six o'clock—let's go!"

Chaim's words faded as I sat on the ground looking toward the hills at the end of the valley. A gentle wind rose with the last vestiges of the morning's coolness. I remembered my Dad always saying, "if only the land could talk." How many times did I hear that expression? Now I finally understood what he meant. In an unbelievable way, I could almost hear voices rising up from the valley on the wings of the cool breeze. Voices that seemed to . . .

"Get up and let's go to the vineyard," Chaim's voice exploded behind me. My whole body shook as my ears opened wide while the deafening morning noises rushed in.

"You look like you've seen a ghost, Ari!" Chaim said as he sat next to me on the rocks.

"Maybe you're right, Chaim, maybe I was hearing a ghost."

"I don't know what you were doing last month, but you've been acting a little strange this morning even for you. First nostalgia, now ghosts, next I suppose you'll want to travel in time!"

"Precisely!" I replied. "What do you see when you look at the valley below?"

"Cotton and rocks and wheat and rocks and grapes and rocks and trees and rocks and rocks and rocks," Chaim rhythmically answered.

"Honestly, Chaim, I've never understood why we became friends."

"Because our fathers were best friends, Ari, and our mothers are sisters," Chaim said smiling wide as the Cheshire Cat.

Our parents—Ayalon Valley—Holocaust—Independence, looking at the valley below, those words lingered in front of me like road signs.

Turning back in time, my first stop was 1200 B.C.E. A fierce battle raged below as a lone soldier, Joshua, cried up to the heavens for help to save his people, my people, do battle against the Amorites. Rocks flowed red as that solitary leader begged and begged for only a few more hours of light; a miracle to save them. An avenging angel not enough, they needed more time, more daylight to do battle. Could the sun stand still? Did he and his people merit such a miracle, such a change of nature?

"Chirp . . . chirp . . . chirp . . ." It was that echo which brought me back to the present. A sound capable of muffling the morning noise could also pierce the millennium. As I looked around for my feathered friend, I found . . .

"Where are your feathers, Chaim?"

"Feathers? Honestly, Ari, I'd swear it was heat stroke, but it's only 6:15 in the morning," Chaim said, accepting the fact that we weren't going to leave anytime soon. "I suppose it really doesn't matter if we are with the workers or not. They only do what they want to anyway," Chaim added in concession. "What feathers?"

"Over there, on the power line above, the bird chirping away, see his feathers, bright yellow breast, grey tail and a black hooded head," I pointed out.

"Looks like a miniature knight in armor up there," Chaim said as he finally boarded my time machine. "Yea, that reminds me, yes, look over there behind the Abbey of Latrun, Ari. Remember the first time we climbed up to the old castle?"

Buckling my seat belt once again, I could see the old Crusader fortress of *Toron des Chevaliers* towering above the Abbey. Built in the twelfth century by men committed to finally freeing the holy land from the occupying infidels, its ruins stood as testimony to their failure.

"Second or third year, Chaim?"

"Second year, Ari, the second spring after we moved to the moshav; a hot day like today," Chaim continued. "Aviva was pregnant again and my little one was walking everywhere except the path."

All I could do was laugh thinking about Aviva waddling in her last stages of pregnancy up the steep hill to the castle. Chaim commented she certainly resembled Hannibal crossing the Alps with his elephants.

Yes, it was our second year on the moshav. We had just finished planting the first one hundred dunams of our vineyard. Emerald Riesling, a light white wine, was to be our first income. Chaim had the bright idea to bring our wives to the vineyard for a picnic since they had never been there before. Besides, as Vickie always said, we spent more time there than home. Nonetheless, she admitted she couldn't see herself getting jealous of a grape. As we sat under the massive oak near our newly constructed shed, she remarked that nothing romantic could ever happen in the wasteland she saw before her.

Sitting down among the crusader ruins, all Aviva and Vickie did was talk about how wonderful it was after two years the regional council had finally constructed a water tank on the hill, where once stood a Jordanian army camp, overlooking the moshav. Aviva laughed thinking of all the times the women had gone with black, plastic pails to draw water from the mobile tank which was brought to the moshav.

Vickie said she always felt like someone out of the Book of Ruth each time she drew her water. That comment had new meaning for our wives since Chaim had shown them one of the many ancient water cisterns which were carved out of the rocks in our vineyard. We thought it pretty funny that Apollo 11 Lunar Module put man walking on the moon and we were just getting running water. Men in space and we discovered water. Oddly it was Chaim that day who introduced the valley's history to my wife.

"Vickie," Chaim said, "do you know how important this piece of land in front of you is?"

"You mean besides all the fighting and killing that went on, I can't think of a thing!"

"Ari never told how our fathers have roots in this valley?" Puzzled, Chaim asked.

"Oh, come on, Vickie," Aviva said. "Ari never mentioned anything about it to you?"

I sought refuge from being the target of their conversation on a high point of the castle where I could see for kilometers the valley in one direction and the way toward Jerusalem in the other.

"He gets quiet sometimes with me when I ask him about things before we met," Vickie revealed.

"Not with us," Aviva said. "You can't shut Ari up when he starts talking about Chaim's and his father's . . ."

". . . and I bet all of this would be boring to you anyway," Chaim said in my defense.

"No, I'd like to hear, Chaim. What's the connection between the valley and your fathers?"

"Okay, Vickie, but I can't tell it like Ari. It all happened before the country gained its independence. Our fathers . . ."

Sitting a few meters away from the rest, I was content to listen to Chaim tell the tale that not only encompassed the birth of our nation, but the rebirth of our people as well. I gazed as he pointed to the old British police station in the distance. Watching Vickie fixed on the police station, I was amazed how she almost appeared in a trance listening to each word Chaim allowed. I must admit, in all the time I was married to Vickie, I never saw her so interested in the events that unfolded into our nation.

While Chaim was telling of our father's first coming to the valley, I couldn't restrain myself from giving a little background to his tale. Slowly I walked down to where they were on the rocks and sat next to Vickie. Apparently she didn't even notice I was there as she sat on edge listening to each word. Hearing in Chaim's tone how intent he was on telling the story, I decided that discretion was the better part of valor. So, I too sat quietly on the rocks.

TWO

Later back on the moshav, I decided to fill in some details for Vickie that Chaim had left out. I took Vickie to the Warsaw ghetto in 1942. Our fathers, like many others, tried to survive the deportations. Thousands had already been rounded up and at risk of death were sent to a fate that would have been worse than the quick bullet in the street.

For several days my Dad had shared a basement with another man about his age he didn't know. Both rarely spoke to each other during the day, lying motionless trying to preserve whatever energy they could. Yet, by night they stalked the ghetto looking for food, scraps of material to keep warm and water potable enough to drink. Together they travelled like twin brothers at play. Around each street corner, however, they knew there could be a Nazi patrol, or worse, the SS rounding people up for deportations.

One day the pair watched as children from an orphanage were stampeded down the street like cattle and literally thrown into waiting trucks. His friend broke the silence that day with tears in his eyes. Mad by the sight, he swore to my Dad that if he survived the ghetto he would never stop having children to help make up for the horror of so many young souls lost. Finally weakening under the strain, he fell to the ground.

Lying on the pavement, he heard noises below. Quickly he composed himself summoning my Dad to come listen. Near a sewer they heard the conversations of men below when suddenly, the sewer cover began to rise above the street line.

"Get over here," shouted a voice from down under.

They scurried toward the opening. No sooner had they arrived at the hole in the street than a hand extended to help them down. Once below, in an instant, shots were fired above.

19

Caught in the momentum of the people below, they started
running with the others down the long, dark corridor of the sewer.
A smell emanated from the swell at their feet that made them gag
and nearly vomit. Flowing down the sewer was something
unbearable to all of their senses. The excrement was a dying people.
Yet, the desire to stay alive a few more moments made anything in
life smell like roses.

Underground, sealed away from the horrors above, the two sat
motionless in the dark among their new comrades. Having survived
for days together, they felt a sense of security given by the fact the
people had arms. One had a German machine gun, two Luger 9mm
pistols, and the rest carried an assortment of knives, scythes, axes,
etc, trophies of their war for survival. Last of all was Yitzchak, their
leader. In his possession were a pistol and a Polish oval grenade. My
father and his friend for the first time were secure enough to get to
know one another.

Alongside my father always was his friend, Chaim's father. He
came from a background similar to mine. Both were from upper
middle class families owning factories. Chaim's grandfather made
dresses while mine manufactured coats. In prewar Poland, they
both had everything, neither, however, had a strong identity with
their heritage. Jews by birth both felt more comfortable with the
Polish workers and customers than with their own people.

In that sewer, all they could focus on was the torment and horror
above being perpetrated on people merely because they were Jews;
Poles, nonetheless, but still only Jews. For the first time they both
realized how lost they were from a heritage that all their lives
seemed so foreign. Chaim's father, being the more practical of the
two, shifted the conversation to the immediate situation.

"Well, what do you suppose we do now?"

"Guess we stay with these people. They have weapons, don't
they?"

Because of the circumstances during the previous few hours, they
had become members of the Irgun. One of the many underground

defense groups of the Warsaw Ghetto, their main philosophy, apart from survival, was of a nationalistic nature. Each member of that motley band talked always of Palestine. Dreams of the future were spoken with such preciseness, such detail; they took on a quality of the present. Dreams that our fathers never dreamt before now fit them perfectly.

"It makes sense," Chaim's father said. "Why not go to Palestine. There is no life for us here and besides our families are lost forever. A war like this can't last much longer. When it's over, does it matter who wins? We've seen what life under the Nazis is like. If they lose, will it be any better under the Poles?"

"Palestine it is then!" agreed my Dad. "All we need to do is figure out one minor detail. How do we get from this sewer to Palestine?"

"Don't worry, that will be easy," laughed Yitzchak the leader from the dark. "We have a plan. All we need to do is steal a German truck . . ."

"Yes, that's going to be really simple," Chaim's father said, challenging the reality of the plan.

Before they finished the debate, someone shouted to look ahead at what appeared to be a light. Quickly Yitzchak yelled for everyone to run in the opposite direction. Run they did as a smell overcame them. My Dad wondered if the stench was finally getting to everyone. Then he realized the light was a poison gas canister the Germans had dropped in the sewer.

For what seemed to be an eternity, they continued to run; each step echoed groans and moans, they were running through a living cemetery. My Dad pondered, as he ran, that a graveyard wasn't really grave. People didn't die they just rested there, but in their sewer was no rest only dying.

Ahead someone yelled they saw another light. Against their faces they felt the freshness of clean air. Like circus acrobats, each one jumped through the opening to the street above. Quickly they scurried to a courtyard across the road and into a small storage building. No one moved or said a word until dark. Even if they wanted to, there was just no energy left in their bodies.

Suddenly, Yitzchak jumped to his feet. Looking out of the window, he saw a German truck driving into the courtyard carrying a Waffen-SS reconnaissance group consisting of one officer and nine soldiers on night patrol. After a brief discussion, the officer and seven of the men left the courtyard on foot. Realizing that only the driver and a guard remained, Yitzchak turned to our fathers and smiled. They watched intently as the two started a small fire and made coffee.

Everyone heard the wheels turning in Yitzchak's head. Chaim's father mentioned he and mine knew some German. Actually they all spoke more Yiddish, a first cousin language and even the two Germans were about their sizes. As evening quickly grew into night, their plan was finalized. Soon one of the Germans became drowsy. Only the sound of what once was a door to the stately house across the courtyard could be heard crackling in the fire. The plan, as it was, only went as far as the road. What they would do after they left the courtyard was left to divine intervention.

In the annals of the great World War many battles were recorded for posterity. Only seconds in duration, their skirmish was minor compared to the ones with which we are familiar. Yet, to the band of desperate survivors, it was a battle for liberation. Proud and brave they were. Our fathers quickly changed into the captured uniforms. Boarding the truck, they heard the gasping of the two soldiers as they lay dying; uneasy with the unnecessary death of the two, but not upset having become soldiers in a war of survival.

Chaim's father drove while mine rode in the back pointing his newly acquired gun at the others. Without notice, Yitzchak shouted to stop in the middle of the road. In a split second, a manhole cover slid from its place. Several men, escaping from their graves below, ran to the truck. Once aboard, Yitzchak motioned to travel again. First around the edge of the ghetto by the cemetery, then directly to the main entrance, they sped.

Steadily Chaim's father drove. Every now and then my father shouted loudly at the others. Yelling at the top of his lungs, his words appeared to be authentic German. Luckily, none of the soldiers on the streets understood him. Sometimes Yitzchak and the others almost burst into laughter as he hurled the collective sayings of our people at them.

Deep inside the ghetto no one expected Jews to capture Germans. Pockets of resistance, but nothing like they had done and it worked to their benefit. Riding down the streets no one gave them a second look. Why should they? A German truck with a group of Jews at gunpoint in the back was common.

At the main entrance to the ghetto, no one even stopped them to check their papers. A right turn and they were out of the ghetto and on to the streets of Warsaw. Yitzchak had said all they had to do was steal a truck. He was right.

Outside the city they were immediately attacked by a band of resistance fighters. One person in the back of the truck was killed before they could make known that they were comrades in arms, united to fight a common enemy.

And fight they did, eventually breaking away from their Polish comrades and forming their own resistance band. Eight months after leaving the ghetto, they had accumulated a total force of twenty-one.

Initially their main purpose was to survive, that in itself a constant battle. However, the desire to reach Palestine and the daily horrors they witnessed forced them to go on the offensive.

They now took extreme pride in their Jewishness. When opportunities arose to make joint raids with Poles, they were instantly turned down. Too many times hadn't they seen the Poles were divided against the Germans, but united against the Jews? Sometimes, in joint operations after successfully defeating the Germans, the Polish resistance turned on them only because they were Jews. Once they even confiscated all of their weapons. Well, almost all, Yitzchak kept his oval grenade in his pants snug between his legs.

Amidst the feelings of helplessness the Jewish people had during the war were a few defiant ones. Most were lead to the slaughter like innocent lambs. Groups, like the one our fathers formed, fought back. Jews defending themselves was not only their philosophy, but of our people for two thousand years as well.

Sons of Bar Kochba and grandsons of Judah Maccabee, they learned during those years one basic fact of life they indoctrinated into Chaim and me as we grew up. When the time comes, the only friends our people can count on are the Jewish people themselves. Two thousand years of persecution and mistrust had taught that lesson. Individuals were to be trusted, but rely on the fact anyone could and would turn against you.

That message was clearly brought home to them; late one evening at their encampment, a group of Polish partisans suddenly walked in. My Dad had recognized one of their members, a foreman in the coat factory. Running through his mind at the time was a false sense of security. Without warning, that man drew his pistol and shot someone sitting by the fire whose only crime was trying to keep warm. Reflexively, my Dad shot dead the man he had known. Why the killing? Months earlier our their group would have all been killed, but that night only two died. Tomorrow hopefully none would have to die.

Each day was a constant battle for survival. Religious Jews say a special blessing each morning giving thanks for having their souls restored. They learned a different blessing, giving thanks each night for having lived another day. One more day was all the life span they could hope for.

Yet, the dream of Palestine was ever present in their minds and daily Yitzchak rekindled it. Everyone believed in him, especially our fathers. He had gotten them out of the ghetto and kept them alive. Six months before the end of the war, my Dad became the leader of the group replacing Yitzchak. Elections weren't held, rather tragedy befell them.

One night they were surprised by a German patrol after coming from a village with food and supplies. A fierce battle raged. As they retreated to safety, Yitzchak stayed behind to cover them. From the hill above, they watched as Yitzchak was surrounded by the Germans.

Without warning, there was a flash followed by an explosion. On the ground lay five dead Germans and Yitzchak. He had always guarded his grenade saying one day it would save him. That night it did by cheating his captors from the night of tortured death that assuredly awaited him.

Yitzchak had saved their lives for the last time. No medals were given nor memorials erected. Yet, our fathers never forgot they lived because of him, his hand the one which extended that day from the sewer below. It was that dreamer who bought his plan of simplicity to reality.

Customarily Jewish children are named after deceased relatives. My name is Ari Yitzchak and Chaim's is Chaim Yitzchak. They never even knew his last name or anything about him, but he was always spoken of in our families with love and respect.

THREE

One day the killing stopped. Peace was what they called it. But for the millions whose lives were shattered, there would never be peace. People who died, ironically, weren't the only casualties. Everyone lost a mother, father, sister, brother, grandmother, grandfather, aunt, uncle, cousin, friend or someone they had known. All that remained were destroyed lives and dreams of a new life in Palestine. That's what kept them going.

Reaching for that star each night for years was all they had. Yitzchak wasn't around to guide them anymore, but they didn't need him either. By themselves they would reach the Promised Land. Both knew it wasn't going to be easy. Under the British Mandate very few Jews were allowed to enter Palestine.

History has recorded many ironies. None, however, was as classic as Jews trying to return to their homeland. Thousands upon thousands of survivors wanted to settle in Palestine dreaming the same dream. Under the British Mandate, they were not allowed to freely return home. Even an international commission in agreement with the United States President Harry Truman recommended the absorption of one hundred thousand souls. The British flatly refused. Ships loaded with refugees from hell were turned back at sea, many dying in those coffin ships.

People who were spared death at sea only ended up in displaced persons camps. After having survived the infernos of Nazi extermination, they were cast into camps again. An entire world civilization made our people displaced persons, but no one cared enough to give them a place to call home.

After dreaming of Palestine, they saw for the first time from the bow of an illegal ship its coastline just as dawn was breaking. What they didn't see, however, was a British patrol boat approaching. Four days later they were added to the ranks of displaced persons.

Men who had suffered more than humanly possible for so long broke finally under the strain. Crying like newborn babies as the guards closed the barbed wire gates to the camp behind them, freedom and its feelings were stripped away and their dreams shattered. Both sat wondering if life itself was worth living any longer.

Inside the Displaced Persons Camp was an underground network. Being former resistance fighters in Poland, they were quickly recruited into its web. Chaim's father surmised getting out of the camp wasn't going to be as easy as the ghetto. He was wrong; constant streams of men were being smuggled out of the camp, Palestine needing soldiers to fight the British and afterward the Palestinians. Since both were veterans as it were, they were prime candidates to be moved out early.

Not many things can readily be counted upon in life. Greed, however, was one of those that could. Within the D.P. camps were a host of British guards who knew that Jews always had wealth. Diamonds, jewelry, gold and silver flowed like water if only tapped, they thought. Duty and honor aside, the guards luckily were greedy. Our people had capitalized upon that fact for two thousand years. What would work in the past would work yet again.

Food shipments were daily brought into the camps, sacks of potatoes, vegetables and salt neatly piled high in supply trucks. The underground effectively utilized that route. Not as spectacular as their escape from the ghetto, the plan of action was to disguise themselves as fifty kilos of potatoes.

Once outside the camp, they were met by members of the underground. Hastily changing into peasant garb, they blended for several days with the local population. Then, at the darkest point in the night, they waded from the shore to a waiting fishing boat. With each full breath of sea air, their lungs were filled with the gusts of freedom once again.

Soon they would see what was snatched from them only weeks earlier . . . Palestine. Within hours they would be going home to a land they had never seen. Yet, each day in their mind's eye they had viewed its splendor and charm. On the wings of Yitzchak's visions they saw the milk and honey flow.

Tears of joy rolled down their cheeks for the first time in years seemingly washing away the pain and suffering they had endured. Our sages of old have written that water has a quality of purification. As each tear fell from their eyes, they regained their innocence; battling to survive shifted to an aspiration of life.

As they jumped into the waters just short of the beach, they felt renewed. A person converted to Judaism immerses himself to gain a new soul. In the waters that day they were born again from the ashes of what they had left behind.

Somewhere on the white beach north of Haifa Bay they finally felt the soil of Palestine under their feet. That instant they both were ready to enjoy the fulfillment of their dreams, but it was not meant to be. Within minutes of landing on the beach, they ran to a waiting car on the cliff above in a flash disappearing from view. And so it remained for the next few days. On their carousel they reached for the brass ring only to have the horse move again and again.

One day life became normal. Refugees running from nothing going nowhere had a home. A small cottage near Petach Tikva was to be theirs for the next two months. However, realizing that they both couldn't run and hide forever, they opted for a chance finally to settle down. One night there was talk of a kibbutz in the north looking for people. The thought of being farmers pleased them; after so much killing and dying it was to be their pot of gold at the end of the rainbow. By the next night they were in the back of a truck headed north. Before dawn they arrived at their new home. Home . . . its sound seemed to ring in their ears.

Rainbows

Kibbutz Shaar HaGalil was only one year old when they arrived. Founded mainly by refugees from a destroyed Europe, it was everything they had hoped for. My father often talked of their first night on the kibbutz. It was raining and very cold when they arrived. All night he lay awake listening to the drops of rain falling on the tin roof over his head. To him it was like a symphony. He thought of all those nights in Poland he was unable to sleep for fear of death. His only friends those nights were the stars.

When dawn broke, he heard a bird chirping away outside. Over his face began to appear a smile. He realized that it had been years since he heard the morning sounds of a bird awaking all of nature. That morning he listened well to the last drops of rain strike their notes on the roof in close harmony with the chirping of the little bird. They had truly come home.

Over the next weeks, both labored as they never had before from sunrise to sunset in the fields clearing rocks and boulders revealing the rich soil beneath. By spring their backbreaking efforts yielded their first crops; they meticulously watched the ground as the little sprouts grew bigger and bigger. One evening they talked about religion. Spellbound, my Dad listened to Chaim's trying to decide if the creator had abandoned his people during the past few years. Or worse, what kind of being could let all of the carnage they witnessed occur?

My Dad, never being a religious man, responded with an answer he had heard once from his mother during a similar conversation. She said it was all because the Jewish people had forgotten they were Jews. Whenever they forgot, the world reminded them, they vowed never to forget.

Chaim's father answered differently, it was all a miracle even though miracles had stopped two thousand years ago. Yet, Chaim's father was adamant. Soon there would be a Jewish State in Palestine. They had heard David Ben Gurion recently talk of it; that indeed would be a miracle and to that end the carnage seemed to make sense. A Jewish state in Palestine may not have been the reason for the suffering, but it most assuredly would be the result.

Soon the peace they had grown accustomed to as farmers gave way to collective responsibility. One evening amidst the talk of partition plans and the possibility of war with their Palestinian neighbors, a meeting was called on the kibbutz. Two people from Haifa, a man and a woman, came to enlist volunteers into the Palmach. Organized in 1941 as a mobile force, it was the first Jewish army in two thousand years. Initially the Palmach consisted of men and women from kibbutzim who took military training while they worked part time in agriculture.

It was to that end the couple were sent to Kibbutz Shaar HaGalil seeking recruits. Long range plans of the Palmach called for an additional reserve of one thousand to bolster its three thousand permanent members. That night they needed as many volunteers as possible. Since they were once in the Irgun, they were skeptical of joining ranks with the Palmach. Yet, as my father listened to every word the woman recruiter allowed, he became totally enthralled with her.

After the meeting was over, my father shyly said to her he would volunteer only if she agreed to let him come to Haifa one evening so they could have dinner. With a blush on her cheeks, she agreed. My father turned to Chaim's, without words passing between them, he nodded he too would join, but added with a smile to find out if she had a friend.

Indeed she did. One month to the day they were married to the woman recruiter from Haifa and her sister. A wedding ceremony at Kibbutz Shaar HaGalil was held. Any event was cause for celebration, but a double ceremony was certainly the event of the year.

Dancing into married life the war that had been so much a part of their lives for over a decade seemingly had finally ended. Peace from war, however, was not meant to be. When the United Nations revealed its plan for the partition of Palestine, the Arab League declared it would carry out whatever measures were required to prevent the plan from being implemented. Quickly they found themselves actively among the ranks of the Palmach in the Galilee.

While all of Israel braced itself for independence and war on May 14, 1948, my parents had other worries. As David Ben Gurion declared the birth of a new nation in Tel Aviv, my father was on the way to pick up the area's midwife. Just as the Sabbath was beginning, my mother started serious labor. A few hours later, during the quiet hours of the Shabbat morning, I was born. Three months earlier, Chaim had been born with the help of the same midwife.

Eight days after my birth they left to fight for their dreams and independence. By June Jerusalem was being strangled by the inability of supplies to reach her. At the center of the problem was the Arab Legion controlling Latrun where they fought bitterly in numerous attempts to seize it from the Legion.

Confusion reigned during those few weeks. Cut off several times from their brigade, they fought with other elements of the Palmach. The scope of their involvement in the War of Independence centered on Latrun. During the middle of July 1948, they fought their last battle of the war. Trying to repel the Arab Legion, the situation had grown desperate, one of the commanders ordering a retreat. At dawn the Arab Legion attacked from all directions. Machine-gun fire, mortars, and armored cars provided a devastating Arab onslaught.

In the first hours of the battle both were wounded; mine in the shoulder and Chaim's in the leg. Under the blistering sun, Chaim's father struggled to pull my father and himself from the battlefield each meter taking precious time and effort. Luckily they were spotted by an officer from the religious platoon and brought to safety.

Settling on the valley of the Ayalon was the dust of a fierce battle. Soon a ceasefire was declared. However, that day at Latrun, forty-four men gave their lives with all the valor and honor befitting a soldier. Tragically the Arab Legion respected neither virtue and prevented the Jewish soldiers from recovering their dead from the battlefield. A centuries old custom was scoffed at by the Arab Legion. For over one and a half years, forty-four bodies lay as they fell on the battlefield. Finally, the remains were removed to the military cemetery at Mount Herzl in Jerusalem.

Fully recovered from their wounds, they attended the internment ceremony. Reflecting on all that had befallen them; they remained silent for what seemed an eternity. A gentle breeze began to cover their faces; above them the flag of the new State of Israel flapped in the wind. As they both gazed at the blue and white flag, they thought of Yitzchak. So much had he wanted to reach Palestine; his dream they shared.

As the honor guard lay to rest the remains of the forty-four, our fathers whispered to each other. Surely there was room for another. Symbolically they interned Yitzchak's spirit and soul on Mount Herzl that day. Yitzchak too had come home.

Four

"Well, Ari, at the beginning of the week I was worried if you would start acting normal again, but getting the tractor stuck up to the axle in the mud this morning in area sixteen convinced me you had returned."

"Very funny, Chaim, maybe you forgot while I was on reserve duty, when you give water and fertilizer to an area, someone is suppose to check the drip irrigation lines for leaks," I said still stiff from the cast like dried mud on my pants.

"I'm just curious, Ari, how does it feel to be back working with our cousins after being in Gaza?"

"Our cousins, indeed!"

Chaim had asked a question I honestly hadn't much time to even consider. Like the Palestinians, our people traced their roots to Abraham. By virtue of our coming from Isaac and the Palestinians from Ishmael, his half brother, we were first cousins.

And so we called our workers when we spoke about them. But since I had been back, I really hadn't given it much thought. Our workers, Selah, Ahmed, Amad, Kalil, Jamal, etc were definitely Palestinians. In Gaza I learned all Palestinians wanted the fulfillment of the Koran's prophecy calling for a jihad against the infidels. We were those infidels.

Never had our workers acted towards us in any way as *those* in Gaza. Selah had been with us for years, practically running the vineyard. We treated him like we would anyone else. Chaim always said he was more like a blood brother to us. Yet, after Chaim's question, I began thinking about our relationship with Selah and our other cousins. Before I went to Gaza I never gave it a thought that our workers were Palestinians. Could they ever become like the ones in Gaza?

While in Gaza I always was the enemy. Around any corner we expected to be pelted by rocks, glass, spikes, etc. from the local population. Always in the foreground were children and women. Out of reach and directing the actions, were the cowardly men. Even if we were just walking down a street in the open air market, the mood could instantly turn against us. We were Israeli and they were Palestinians which in itself was enough.

"Chaim, how long has Selah worked for us?"

"Oh, I guess about five seasons give or take a few months, Ari, why do you ask?"

"What do we really know about him?"

"He works as hard as we do and much of the success we've had with our grapes has been due to him. What else do we need to know?" Chaim answered sounding like a defense attorney.

"Is he married? Are his mother and father alive? Does he have brothers and sisters?" I questioned. "And does he hate us because we are Israeli?"

"Don't be ridiculous, Ari," Chaim, losing patience, yelled back to me, but come to think of it, in five years I never bothered to ask if him about his family. Some cousins we are!"

"You are right, Chaim, but what do you think his feelings toward us are because we are Israeli?"

"Intifada or no Intifada, Ari, he could never be like those Palestinians. Last night he and I stayed up till three in the morning spraying. When the tractor broke down, he spent an hour under it trying to get it going. I don't think you would find many members of our moshav who would work so hard."

"I guess you're right, Chaim, but I've become a little paranoid ever since I was in Gaza. Your question just shook me up a little."

Within minutes I had left Chaim and started walking down the rows of trees in area twelve wanting to see how the workers were doing tying the branches. Tying was necessary to expose the grapes for spraying. If the branches were left to grow naturally, they would cover the clusters of grapes inhibiting the spray from reaching the fruit.

Grapes were extremely sensitive to powdery mildew and a host of other insects and parasites. We sprayed on a routine basis trying to arrest those problems. In all my years growing grapes, I can't remember a season without something affecting the grapes. So, many late nights had to be spent doing spraying.

Most of the chemicals we used had a limited effectiveness in extreme heat. Once the Israeli sun went down, however, the winds begin to blow and cool everything off. Cool nights were ideal for the grape's development, not to mention enhancing the effectiveness of the sprays.

As I inspected the job our workers had done, I began seeing small puddles of water evenly spaced among the rows. Leaks were not an uncommon sight, but those seemed to be too much of a fixed pattern to be coincidental. Rabbits were attracted in the evenings to the drip irrigation lines for a source of water, their rodent like front teeth easily slicing the lines. Unlikely, I thought, a group of rabbits would bite the lines at five meter intervals. I picked up a line and ran my fingers over the black, plastic pipe feeling unmistakably it was cut by a knife.

Sitting on the ground under the shade of the grape vines, a bolt of fear struck my senses. Was it now beginning in our vineyard too? No accident, that menacing vandalism was the kind of action the leaders of the Intifada called for. Inflicting major damages were readily remedied by an insurance claim. A prank like the cut lines costs extra time and materials to repair. I thought of how many such actions happened daily around the country, untold thousands of shekels worth of time and materials being wasted.

My first thoughts were does Selah know about it? Of course he did. They were *his* workers from *his* village after all. The more I thought about it, the more I was convinced he had orchestrated the action. All of a sudden I heard screaming.

"Give me that knife!" shouted Selah.

Approaching, I saw he was holding the left hand of the kid with reddish, curly hair and blue eyes he brought back last weekend. Most of our workers were young boys. Since schools had been perpetually closed because of the Intifada, we benefited with a constant supply of cheap labor.

"I said drop it!"

Within seconds the knife dropped landing on the ground near Selah's foot. The boy was forced to the ground with Selah's knee securely on the back of his neck as I approached.

"Owe you money?" I asked Selah trying to give him an opportunity to confess what really happened.

"No, Ari, he said something about my sister I didn't like," Selah quickly answered.

As Chaim would say, now we knew he had a sister. It sounded good. Our cousins were always fighting among themselves over things less sensitive and much more trivial. Should I mention the cut lines? I decided not. During the drive home, I told Chaim the events the day.

"Sounds to me like Selah was telling the truth; he probably doesn't even know the lines were cut. Boy, he must have some sister to almost kill a kid over her and I'll bet she's even good looking."

"C'mon, Chaim, have you ever seen a pretty Palestinian girl? Most look like the dried leather of our commando boots."

"On the other hand," Chaim smiled, "how do we know his story wasn't a cover up. He could have seen you first, Ari. Quickly sizing up the situation, he decided to throw the kid to the lions. When you didn't come right out and accuse anyone, which is your nature, he made up the story about his sister. That should fill your paranoia!"

"Thanks, Chaim, just what I needed."

"And he probably doesn't have a sister either."

FIVE

As we pulled into the parking lot by the office after our day in the vineyard, Moshe, the moshav's business manager, came running toward our truck. "There's going to be a meeting of all the agricultural branches tonight in the community room at eight p.m. and you *both* have to be there!"

"Why are we having a meeting?" Chaim asked.

"Today one of our cousins set fire to the wheat fields near Beit El-Safa," Moshe said.

Chaim and I just looked at each other as Moshe walked back to the office continuing to let people know about the meeting. On our faces were a thousand questions. Were the incidents in the vineyard and in the wheat fields coincidental or a coordinated effort of the Intifada?

"I guess this means Selah doesn't have a sister," Chaim added with his typical understatement.

Although called for eight p.m., most of the people didn't come until around nine. Chaim filled in the others on circumstances in the vineyard. Luckily, the damage to the wheat was minor. Only the grass surrounding the fields caught fire. At that time of the year, the wheat plants were green and dirt doesn't easily burn.

Forever everyone gave their opinions on how we should react. Calm and level headedness prevailed. There was no doubt that the perpetrators of the fire by the wheat fields were from Beit El-Safa. We decided that no retaliation would be carried out and the events of the day were merely coincidental. Our workers in the vineyard came from the village of Deir El-Salam near Hebron too many kilometers away from Beit El-Safa.

Protection for us at work was of major concern; unanimously it was decided that we had to carry weapons for self defense. Reports from other parts of the country gave us reason to be concerned. Several members of other collective settlements had been attacked in recent weeks. One person in the Jordan Valley was even stabbed by one of his long time workers while he was inspecting his fields. The reasoning behind all of those incidents as coined by the news media was nationalistic motives.

Since the Intifada had begun, world attention was focused on the plight of the Palestinians who lived on land Israel captured during the Six Day War. "National aspirations of a country of their own" as the media called it. However, in my opinion, national aspirations had become an umbrella phrase for any terrorist act aimed at harming innocent Israeli men, women and children.

Usually I never had trouble falling asleep, working ten to twelve hours in the vineyard insuring I would be tired. That night, however, I was restless and the mere thought of what troubles could lay ahead in the vineyard kept me awake. I never slept in Gaza either. All I could do was lay in bed and think, musing myself by counting grapes. Sheep were too smelly, I thought. The humor of it broke the tension and soon I fell asleep.

"Good morning, sweetheart," softly entered my ears. I was at the point of waking between dreamland and reality.

"Make your breakfast before you go to work, sweetheart?"

I opened my eyes wide and saw it was Chaim kneeling by my bed.

"Very funny . . . very funny," I said as I picked up my jeans from the floor and put them on.

"Well, its 5:30 a.m.," Chaim laughed, "okay with me if you want to only work half a day."

We were about to leave my house when Chaim reminded me weapons. Most of the people on the moshav had private handguns. In addition, we were issued arms by the army for use during guard duty at night and to defend the moshav if need be. Chaim said we needed to check out guns at the armory before we left.

"If you think I'm going to walk all day in this heat with an Uzi or an M-16 you must be crazy," I said.

Instead I got my hand gun, a 9mm semi-automatic revolver. When I made major in the army reserves a few years ago, I bought it as a present for myself. Yet, the thought of having to carry it daily gave me concern. After surviving three full scale wars, I always grew apprehensive every time I held a gun.

"You're right," Chaim said, "I'll get my forty-five."

Speeding toward the vineyard, we passed the remnants of burned tires on the road through Beit El-Safa; the sight was becoming common place, black donut impressions left in the road from burning tires too numerous to count. Gaza was all I could think about.

"Well, what do you think our cousin's reaction will be when we turn up with our guns?" I asked.

"Probably betrayal," Chaim said as if we were the ones who had violated a sacred trust. I chose not to pursue the conversation.

Once we reached the vineyard, all thoughts of guns and burning tires disappeared. We were behind with spraying and tying the branches would take another few days to complete. Plus the electricity to the pump house had been off for several hours. Without electricity we weren't able to give water or fertilizer. I just hoped by the weekend we would be caught up.

Pulling up to the shed, Amad came running over to the truck before we could get out. He told us Selah had gone back to Deir El-Salam to bring more workers to finish the branch tying. I was pleased with that news because I didn't want to confront him after yesterday's incident.

"Do you think he left because of yesterday?" Chaim asked.

"Now look who's getting suspicious."

Selah going back to his village during the week was a very common occurrence. Every couple of weeks he would return for a day or two. As long as he left someone in charge we didn't care. Amad was basically capable enough. His only problem was that he liked to joy ride nights with our tractors, usually to Abu Ali's encampment.

Abu Ali was an old Palestinian who had lived in the area of our vineyard for at least five decades. Somewhat of a sheep baron, no one knew how many herds he had or for that matter how many wives either.

Getting out of the truck to get more string for the workers to use in tying up tree branches, Amad spied my gun. Chaim saw his puzzled reaction first. Just as Amad's mouth began to open, Chaim jumped out.

"Yesterday Ari saw a big snake in area four while he was relieving himself," Chaim quickly said, "and you know how afraid he is of snakes."

Chaim's answer seemed to have worked. Snakes of all description roamed the vineyard and our cousins were equally scared of them.

All day it was blistering hot. Changing from season to season, the weather easily wavered from one extreme to another. As the hot winds blew in from the Arabian Desert over Jordan, they arrived in Israel ready to bake everything in sight. We worked under that sweltering heat normally drinking four to six liters of water a day.

On the other hand, the hot weather was ideal for grapes. Hot days and cool nights were the perfect climate for the grapes to peak with the proper level of sugar to enhance its sweetness. If the summer was not hot enough, it could delay harvesting until the early fall. Extending our harvest would be bad for our profits since it meant operating longer. While we sweated and baked in the sun, we prayed it would get hotter. Medicine that's good for you I guess always has a bitter taste.

Counting heads, one boy was missing, the curly topped kid who fought with Selah. He'd gone back to their village with Selah. I sighed with relief to know he was gone. Chaim was right that Selah probably didn't know anything about the cuts in the lines. Maybe he had a sister after all.

I grabbed a black bucket filled with pipe connectors and walked to area twelve to repair the cuts in the drip lines. Approaching, I grew pale. All of the leaks were repaired leaving no trace. I began to wonder all over again.

Around noon Chaim and I met on the hill by area seven to have lunch under the carob trees. Or rather, I should say, Chaim ate while I just laid on my back resting my head on a rock, the day's sun taking its toll on me.

"Well, are you going to see your parents this weekend?" Chaim asked as he too reclined under the carob tree's shade.

"I really don't know. My parents have been nagging Vickie that I hardly take time to see them. I think I might drive to the Galilee. I guess I can all use a couple of days of being spoiled," I said, "besides, it will keep Vickie quiet."

Happily the conversation shifted away from Vickie to the immediate problem of spraying. Amad wasn't as reliable as Selah at night by himself. We drove the plow leaving furrows along the ends of the rows so we could tell where he sprayed. The next day we could see the tractor tracks where he had ridden over the freshly plowed rows, but that wasn't always enough. Once I caught him just backing the tractor into the ends of the rows to cross the furrows.

Both Chaim and I had to be in the vineyard the next day. Our advisor from the Ministry of Agriculture was coming. Chaim suggested we contact Moshe on the radio to ask if someone else from the moshav was available to spray for us. That was one of the very few advantages of the collective living on our moshav.

Chaim walked down the hill to the truck to call Moshe. While he was gone, I closed my eyes and without warning began thinking of the first day I met Vickie. I could almost feel the coolness of that December evening.

SIX

For Jerusalem in the middle of December it was a day of decision. The entire country focused on whether the Prime Minister, Golda Meir, would ask the president for a time extension to form her coalition government. Also on that day were the funerals of yet more Israeli soldiers who had fallen. Above all it was the eighth and last day of Hanukah, the Jewish festival of lights.

All week I had busily attended endless holiday parties given by my fellow students at the Hebrew University. By week's end, I looked and felt over stuffed. My diet staple consisted of a steady supply of the two traditional foods of Hanukah, the potato pancake and the jelly donut. I was gladly looking forward to the return of my normal eating habits.

Hanukah celebrated the rededication of the Jewish Temple in Jerusalem by Judah Maccabee. Judah, his brothers and their followers, against all odds, courageously rebelled and drove out the vastly superior Syrian army who represented the Roman Empire in 165 B.C.E. During the rededication of the Temple, a miracle occurred. The menorah, the seven branch ancient Hebrew lamp stand made of pure gold while having only enough oil to burn for a single day, burned for eight days until more oil could be secured. In commemoration we lit an eight branched Hanukah lamp, one candle each night progressively for eight days.

Since the creation of the State of Israel, Hanukah, because of its nationalistic nature, has been universally celebrated by both the religious and non-religious alike. That December it held for me even more significance because it was my first Hanukah in Jerusalem. United during the Six Day War in 1967, she had once again become the eternal symbol of our people. Although not religious, my friends and I made a point of going each night to the

Western Wall, the last vestige of the Holy Temple, to light our menorahs.

Thousands of people crossing the entire spectrum of Israeli society were there praying, singing, dancing and crying. At half past four the Chief Rabbi of the State of Israel kindled the eighth and final light. To say the least, it was moving to one's soul to be by the Western Wall.

Lighting my last candle, tears filled my eyes. Within the flame I saw the fiery souls of my friends, comrades in arms, who died during the Six Day War. My flame flickered, a memorial to the fallen while emotion filled the air. Jerusalem never looked more beautiful.

Standing near an open area, we had just finished lighting our last candle. To my left I could see a group of older students performing the same ritual. Suddenly, I saw a strange sight. One coed had nine candles burning instead of eight. Presuming her ignorance, I decided to wander over to see why she lit nine. *Curiosity killed the cat.*

"Excuse me," shyly I said, "I couldn't help but notice you got a little carried away and lit nine candles instead of eight."

"Oh, it was no mistake," she snapped as she turned to re-enter the conversation with her friends.

Dismissing her arrogance, I too turned to join my friends. However, after the first few steps I pivoted on my right heel and headed back. Glancing at that girl from a distance, I took notice. She was unmistakably small with hair deep brown in color cut stylishly short. And her face, well, it was the most beautiful I had ever seen.

I felt sudden warmth as apprehension filled me. Should I say something to her again or be quiet? Certainly she was with someone else and probably wouldn't take notice of me at all. Alas, I resigned myself to rejoin my friends. As I started walking back, I heard a shout.

"You're not even the least bit curious why I lit nine?" a voice behind me asked.

Slowly I turned around. One quick glance and I knew I really didn't care why she did it. All I wanted was just to hear her voice explain. We walked over to the edge of the courtyard by an old building almost without saying a word. Sitting on the ground, I began to experience a relaxed mood I'd never felt before thinking my eight candles would burn indefinitely while time seemingly suspended itself.

"I do it as a reminder of all poor African people who still live on the other side of freedom in my native South Africa," she continued, "as long as a people are deprived of liberty and their right to a life of their own choosing, I'll burn the ninth candle."

In my entire life, I had never encountered a more serious expression of belief and conviction as I did in her voice that night. Spellbound, all I could think was from those beautiful little lips. Her deep brown eyes searched mine for a response. Seconds felt like years as my life was held in balance on my next few words. They had better be good, I thought to myself.

"I guess you're right," I finally said, "That's the message of Hanukah. The pursuit two thousand years ago of life and liberty for our people, rebellion against the tyrannical suppression of our beliefs and someone else being master of our destiny. Each of the eight candles rededicates us to those ideals. A ninth candle could symbolize the common struggle of the other peoples of the world."

Did I pass? Was it the right thing to say? I searched her face for an answer. Nothing. Maybe I should have thought more before I spoke? The silence seemed deafening. Without warning, she leaned forward and to my surprise gave me a kiss. In the silence that prevailed neither of us spoke. We didn't have to.

Our sages of old have written before a person is given life, angels in heaven look into the souls of newborn children. Matchmaking of souls occurs at that time determining which souls will be married to each other. Hence, the expression, marriages are made in heaven.

No truer proof of that could be found anywhere greater than Vickie and me. From the first moment when our two souls met by the Western Wall until today, no greater love has ever existed. It was once said of a great contemporary rabbi of Jerusalem that while accompanying his wife to the doctor, he explained his wife had a pain that hurts *us*. This too was Vickie and me. Each new day brought about a metamorphosis until we became as one thinking, sharing, living and loving being.

But we came from different worlds. Vickie had only recently settled in Israel with her family from South Africa. Like my Dad, Vickie's was also a refugee searching for a place to live a life without fear. While my mine ran from physical persecution, hers fled as a result of his principles and ideals. Scared men looking for a place to pursue unmolested lives, both searched until they reached a common place. Yet, they were to imbue each of us with a different value system, an eternal wedge between the quintessence of our true love.

Vickie grew up in Johannesburg, South Africa where her attitudes and beliefs were formulated. Her father was an extremely successful lawyer by any standard. His formative years were spent at the University of Witwatersrand. At Wits he was to experience his first doses of liberalism. From an old establishment family, in his house growing up were always represented the most conservative of views on the politics and economics of South Africa.

After graduation he began, with a schoolmate, a small law practice. During his first year, as he always put it, he was lucky to be in the right place at the right time. Although small, his firm began dealing with one of the two principle industries in South Africa, gold. Through insider knowledge he was able to successfully speculate in land, diamonds and of course the mining of gold. It was his contacts in the gold industry that bore his wealth and nurtured his liberal views.

Dreams once fulfilled were dreams not dreamt again. With a large office on Rissik Street and an exclusive house in Lower Houghton, he couldn't have dreamt of more. Vickie's father had achieved what, in his youth, was further than the nearest star. A great philosopher once said that man had to be in comfort before he could be moral; he had reached the epitome of life's comforts.

Once, while enroute to the mines for a meeting, a group of police cars stopped on the road side drew his attention. Getting out investigating, he saw the bloody body of a grey haired black man lying motionless on the grass. He knelt down to the man to see if he was alive. As he was about to rise, the old man slowly opened his eyes. Vickie's father inquired as to what had happened. The old man cried the police had beaten him. Walking over to one of the officers, he asked what the old man had done to deserve such a punishment. Before the officer could answer, a rather larger officer broke in with an insulting term for a black African. "The *kaffir* was black. Wasn't that enough?"

Fashions changed on the winds of taste. Until then it had been fashionable for Vickie's father to be liberal. At Wits it was the thing to be. Liberalism meant only sympathy; involvement, however, was another story. On that day he stopped being a liberal, unable to resist becoming involved.

Totally assimilated, he was given almost no inkling of Jewish values. Mere coincidence resulted in Vickie's mother being Jewish. Yet, from somewhere in the recesses of his soul, he mustered one thought. Millions upon millions of people were persecuted and killed in Europe only a few years earlier because they were Jews. In South Africa it happened to people because they were black. Would the Jews remain untouched at the end?

An exclusive school for most of her education, Vickie wasn't the only Jew, but the few Jews in her class tried to forget that fact. It wasn't in vogue to be Jewish in her school she would say. At the end of the day I was the first Jewish boy she ever dated.

Like all people of South Africa in the middle of the century, Vickie's family lived under a bubble. Their world existed within its white controlled shell, blacks being merely a commodity. And for the Jews, their lot was mingled with the whites. More liberal than their Christian counterparts, they gladly reaped the benefits of living under the bubble. On the outside were the blacks always looking in.

And then the bubble burst! Like a child's balloon, the pop was so abrupt that it has resounded until today. What made the bubble burst? Pins such as the Sharpeville massacre and the Rivonia Trial that led to the imprisonment of Nelson Mandela and others accused, convicted of sabotage and sentenced to life were to pick at the fabric of South African society until it frayed.

Vickie's father began to champion the cause of "the Africans" as they called them. Two phenomena occurred occupying the remainder of his professional years in South Africa, house arrest and detention without trial. Gradually he shifted from the lucrative world of gold, land and commerce to the rights of the individual.

First starting by defending unknown blacks, soon he graduated to members of outlawed African committees. At that level he travelled frequently to Robben Island prison. Always at the disposal of the government was the Suppression of Communist Acts. On the side of his clients were the ideals of truth and justice, battle lines being drawn.

Not one to involve herself, Vickie's mother even began to become a silent member of women's groups dedicated to helping "the Africans." Organizations, such as the Black Sash, came to the foreground of the struggle that seized South African society. Her silence broken, she became more vocal with each day.

Then, early in the summer of 1966, Vickie's father was caught during a secret meeting with members of one of the outlawed committees. Released on his own recognizance, he was sure what lay ahead of him was a future of unpleasantness. For some time he had known he was targeted by the authorities for being an outspoken critic of the government's policy of apartheid. Quietly he had been liquidating his vast holdings under the reality that he might one day have to flee the country.

Two days after his arrest, Vickie's father returned home early one morning while only she was at home. Vickie was very much surprised to see her father home, acting strangely upon entering as if he were lost in another world. She followed him into his study and watched him leaf through the pages of his stamp collection.

Queer, she thought to herself, that as busy as he was he could find time to come home just to look at his stamps. Intently watching him, she realized he was selecting specific stamps, steadily removing them one by one. Turning the pages of *The Jewish State* by Theodore Herzl, he positioned each stamp securely in its place within the pages of the book.

Never did he ever utter a single word that could be construed to be Zionist rhetoric. As she watched the contradictions unfold, she could hold back no longer. What on earth was her father doing? Without a word, he rose and walked over to her. Embracing her as he had never done, he kissed her on the forehead.

"Tonight," he sighed, "we will begin a new life. Now go upstairs and pack a small bag. We're going on holiday."

Vickie had already started to take leave from him when he added to pack only summer things. Summer things? It was winter in South Africa. Where could they be going? And why was he reading, of all things, *The Jewish State*?

Immediately after sunset, Vickie's family drove away from their home. Her mother whispered in her ear not to look back. Was she ever going to see their home again? Why were they leaving? Where were they going? All the confusion made Vickie cry and soon she fell fast asleep.

Her father drove all night stopping only to refuel. Near the breaking of the dawn, they reached the northern border with Southern Rhodesia. After a brief conversation with the South African border guards, he came back to the car for a small black bag. Within minutes they had stolen away into Rhodesia across the Beit Bridge heading in the direction of Salisbury.

Once in Salisbury, he explained soon they would board a plane which would eventually take them to Israel where they would make a new life. Vickie's first reaction was that she couldn't possibly go. She had already started studies at the university. How could she ever get an education in a country where she couldn't speak the language?

Her father had been, over the course of several months, converting hundreds of thousands of Rand into priceless stamps. These could be sold on the world market for an appreciable profit. Almost impossible to smuggle one's wealth from South Africa, stamps were easily hidden. In his black briefcase were rolls upon rolls of 2 Rand gold coins. Israel would offer them a new life while wealth would insure their easy absorption into the new country with its difficulties.

Vickie's family eventually settled into a large apartment overlooking the Mediterranean Sea in northern Tel Aviv. Quickly her father entered the economics of the growing state. Fortunes once made were fortunes made again. Success seemed to follow her father where ever he turned. He never forgot the struggles he'd left behind in South Africa, but his attention focused primarily on Israel, soon championing the plight of Palestinians.

SEVEN

June 1966 was a turning point in both our lives. Leaving South Africa forced Vickie to begin a new life away from everything she had known and held dear. Already nineteen years old upon immigration to Israel, she was only slowly shedding her youth. For us Israelis, we too were stripped of our downy fur joining ranks with others under Israel's compulsory military service. Believe me; a person's time in the army by itself can have a maturing affect. No one, however, was prepared for the sobering experience that lay ahead of us.

Like all high school students our age, Chaim and I became active in a program that facilitates service in the Israel Defense Forces. The year prior to induction, we would meet together, go on trips around the country and do other activities with the intent of molding its members into a cohesive unit, remaining that way throughout our initial army service. So, at eighteen we became members of the Israel Defense Forces. Grueling as it was, the training we received did more to foster our maturity than we ever would have imagined at the time.

Vickie came from a country which also had compulsory military service, however, with two major differences. First, Israel drafted women. From before its birth, Israel discovered that women could play an active role in her defense. While noncombative, women filled primarily support and logistical functions. Many times women had proven themselves to have made a decisive difference.

Second, South Africa, during the mid-1960's, was a country at peace. Compulsory service was at best less than a year. No one even thought of consciously objecting to induction. Often young recruits looked forward to it as a time to make friends who would be useful to know in later years. Army service in a nation at peace was hardly anything to worry about.

Service in defense of Israel at the time was another story. Not even two decades old when we entered the army, Israel had survived two major wars and years of border skirmishes. Although officially not at war during the immediate years prior to our induction, Israel was anything but at peace.

To the north raged a major civil war in Lebanon. Political assassination ruled the day in our other neighboring Arab countries creating tremendous instability and uncertainty. On the Syrian front were threats by the King of Jordan to invade her. Later, however, with their differences settled, they both became active with shelling of our settlements to the north and infiltration of terrorists from the east.

As if the Middle East wasn't volatile enough, the Arab Summit in 1965 established the Palestine Liberation Organization with its covenant stating explicitly its purpose, the destruction of the State of Israel. As a result, the PLO tried to create an environment whereby our border states would be drawn into war. Our defense forces were constantly in a state of readiness. Too many precious lives were lost during that period of relative calm.

Upon her arrival, Vickie, opted for a year of national service; primarily geared for those women who, for various religious or ideological reasons, could not comply with induction into the regular army. They worked in hospitals, schools, and other institutions of need.

Vickie luckily was a teacher's assistant in a development town of refugees from mainly Arab countries such as Yemen. I say lucky because not only did her language skills improve, but her experience to the side of Israel that was not all tinsel benefited her later on in life.

Myself, on the other hand, I was doomed to the endless hiking, running etc. of the physical side of the army. I remember almost at the end of a five kilometer run Chaim, who was lying on a stretcher holding on for dear life, was dropped by the *klutz* bringing up the rear. Our drill officer, after explaining how in a real battle situation we could have killed a wounded soldier by that action, decided that more practice was needed. Being that *klutz* who dropped the stretcher, Chaim, Alon and me had to march and run with the stretcher for almost a kilometer. At the end it felt like its poles had grown to my hands.

Our training was geared to winning the next war of survival, the battleground always our homes and fields. To give an inch was to lose what we had waited two thousand years to gain. So train we did, day and night.

Chaim, always one to open his mouth once too often, had the bright idea it would be fun to jump from an airplane. Before I knew it, we had volunteered to become paratroopers. When a person's young, he becomes a bit more daring than common sense allows. Constant training gave us the razor's edge, but no war could be more perilous than that first jump from an airplane. Seconds felt like hours and minutes like an eternity. Soon events turned our jumping games into reality.

Spring of 1967 saw the Syrian forces shelling our farming settlements across the border. To our west, Egypt amassed troops in the Sinai while President Nasser closed the Straits of Tiran to Israeli shipping. Our government had publicly declared in advance that we would consider that action to be an act of war. With Arab troop buildups on all of her boundaries, Israel was left with no alternative but to defend her populace. On June 5, we launched pre-emptive strikes at our neighbors. Successes beyond the wildest dreams of the world were in our hands.

Chaim and I, barely nineteen, dropped from the sky in the midst of the hot Sinai sands fighting in various battles and skirmishes over the next few days. Unlike our fathers before us, we luckily escaped our first taste of war unharmed.

Luck would not be, however, on the side of a great many we knew. A very high percentage of the dead were both commissioned and noncommissioned officers. Our defense forces were lead by courageous men whose words to their troops during battle were always "follow me." Honor always pays with the highest of payment.

When it was all over, our nation had changed. She had become a major military power resulting from unbelievable victories and our land greatly expanded on her frontiers. And the attitude of our people reflected a well deserved sense of pride. None of our lives would ever again be the same. We had experienced so many lessons of life in such a condensed period of time that it would take years for each of us to digest them.

Vickie, at the outbreak of the war, immediately volunteered to work in a military hospital in the Negev, seeing hourly the mangled bodies of our wounded. Within herself she searched in vain for a justification to the carnage as she put it, no gain worth that price; young men torn to bits before they had a chance to taste the sweet nectar of life, for what she cried?

Night and day she worked without stop. Vickie, like others, made a difference to the soldiers who needed immediate comfort. A cup of water, extra pillows, or just a hand to hold easing the pain were simple, but important beyond compare to a soldier wounded in battle. Vickie's heart poured out ever so freely and until this day it hasn't stopped.

Chaim fell in love with a girl he met at a base while we were picking up supplies. He came running out to the truck for me to come inside. Pointing her out he said, "That's the girl I'm going to marry." Our supply order completed, Chaim made a ruckus that we were shorted. When the clerk came out, Chaim yelled a certain group of boxes in the back of the truck were wrong. She climbed in to see for herself. Moments later, Chaim and she came out giggling like school children. I never knew what happened, but it seemed to have worked. Chaim and Aviva were married in August of that year. Aviva only had brothers, so much for family traditions.

Rainbows

Next to Chaim, my best friend in the army was a young lieutenant named Yigal, our immediate commander. Our friendship began on the day of my first jump when I stood in the hatch of the airplane rationalizing I probably would die with the parachute on my back. Yigal, a veteran of first jumps, gave me the encouragement I needed, his foot swiftly connecting with the rear of my pants. Next thing I knew I was falling helplessly to the earth below. By what seemed at the time a miracle, my chute opened and I lived.

During a tank battle on the second day of the war, we were riding on the backs of half tracks. Yigal was ahead of us by about twenty meters when suddenly his half track burst into flames. He along with four other men died amidst that flaming coffin.

Our defense forces lost the cream of its new leaders. To foster Yigal's legacy, I extended my army service and entered officers training. It was just something I had to do. Things like that always are.

We all had survived. Circumstances thrust us from adolescence to adulthood within days, but it was time to get on with our lives. Yet, our lives would never be the same again. Life's that way. What would war be like for us next time? Would we die while others lived? Maybe our country would not be so lucky? Those were questions we thought, but none dared not to ask. We prayed there would be no next time.

EIGHT

"I say it every time someone else, besides us, does the spraying, but this is the last time anyone and I mean anyone else will," Chaim fuming kept saying over and over again.

"Chaim, it's not their fault. It was a mistake, that's all," I said trying to calm him down.

What had gotten Chaim so upset was that the two people from the moshav who did the spraying for us forgot to check the oil in the power take off unit of the tractor. As a result, the gears froze up causing the spraying machine not to work. Chaim had good reason to be upset. Mildew already covered more than half the vineyard.

"We'll have to tow the tractor into Ramle to get it fixed," Chaim said with his hands on his head. "While we're at the garage, you phone around and borrow someone's tractor. It'll be a couple of days at least before ours can be fixed."

Chaim was more than optimistic. Last time the tractor broke, the parent company in Tel Aviv ordered parts from Spain which took more than five weeks to reach Israel. Only left with one tractor in vineyard, we potentially faced a dangerous situation. If our old tractor stopped running it would completely halt our whole operation. But I was sure I could borrow a tractor from one of the other settlements around the valley. We'd done it before. Thankfully in Israel there was always a great spirit of cooperation.

Arriving in Ramle, our tractor in tow, I was overcome with a strong desire just to goof off the rest of the day. My attitude only added to Chaim's frustrations. Chaim compromised. If we finished getting everything done and I agreed to spray, then he would spring for falafel and beer.

Ramle. Not your typical city on the itinerary of the standard holy land tour by any means. Said in Arabic, the city was built by Caliph

Suleiman more than twelve centuries ago. Ramle also had the distinction of being the only city in Israel to be originally founded by Arabs.

Rule of Ramle bounced back and forth between various groups. Sunnis, Shities, Crusaders, Mamelukes, Christians and even Napoleon on his way to Acre all had control at one time. During the 30's Ramle was the scene of anti Zionist rioting which caused the Jewish population to flee. The War of Independence saw times reverse themselves with almost all of the town's Arab residents fleeing.

With all of our tasks accomplished, I took Chaim up on his lunch offer. We bought our falafel in the open air market and sat nearby in the square just off Herzl Street. Under the shade on the grass, we both were overcome by an extremely relaxing mood.

Surrounding us were dozens of retired people talking about politics, pursuing the occupation of pensioners, conversations centered on the Intifada. I thought it interesting the older people held very right wing views. Chaim pointed out since it appeared most were either refugees from Arab countries or had lived in Israel during the independence years, what did I expect? He was right as usual.

Yet, there before us was a micro view of Israel before the Intifada. Alongside the older people were many of our cousins who had come either to buy or sell in the market. As we watched the interactions, there were no signs of brotherly love, but peacefulness prevailed. Or rather it was a peaceful coexistence with both ways of life different, but neither interfering with the other. I began to relax even more since I finished my beer. Closing my eyes I saw Chaim and me playing with Palestinian kids our age from the village nearby Kibbutz Shaar HaGalil. I was drifting . . .

"I said lunch not the whole day. Let's go!" Chaim said rippling my pool of calmness.

"Why do I always have to listen to you?" I asked. "Who put you in charge anyway?"

"You did years ago when you left the vineyard to become the moshav's business manager," Chaim snapped back with a smile, "one of your better decisions I might add."

Chaim was correct. I had left the vineyard for a little over four years to manage the affairs of the moshav. Being in charge of a collective farming community in Israel was like having a perpetual headache. A drunk had it better. When he awoke in the morning, he knew as the day progressed, he'd feel better. That was the best I was to feel the whole day.

Work always lasted from before dawn until the wee hours of the night. Under normal times it would have been complicated enough. Added to it, however, fact Israel was encountering hyperinflation made daily matters unreal. It was a joke to plan the economics of the moshav. So much money, so many zero's yet, nobody laughed. At the end the moshav survived both the economy and my stint at its helm, but the toll it took on Vickie and I could never be repaired.

Vickie and I desperately wanted children. While fertility rates ran rampant in the midst of the moshav, Vickie remained a barren desert; exposing the thin soil, sand, and rocks of our life. One day she said that she wanted to try the basal body temperature method of getting pregnant. It was a simple method. The basal temperature is when your body is fully at rest. Slight increases like ovulation raise basal body temperature. Vickie would be most fertile during the two to three days before her temperature rise. Tracking her basal body temperature each day, she might be able to predict when she'd ovulate; when she'd most likely to conceive, and the best days to have sex.

The inherent problem was my working in the vineyard. What man wouldn't relish his wife saying he had to be nearby to make love instantly when her thermometer said, GO?" Vickie suggested I ask to be the moshav manager so I would be close at hand. Chaim agreed and I submitted the request. But being the manager of the moshav was not the stay in the office job we both envisioned. It seemed that for the first two years, I was always in Tel Aviv, Jerusalem or in the fields with government officials every time the thermometer beckoned.

In desperation, we started in vitro fertilization, a process where an egg is combined with sperm outside the body. A very expensive procedure; treatments in Israel are fully funded by the healthcare system for couples who have no children from their current marriage. IVF treatment was as stressful for Vickie and me as the thermometer method had been.

After two failed attempts, we unsuccessfully slowly tried to resign a life without children. But we together we couldn't. I went back to the vineyard as if nothing that taken place in our lives. After a struggle, Vickie started working with her father on his crusade to free Israel of the apartheid it perpetrated on the Palestinian people. She became quickly the noble Vickie Quixote. Two years later we just both seemed to slide away from each other until the day she finally left the moshav.

Driving back to the vineyard, I fell asleep in the truck. I think it was more the falafel than the beer which had the sedative effect. As soon as we turned off the paved road leading to our vineyard, I was abruptly woken up. Who could sleep bouncing around like a roller coaster? The roads in our vineyard were planned and constructed by the same company who laid the surface of the moon.

Before returning to work, Chaim wanted to ride up to Abu Ali's encampment and discuss water for his sheep. We gladly supplied him with all the water he needed. But in the last couple of weeks his kids had done extensive damage to our water taps by bringing their tractors and wagons too close. It took Selah and I the better part of a day to make the repairs. I began to wonder if the damage was accidental or not.

Abu Ali's camp was on the tallest hill overlooking the Ayalon Valley. From his tent was a most breathtaking view. Once I was at his encampment before morning. When the sun peaked over the hills driving away the morning fog, what lay in front of me was a sight that was beyond description. A magnificent array of color and light filled the valley. So inspiring, I paused to give my compliments to the artist.

Coming first to greet us from the camp was Rothschild, Abu Ali's dog, the mangiest creature I had ever seen. Next came one of his wives or daughters with an array of children of all sizes and shapes following behind. Finally Abu Ali approached, tall and thin for a man of his years with his countenance gracefully proper in his long white robe and *keffiyeh*, a checkered black and white scarf worn around his head, a symbol of Palestinian nationalism dating back to the 1936–1939 Arab revolt in Palestine. On his face was always the look of an almost beard usually brought on by the fact Abu Ali, in his later years, was just too lazy to shave or most anything else for that matter.

Under his main tent one of his wives was boiling water in a *cezve*, a small copper engraved long-handled pot with a pouring lip designed specifically to make Turkish coffee over an open fire. We sat on the ground with our legs crossed and folded under us. Even though it was exceedingly hot, we drank thick, black Turkish coffee, which was more or less the consistency of mud that was poured into my cup. Added to the hospitality were several thick, hard cookies and an assortment of dried fruits and nuts. Drinking coffee was just what I needed to reawaken my spirits.

Abu Ali, being always agreeable, said he would control the driving of his people and offered a thousand pardons for any damage they might have caused, pulling out an extremely large roll of currency. US dollars, Jordanian dinars, and Israeli shekels were rolled very tightly together. Just about anything you would want in a nice neat package. Offering to pay, I said just to forget about it. Chaim, on the other hand, quickly added that it would be only fair to reimburse the moshav for the expenses. Abu Ali began peeling off crisp one hundred shekel notes, one at a time, until Chaim stopped him at five.

Business over, Chaim said we really needed to check on what was happening in the vineyard since we'd been gone all morning. Abu Ali informed us Selah had returned while we were in Ramle. Getting up to leave, I asked Abu Ali how he came to call his dog Rothschild. His answer was somewhat unsettling to Chaim and me.

"Because," he said, "Rothschild was the one who enabled Jews to establish a home in Palestine."

Not an answer motivated by the Intifada, his was purely historical and personal. Abu Ali's family for generations had been wealthy landowners in the area. Once Jewish settlement occurred, Arabs began selling their lands. Although they received handsome sums, the monies were quickly spent. The land remained, however, not in their hands. By the fact he called his ugly dog Rothschild showed he still harbored a lot of bitterness.

Unmistakably, Abu Ali knew the history of Israel's settlement and the roots of the wine industry having lived both first hand; what he didn't personally see he heard from his father. In fact the moshav's vineyard was on land that once belonged to his family. That, I guess, was why Chaim and I were always so accommodating to him.

More than a century ago, waves of settlers mainly from Europe tried their hand at farming the frontiers of Palestine. Early attempts for a variety of reasons failed appearing that populating Palestine was doomed. Most of the first Zionists returned to the continent with their idealism in tow.

At the beginning of the 1880's, Baron Edmond de Rothschild was determined to assist the new Zionists establish a foothold in Palestine, feeling the Holy Land well suited for viniculture. One of the main reasons for the Baron's interest in grapes stemmed from the fact he was the owner of large, quality vineyards in France.

Palestine lacked men of knowledge in viniculture to say the least. So, the Baron sent his own specialists to advise the settlers. All expenses of that most industrious project were borne by the Baron.

He paid for large scale plantings in the center of Palestine. Until the vineyards yielded fruit, the Baron even provided financial support directly to the farmers. His plans seemed to work and by the end of the 1880's thousands of dunams of vineyards were planted. Most of all, the success began to attract many new immigrants. The new Zionists were finally given hope for the future.

But just growing grapes wasn't enough. Among it all, the Baron promised to build wineries in Rishon le Zion and Zichron Yaakov. Until the wines of Palestine could be competitive on the world market, once again the Baron gave price subsidies. To complete the Baron's plan, Palestine needed to gain a preference for export. Everything was going right. By the 1890's hundreds of thousands of vines had been planted.

Late in the 1890's, however, problems began to occur worldwide with a major overproduction causing prices to drop compromising the Baron's subsidy program. What resulted was a large disparity in what the Baron received for the wine and what he actually paid locally. All of this was further complicated by the fact that with the successes of grape growing, Palestine remained a single crop country.

Trying to recover from a bad situation, the Baron investigated what had gone wrong and soon found many tragic errors had occurred. First, the advisors he sent to Palestine gave technically bad advice. Second, for its climate and soil, the wrong rootstocks and varieties of grapes had been planted.

Even though cooperatives and joint ventures among growers were undertaken to develop other markets in the Middle East and Europe, it became self evident that change was needed. After two decades of success, there was no choice but to uproot large scale vineyards and plant alternative crops. A project of that magnitude would be extremely costly. The Baron, feeling somewhat the cause, agreed to finance the crop replacement.

Throughout the country, vineyard after vineyard was uprooted and replanted with almond and citrus trees. The irony of it was that one of Israel's major export items, citrus, resulted from the overproduction problems in viniculture. Our own vineyard had come full circle beginning as a vineyard, shifting to an almond and lemon orchard, finally returning to a vineyard once again. Abu Ali was right. Without Baron Edmond de Rothschild, the Jewish people may never have been successful at settling Palestine.

NINE

"If you're going to spray tonight, you'd better get some rest," Chaim said as we got in the truck to leave Abu Ali's encampment.

"Okay, Chaim, I can sleep under the shady oak by the shed. It's very quiet there."

"I'll take you back to the moshav if you want, Ari."

"No, it will be all right, besides, I wouldn't feel comfortable leaving you by yourself," I said trying to reassure Chaim I'd get plenty of rest and wouldn't fall asleep on the tractor. Even though I was full of the mud we drank at Abu Ali's, I was still very sleepy.

"And spraying alone tonight makes me more comfortable, Ari?"

"Relax, Chaim, I'll have Selah to protect me," I smiled.

Chaim dropped me off on his way to area four to check on how things were going and I walked up the hill to our shed. Upon the tall oak, where our cousins lived during the season, they had built a sort of tree house around the base of the tree. Constructed of old scraps of wood and steel, it looked more like something a group of kids might make. Then I caught myself. Almost all of our workers were young teenagers.

For very practical reasons they chose to sleep there. First, it was much cooler at night under the tree than in the shed. Second, snakes and scorpions couldn't get to them as easily. And last, they could hear if anyone approached during the dead of the night. A few years ago, while they slept in the shed, someone broke into the adjoining room where we kept our sprays, fertilizers, tractor and water system parts. Selah and the others were scared and kept quiet. Since then they have preferred to sleep outside and that's been fine with us.

I made my way up the tree house. Moving from mattress to mattress trying to decide which one to pass out on, I just had to laugh out loud. There I was a cross between Robinson Caruso and Goldilocks. My laughter seemed to echo as it bounced off the walls of the shed. And sure enough, the bed that Baby Bear slept in was just right. It didn't take long for me to journey to dreamland . . .

Looking at my watch, I couldn't believe I had slept less than an hour. My entire body was drenched and as I stood up, my shirt literally dripping from the sweat. Climbing down, I decided to go to the water wagon behind the shed and wash in order to cool off. It was an old wagon on which we placed a black, plastic, five hundred liter tank previously used to store ammonium nitrate, a fertilizer for the trees. Water placed in the tank still had its residual taste.

We kept the wagon under the pine trees behind the shed in order to keep it cool. During the night when the sun went down the temperature inside drops cooling the water considerably. I knew it would, however, be already very warm. As long as it was wet, I didn't care.

Taking my shirt off, I opened the valve to the tank. As the water poured out, I placed my head under the tap for a few moments just to soak, contorting my body under the wagon to take a half shower. Although warm, it was pleasantly refreshing. Before closing the valve, I decided to splash water on my face when the strangest thing occurred.

Facing the sun with my face covered with water, I slowly opened my eyes. Rainbows! All I could see were rainbows. More correctly, not really rainbows, but water refracting in my eyes causing everything to look prismatic filled with color, blues, reds, yellows and greens everywhere. The whole vineyard appeared to be covered in rainbows. Truly, I thought, it was the strangest phenomenon I had ever seen.

Could I do it again? I bent down and splashed water on my face. Directed toward the sun, I opened my eyes. Rainbows clearer and brighter than before, this time the illusion remained in my eyes. "Chaim's never going to believe this." Turning in the direction of the shed, to my surprise, I saw the silhouette of a person . . . a young girl.

"My eyes must be playing tricks on me," I said out loud, "there are no young girls out here, but there is one in the midst of my rainbow."

Blinking my eyes, the rainbows vanished, but not the image of the girl. She sat motionless on the ground staring at the sky. Covering her form were layers of purest white. Her face blended into the clouds while her eyes so blue seemed to vanish from her face into the sky. Beginning to blow, a breeze quickly picked up each strand of her hair and wistfully moved it around partially covering her face and ears.

Suddenly my shirt fell from my hands into a puddle of water below instinctively bending down to pick it up. Only for a split second were my eyes removed from her, but when I looked in the direction of the shed again, she was gone. I kept staring at the spot waiting for her to reappear. Vainly I looked around the whole area including the pine trees behind the shed and the rows of grape trees in front to no avail as she was nowhere to be found. Without thinking, I ran to the tree house, feeling certain she must have gone there. My heart sank seeing she also wasn't by the tree.

Buckling, my legs just gave way under me and I fell to the ground under the quiet oak. I sought solitude in the silence. Who was she? Or was it more appropriate, what was she? An illusion? A figment of my imagination? After all, wasn't I seeing the world through rainbows only moments before? No, she was real all right. Living flesh and blood wrapped in the most beautiful girl, woman, I had ever seen.

Her image played through my mind like a video over and over again. Within moments I had committed to permanence her ever being; the contours of her lips, the angle of her chin, how her eyes blended perfectly with the color of the sky and the reflection of the sun glistening on her hair as each strand fluttered in the breeze. Like a general bending over a battle plan, I committed it all to myself.

Someday, somewhere I knew I was going to find her again. Next time she wouldn't slip away.

Maybe she was a leprechaun? Weren't they keepers of the pot of gold at the end of the rainbow? Who said they had to be funny looking little men dressed in green? I mused myself by thinking she was a leprechaun. If I found her again, I would certainly get my pot of gold. What better place to find her than at the end of a rainbow? The comedy of it all got the best of me. I began to wonder if the trick with the water could happen again. More rainbows?

I walked back to the water wagon and feverishly splashed my face with water again and again thinking to myself when I opened my eyes there she would be. Then, I thought, I probably wouldn't even see rainbows.

As I stood there debating, I felt like keeping my eyes shut indefinitely being unable to bear not finding her in another rainbow. Realizing I was being very immature, I asked myself how I could act that way about the image of a girl I didn't know and only saw for a precious few moments.

Slowly I felt the sun baking my face as I turned toward its heated rays. At least, I thought, I would see the rainbows again. With trepidation similar to my first jump from an airplane, I just couldn't open my eyes. Quickly, however, I regained my composure ever so slowly I opening my eyes. As the light creped in, I began to focus on an image of a person while my heart raced. Was it an optical illusion? I continued opening my eyes. Suddenly I saw . . .

"Chaim, what are you doing here?" I screamed with all the disappointment my heart could muster.

"I wanted to see if you were okay, Sleeping Beauty," Chaim said, "pardon me for being concerned."

"I'm sorry, Chaim, it's just . . . well, you won't believe me.

"Try me, Ari."

"It all started when I saw the first rainbow . . ."

"Rainbow?" Chaim questioned with a characteristically puzzled look on his face. "I do believe you should lay off either the falafel or the beer. One of them has affected you, Ari!"

"No, Chaim, really there were many rainbows and strangest of all I saw . . ."

"Forget it, Ari," Chaim said, "I solved a mystery for us?"

"Mystery?" I asked being the puzzled one, "what mystery is that Chaim?"

"Selah has a mother. He brought her back with him and she's working in area four with the others tying vines."

"I'm glad he has a mother, but Chaim there was this image at first. Then I realized it was . . ."

"And a sister too, Ari!"

"Sister!" I exclaimed as I sat on the ground unaware I'd landed in the puddle under the water wagon.

"Yes, he has a sister."

"What does she look like Chaim?" I desperately asked.

"I don't know. Selah said she was sitting under the carob trees, but when I looked I didn't see her. We'll probably meet her tomorrow," Chaim said. "Come on; let's go back to the moshav. Aviva wanted me home early today."

So Selah had a sister after all. Could it be my little leprechaun was his sister? No, she couldn't be a Palestinian. The girl I saw was beautiful and I never saw any Palestinian women look that beautiful. But then I haven't been around many Palestinian women either. If she was Selah's sister, my fantasy ended there. I'm an Israeli and she's a Palestinian. Oil and water. Yet, the last time I felt like that was the night I first met Vickie. Boy would I be wading into dangerous waters. Just thinking about it was wrong. If my Dad ever knew that for even a fleeting moment I had designs on a Palestinian girl . . .

Riding back to the moshav, I told Chaim all about the rainbows. As I expected, he said I was a little nuts. I chose not to tell him about the encounter with my little leprechaun even though all I could think about was her. Hopefully I would see her when I returned to the vineyard to spray.

Staring out the window of the truck, I had a strange thought that if the girl I saw was indeed Selah's sister . . . suppose also the feelings I had reappeared once again . . .

"Since Selah's back it looks like you'll be able to visit your parents," Chaim said intruding on my thoughts. "I want you to take a package to my mother. Aviva started knitting her a sweater last September and she just finished it this week."

"No problem, I'm sure your mother can use a sweater during this heat wave," I gladly said to change my thoughts.

"Funny aren't you, Ari. I remember Vickie making your father a sweater for two years. She procrastinates even worse than you."

For the rest of the journey home I thought about our first two years on the moshav. Vickie started knitting my Dad a sweater on the first night in our new home, Aviva teaching her how. Vickie thought it would be a nice gesture because for some reason she felt he didn't like her.

I could never get her to understand it was her liberal father that annoyed him, not her. His only fear was the "the left," as he called him, would corrupt me. I had always remained steadfast to the political views of my Dad. By the shed was my only slip. I regained my senses and would make no attempt to meet Selah's sister. Instead of rainbows, leprechauns and pots of gold, I concentrated on mildew, spraying and the Intifada.

All of a sudden, I heard a loud crash. Glass from the passenger side window next to Chaim exploded. Chaim's face was covered in blood. An instant later a loud bang reverberated within the cab of the truck. We were half a kilometer before the village of Beit El-Safa driving down a section of road covered by olive trees. I immediately stopped the truck, withdrew my revolver and shot two rounds into the air. As the sound echoed among the trees, the rock throwing stopped.

"Here, take this," I said handing Chaim a roll of toilet paper that was on the dashboard.

"I'm okay, I'm okay," Chaim said, "let's just get the hell out of here, Ari!"

Luckily Chaim's cut on his right cheek was minor. It could have been a lot worse because I was going ninety kilometers per hour. When a rock hits a car moving at that speed, it strikes with the velocity of a bullet shot from a gun. All I could think about was the rest of the world not understanding a rock in the hands of a kid was a deadly weapon. I too suffered an injury. That rock shattered my fantasy.

TEN

Returning to the vineyard that evening, I avoided going near the shed. Selah heard the tractor by area three and came to see if I needed help. After the events of the week, I really didn't know what emotions would come out of me as Selah approached. Pretending I didn't see him, I climbed on top of the sprayer to mix the chemicals.

"Let me do that for you, Ari," Selah said with a smile, "you have a lot of night ahead of you."

"Okay, you check the pesticide mix. Be careful you don't breathe too many fumes."

Only hours since Chaim and I had gotten caught in a hail of stones, I felt deeply rooted anxieties about dealing with Palestinians. Selah and the others, I kept telling myself, were after all only Palestinians. I just wanted to be rid of them all. Chaim hopefully would see it was us who were betrayed. But when Selah climbed upon the sprayer, I realized people were not stereotyped groups. A person was an individual, nothing more. If there were good and bad Israelis then most assuredly there had to be good and bad Palestinians.

Deeply I looked at Selah, the same Selah I had known for years. Hard working and dependable, Selah was someone you could count on in a pinch. I was confident his whole family must be like him and would like one day to meet his father, sure that's where he got his character. The apple never falls far from the tree.

"I forgot to say welcome back, Selah, everything okay in your village?" I asked with a sense of relief.

"Some things changed for the good and some things changed for the bad. Most things, however, remained the same," Selah answered unsure why I had a sudden interest in his village.

"I'm just curious, but Chaim said you brought your mother back?"

"Oh, that," Selah answered, "Circumstances with my father presented themselves in a way she couldn't live at home anymore. You don't mind if she stays here for the duration of the season do you, Ari?"

"No, why should I. At least you'll eat better," I said laughing myself back into our old relationship.

Selah finished mixing the chemicals and filled the tank with water to make the proper dilution. As he started to walk back toward the shed, he turned.

"My sister also, Ari?"

"Your sister?"

"Chaim didn't tell you. I brought my sister to keep my mother company. Can she stay too?" Selah rhetorically asked.

"Just don't get in anymore fights over her."

"Any more what? Oh! Fights, no that kid's gone. There'll be no more trouble."

Watching him walk away as the sky grew into twilight, I became uneasy again. I didn't like his answer. He should have remembered immediately the fight over his sister, if indeed it was really over his sister. I felt ashamed. To relieve my feelings, I had to say something to make me regain that trust.

"Selah, if you are wondering why I have a gun it's because . . ."

"Snakes," Selah quickly answered, "I know Amad told me. Just be careful you don't shoot your toes off . . . or mine!"

I felt better once again. A silly idea ran through my head. Selah could end up being my brother-in-law. With that thought I was brought crashing back to the world of realities. All I saw before me was again oil and water.

I still wasn't sure if my leprechaun was his sister. Besides, I wasn't supposed to have designs on any girl unless she was Jewish. Christian, Moslem, Hindu, it didn't matter. Neither my mother and father nor the world in which I lived would approve; besides the fact she was at least half my age.

Since I sprayed nights, I successfully made it to the end of the week without meeting Selah's family. I returned to the moshav early in the morning just in time for Chaim to leave for the vineyard literally with the engine running in the truck. Really I hated the change of schedule because I never got adequate rest during the daytime, but that week it served its purpose well.

What would I do next week? We sprayed one week on and one week off to give the fruit on the trees an opportunity to feel the effects of the spray. Next week I would have to meet his sister. After going to my parents, I'd be able to survive our first encounter. Being around my boyhood roots, I was sure would rekindle my values and beliefs. Might I even tell my Dad about my leprechaun was Palestinian? That, however, I feared would be tantamount to committing suicide.

Vickie drove up to my house, our house, on the moshav, bringing a present for my parents. As she got out of the car, I was stunned. She looked imperially dressed from head to toe. No matter how hard I tried, I couldn't turn my eyes away from her.

"Aren't you a little overdressed for a visit to the moshav?" I asked having great difficulty saying anything.

"Funny, Ari, very funny. I am going to the Mann Auditorium in Tel Aviv for a concert in a couple of hours," Vickie answered with her characteristic curtness.

"Date?" I sheepishly asked.

"Yes, as a matter of fact I do."

"Oh!" I quickly answered not wanting to think about the rest of the information I would receive.

"My parents Ari, I'm going to the concert with my parents."

Normally that kind of answer would leave me elated. Ever since our divorce, though, I shuddered to think Vickie could fall in love with another man. Ours was the perfect marriage for a very long time and in the end it was even the perfect divorce. No disputes about community property, we were just two people who loved each other too much to hurt one another anymore. Staying together would have done just that.

Ours were different worlds. Vickie, the sophisticated, debutante girl who had everything daddy could give her. Myself, I was the poor son of a kibbutznik who felt more comfortable milking cows than wearing a white shirt. For us, clouds with silver linings shined in the sky no more. Before the magic disappeared completely, we decided to part.

When we obtained our Jewish divorce, the rabbi said it was the first time he'd ever seen a couple embrace and kiss after the divorce ceremony. Bring their lawyers, their parents, their girl friends and their boyfriends, fight, scream, and swear, but never muster emotions of passions. Till this day I haven't fully understood why we let each other slip away.

Vickie's had many suitors pursue her over the last few years. I guess none could measure up to her high standards. With a certain degree of sadness, I wished maybe she would get married again. She had so much love to give. Knowing she was still single continually gave me false hopes. Dreams of our reconciliation from time to time kept popping into my head. I wasn't unhappy not being married to Vickie, but then I wasn't really happy either.

As I looked at Vickie sitting in my living room, our living room, I just couldn't stop thinking of my little leprechaun. What was it about her that reminded me so much of Vickie? How had I mustered feelings toward anyone else like I did for Vickie? Then, I realized my vision didn't remind me of Vickie. Those feelings were feelings anew. I wasn't the same person anymore.

I remembered my Dad always saying to me I was young and foolish. "One day," he laughed, "you'll grow up to be old and foolish." Yes, I grew older, but not foolishly. Our breakup had taught me many painful lessons of life. Most prominent of which was you never appreciate the people close to you until they are gone.

Bursting from within me when I first encountered my leprechaun were not old desires for Vickie. Rather, they were relative to what I wanted and needed as a new person. So much time had I reflected on the past that I was ready for the future and what it might have in store. One can never go back I learned, going forward, on the other hand, was limitless.

"You look thin, Ari," the Vickie of my past commented. "Are you still eating only tuna fish sandwiches and potato chips?"

"No, sometimes I make myself French fries."

No matter how much I felt prepared to venture forth to a new life, it was always comforting to know Vickie still cared about me. Vickie's voice seemed to cause the vision of my leprechaun to fade.

"You're starting to look a little chunky yourself. I thought Chinese food wasn't fattening," I smirked as I won the round.

Every time Vickie and I were together, it was always the same, an atmosphere prevailing as if time were suspended. Our lives for that moment had not changed. Vickie was the same Vickie and I was the same Ari. Together we joked, smiled, and laughed like always. Suddenly Vickie looked at the wall clock and realized it was time for her to leave. Time began its pacing march forward once again. It always ended that way. We said our canned goodbyes.

ELEVEN

"From the looks of it, you could do with some real food," my mother, being a mother, smiled.

"Where's Dad?"

"He's at the dairy. They're installing some new milking equipment today and you know how he's got to be there to make sure every thing's done perfectly."

"But it's been ten years since he left the dairy? What does he know about modern equipment anyway?"

"Maybe so, but he spent over thirty years working there. Ari, you should understand because you're just like him," my mother said giving me one of those famous hugs. "He's been waiting for you to come all day."

Walking through the kibbutz to the dairy, I began to experience a very pleasant feeling . . . coming home. At the dining hall in the kibbutz center I refreshed myself with a cold glass of sparkling soda with a twist of orange. Sitting on the front steps, I engaged in numerous half conversations with people busily going in and out.

"How's your moshav, Ari?"

"Good to see you again, Ari."

"You're mother's been baking all day," etc.

Then all of a sudden, I got a jolt from the rear so strong that I dropped my glass.

"Keeping my son out of trouble, Ari?" Chaim's father said as he helped me pick up the broken glass from the steps. We talked of insignificant things until he said, "doctor says his heart isn't doing so good."

"Another heart attack looming?" I asked.

"No, it's the old story. He neither watches what he eats nor does he exercise. You know, Ari, I don't have to tell you. Maybe you can talk some sense into him while you're here. Just don't say anything that will excite him, okay?"

"How about I'm in love with a Palestinian girl?" I mumbled.

"What's that you said, Ari, I didn't hear you?"

"Oh! Nothing, nothing at all."

But it wasn't nothing. All the way driving to the kibbutz I drifted from one daydream to another. In each, I saw myself and my fantasy laughing, playing and just being in love. Image after image brought me closer to the reality of it all. I was ready to love again and most importantly, I was ready to be loved.

One thing's for sure, before you reached the dairy, it reached out to you. The aroma, to put it mildly, was heavy. Approaching, I saw him standing there dressed in the traditional kibbutz blue work clothes wearing knee high, black, rubber boots. His stature appeared to be a little bent owing to the weight of his years; a crowning full head of silver gray topped his majestic figure. Looking at him directing a cast of characters unloading and installing, I marveled that he could have been one of those larger than life movie heroes. Then I smiled.

Boys growing up usually attach themselves to a myriad of fictitious heroes they could admire and emulate. Israel, during the early fifties, had no great assortment from which to choose, most of us identifying with Biblical heroes. To be a King David, Joshua or the wise King Solomon was indeed desirable. As our nation grew, men who had proven themselves during battles defending our land were added to the list.

For me, I sought no other larger than life figures. My Dad was the only hero I ever needed. A kind, quiet man gentle to all he touched, however, instantly mustering all the rage and anger a given situation might demand. He was drinking coffee when I finally reached the milking parlor.

"Gaza seems not to have harmed you," he said.

"Not outwardly, anyway," I answered with both of us knowing exactly what I meant.

"Come; let's go back to the house. We'd better start eating now if we're going to finish all the food your mother prepared before you leave."

Turning to walk away from the milking parlor, my Dad put his arm across my shoulder. Mystically, like a magician's wand, his grip quickly healed all that had gone wrong inside of me. Vickie, my leprechaun, Gaza and the Intifada all faded away. The strength from his arm transferred itself to my very soul giving the inner peace I sought for so long. My hero had once again saved the day.

Friday night on kibbutz was a time of gaiety and togetherness. Not unlike the homes of the more religious, we sat down to enjoy a festive meal befitting the Shabbat. A couple of years ago the kibbutz, for economic reasons, closed the central dining hall on weekends. My mother, true to form, presented us with a meal fit for a king.

Remembering Chaim's father's words, I was determined not to excite my Dad, but I guess the formula of fathers and sons always makes for something volatile. My mother, however, was who I feared most. I knew she would start . . .

"Have you met any interesting people lately?" my mother slyly asked.

"No, I haven't dated anyone at all!"

"I wasn't asking . . ."

"Mother, one day I will, but not now. I'm enjoying myself too much."

"You might be able to fool Chaim and Aviva, but I'm your mother, Ari, and I . . ."

"Just listen to her," my hero again saving the day said, "Let Ari be. We haven't spoken to him since he was in Gaza on reserve duty. Tell us, Ari, what's the so-called Intifada really all about?"

My Dad had asked the paramount question which puzzled an entire nation, if not the whole international community. In his eyes my being in Gaza made me somewhat of an expert. It would be, hopefully, as close as he would come to the Intifada. His question was a frank and harmless and I thought my answer would be the same.

"It's about confusion, nothing more, nothing less," I answered with a deep breath.

"Confusion! Ari what on earth could be confusing about Palestinians wanting to take land away from us. We were the ones who sweated, lived and died to make this land produce like no place in the world. For half a century it lay fallow with neither the British nor the Palestinians being able to do anything but occupy its desolateness. No, not until we came and nurtured its very essence did life spring forth. Now they want it back . . . a lot of nerve I say, they speak of Palestine not meaning Ramallah and Hebron. What they really want is Palestine with Haifa, Tel Aviv and Jerusalem. Confusion! Confusion . . . !"

"Please calm down. It's not good for you. Ari didn't mean anything by it, I'm sure. Go ahead; tell your Dad what you meant."

"To me it is very confusing," I began, "each and every day I work with our cousins. Freely and openly we act like true friends. Yet, in Gaza, I was scared to walk down streets and passageways. I don't hate Palestinians because they are Palestinians, but I felt honest hatred from them solely because I was an Israeli. What did I do to them? Nothing! We didn't create the Gaza Strip, the Egyptians did. My being an Israeli was more than enough cause for them . . ."

"At least this should come as no surprise to you," my Dad said. "Haven't I taught you time and time again because you are an Israeli, a Jew, you will always get that feeling. Sometime, somewhere it will surface and become ever-present."

"But does that mean I'm suppose to hate them back just because they are Palestinians?"

"No, not necessarily."

"Take Selah," I said, "he's sometimes as much of a brother to me as Chaim. Now I look each day at him with suspicion. Will he . . . could he do something to harm me?"

"Ari, when the time comes you can only count on your own people."

"But, Dad, don't you think that Selah's parents probably tell him the same thing?"

"I'm sure they have and that proves I'm right. Tell me, have you or Chaim been seriously threatened by our cousins at any time?"

"Very recently Chaim and I were caught in a hail of stones. Chaim got cut slightly on the cheek."

"And what were your feelings at that time, Ari?"

"I could have killed. If I could have seen any of them, I would have shot."

"See what I mean!"

"I don't want to go out and shoot at people just because they are Palestinians."

"You will, Ari, you will."

"I don't know about you, but I see why Ari is so confused," my mother interrupted. "He hasn't seen what we did growing up."

"You don't understand either, Mother. Chaim and I grew up playing with the kids from the neighboring village as much as the kids from the kibbutz. They never reacted to us in any way other than friendly. They would never . . ."

"Ari, now you're being naive. Don't you think I grew up in Poland having many more friends among the Poles than the Jews? Yet, when the time came, they all turned very quickly. The major difference now is we are the majority and it's our country and that's precisely what we've spent more than four decades doing. We've built a nation for our people and succeeded beyond even our own expectations. Within our boundaries has always been room for our cousins, but they must realize one important fact. Israel is our country, not theirs. We make the laws and they have to live by them just the same as we do."

"Now you're sounding like someone who is trying to justify life in South Africa not Israel," I said. Sometimes a person says something and immediately knows it was a mistake. At that moment the words can't be stuffed back into your mouth. So, the only thing to do is batten down the hatches and try to weather the storm.

"He finally won you over that no good father-in-law of yours . . . All his liberal ideas . . . I knew it couldn't be you talking, Ari. Now I know it was him. He won't . . ."

"That's enough you two. If you continue I'll be the one with the heart problem not your Dad," my mother said placing her name in nomination for the Nobel Peace Prize.

My Dad was more interested in how our moshav was doing financially. Most of the collective farms in the country were experiencing bad times. Endless debate was going on in the country like a ping pong match trying to assess the causes. Among the reasons given were government policies failing to control the economy, poor management of the farms themselves and a shifting of national philosophy.

Dry as the subject was, my mother made her apologies and went to sleep. My Dad too grew tired. I knew our argument had taxed his capacity a little too much, but he was strong. As he always said, "only the good die young." He planned to outlive us all.

Walking outside at the crisp part of the night, I found the old tree where Chaim and I spent many centuries of time at play, the focal point of our world of make believe. In front of the tree was the field where we played football with the Palestinian children from the village near the kibbutz.

Looking back, maybe my Dad was right. Those times were, indeed, a world of make believe. We were just children, Israeli and Palestinian, happily playing together, but what of the grown up world? Each day thousands of Israelis and Palestinians worked together. Maybe that too was artificial?

Could it also be possible my Dad was right concerning my attitudes? Was I unwittingly influenced by Vickie and her father's ideals? Not to mention my fleeting fantasy with a Palestinian leprechaun. Or were those truly my feelings? I couldn't even sort out how I felt in Gaza. Too much had happened since to cloud my mind.

Sitting by the tree, I reflected on the first weekend I brought Vickie to the kibbutz. My parents were a little too overbearing for her. So, we retreated to the safety of the tree. Beneath it we laughed because Vickie got the impression that my mother had already started to knit booties for a grandchild. We had only known each other less than a month.

Time, under the tree, seemed to whisk away. Since my internal clock was upside down from spraying nights, I sat beneath for hours. Finally, as the sky grew more intense with its mosaic of light, my thoughts drifted to other natural phenomena—rainbows. All I could think about were those silly rainbows.

I so wanted to tell my parents about that strange occurrence. My mother, most of all, would enjoy the tale, but I would be less than honest if I didn't tell them about what filled the pot of gold at the rainbow's end. How could I ever tell them? The more I tried to put it out of my mind, the more it entered. Soon I found myself confusing fantasy with reality.

As the night air blanketed me with the morning dew, I grew to a realization. Within the next few days I would have to face up to a lot including meeting Selah's sister. What if it was love I would feel for her? What could I do? Oh! What should I do? Never one to shy away from anything, I just wished I could stay on kibbutz with my parents and not face my reckonings. Soon I nestled under the blanket of dew and fell asleep.

TWELVE

Riding to the vineyard, I began to experience something I had not felt since I was a teenager, butterflies in my stomach. Like the anticipation of a first date, I was squirming all over the front seat of our truck. I couldn't believe my reaction. She was just a girl and I a grown man. Forget for the moment, if I could, the fact she might be a Palestinian, I must have been twenty years her senior; if she was Israeli that would complicate matters enough.

"Hear what happened in the territories yesterday?" Chaim asked with his perfectly wrong sense of timing.

"No, I was just too wrapped up my parents to bother to listen to the news. What are you talking about?"

"A four year old boy from one of the religious settlements got his head split open by a rock. His father was nearing a Palestinian village behind a border police jeep escort when from out of nowhere rocks started flying. Caught off guard, the border police hesitated. Their commander, fearful of repercussions, failed to fire or give chase."

"What about the boy?"

"Well, it seems he was sitting in a safety seat in the rear with the window down. One of the rocks sailed into the opening and struck him in the front of his forehead. He's in a hospital in Haifa in poor condition. After what the news described as a grueling operation yesterday, the doctors are going to operate again this morning."

"Did they say what his chances are?"

"Aviva heard late last night the part of the brain that gives signals for speech might have been affected. You know, Ari, maybe you have the right idea about the Intifada and my approach is wrong."

Could I believe my ears? Chaim was changing his mind to agree with me. I wanted to scream out to him those were my views last week. Since the weekend, I'd changed to the way he felt. And my Dad couldn't understand my confusion.

For the first time maybe I saw my Dad was right. All I felt was rage at whoever could possibly do such a cowardly thing. No reason in the world justified harming an innocent little boy like that.

Consumed by thought for the rest of our trip, I was totally oblivious to Chaim and my surroundings. It was that kind of trance where a thousand thoughts run through your mind at once melting into one. Occasionally I nodded or grunted a response to Chaim while he carried on conversation after conversation with me.

"Today's the day; you get to meet Selah's sister."

Like a child caught with his hand in the cookie jar, I blushed red all over. Eager to divert Chaim, I desperately searched for a response and for the life of me I couldn't believe what came out.

"Chaim, do you remember the night everyone came over to our house to watch Maccabbi Tel Aviv play in the European basketball semifinals?"

"Remember! How could I forget the first time I ever saw you fight with Vickie? Why on earth are you bringing that fight up now, Ari?"

"Not our fight, Chaim, remember how drunk you and I got after they lost by one lousy point in overtime?"

"That is the last time I ever put brandy near my lips. We went to the office at one o'clock in the morning and turned on the air raid siren. Boy was everybody pissed."

Why did I bring up that night? Chaim continued on reliving our escapades of that evening. Perhaps it was a mental block, but I had forgotten our first fight. We never even fought. All I did that evening was ask Vickie to please serve my friends and me some sandwiches while we watched the game.

"Chauvinist," was what I got back. "Do I look like the barmaid around here?"

"All I wanted was little pita bread."

Later, when we finally made up, Vickie said she had been getting frustrated about my developing attitude toward women in general. Quietly she listened and observed for what was, according to her, a very long time. My request, although harmless unto itself, was the straw falling on the camel's back.

Not that Vickie was a feminist or I a true male chauvinist; we were just accustomed to different home styles. My mother always waited on my Dad like he was a king. Old world traditions she learned from her mother. To me it seemed only natural to have one's wife in the same role. I even asked my secretary in the office to make me a cup of coffee at least a dozen times a day when I was the moshav manager.

I guess, looking back on it, Vickie equated my attitude with taking advantage of the black peoples in South Africa. She said later my being drunk exacerbated the problem because my voice carried with it a tone of superiority. To this day I still don't see anything wrong with the way my mother and women like her treat their families.

"And when they finally wrestled us both down in the mud at four am, Ari, you looked like a creature from a horror movie when you raised your head."

To my amazement Chaim had relived that entire night without me hearing one word. All I could feel was something inside of me getting ready to snap. My thoughts simultaneously were thoughts of Vickie and anticipations of my leprechaun. Boy was my . . .

". . . head splitting in half the next day from the hangover you had. Remember, Ari?"

Chaim and I burst out laughing. With his simple knack, he seemed always to soothe my most sensitive situations. Chaim was made of the earth while I was made from the winds. Those elements governed our lives and in turn revealed a lot about our personalities.

Once we arrived at the vineyard, I told Chaim I was going to walk down the rows of trees to look for leaks in the drip irrigation lines. Working in the vineyard insured we got more than our share of exercise. The typography of our vineyard was such that water always ran down hill on one side of an area. All we had to do was walk along the end of a row and look for water accumulation. Up that row we knew would be a leak. And walk kilometer after kilometer after kilometer we did.

I started in areas six and seven where our cousins were to be found and I was sure Selah's sister would be with them. Rather than stalk her like a hunter after his prey, I decided to let our second encounter be natural. Beginning the mundane task of checking the drip lines, I didn't have to wait long to find a leak; the fourth row's end a bubbling pool of water. My thoughts concentrated on the immediate problem of water leaks. Our rendezvous would have to wait, water too precious an item to waste.

For about hour and a half I had fixed what seemed to be an endless amount of leaks. I was sure the previous night all of the rabbits in Israel dined in area seven. Walking along each row, I began to notice the growth and development of the vines. The spraying was apparently working on the mildew.

Basically powdery mildew dried out the grape resulting in its skin cracking or remaining small. Since we got paid for not only the weight of the grapes, but the quality of the juice as well, its effects could be devastating. As mildew spread, the potential yield per dunam plummeted.

Approaching the last row of area seven, I realized soon I would have to meet her. Since the young kids were working in area six that was where our rendezvous would have to be. Walking toward six, I heard water spurting onto leaves. That, I knew, would be a big leak and sure enough, the whole bottom half of the second row was mud.

Evidently when Selah was doing cultivation yesterday, the plow blade nicked one of the main feeder lines of the water system. We didn't notice the leak immediately yesterday because we gave water to a different part of the vineyard. Now that we were giving water to area six, the booster pump provided a pressure of more than seven atmospheres. Fixing a leak under that kind of pressure would be like working under a waterfall.

Finally finishing the repair, I decided to move a couple of rows over and rest. No leak for the next three rows was a good omen. The ever-growing vines provided plenty of shade as my head lay on the ground and began to doze a little.

About ten rows over I heard our cousins working. Realizing they would reach my Rip Van Winkle row in approximately twenty minutes, I chose not to move and enjoyed the next few moments of uninterrupted rest.

After a too brief period I heard them only two rows over, lazily rolling over to see them. To my surprise, I saw a woman's golden tanned feet covered in somewhat worn sandals protruding from under a traditional Arab dress light blue in color, extensively embroidered. And . . . and that's all I could see under the trees. My heart raced faster and faster.

Lying there I honestly had no idea what to do. Should I get up and walk to the end of the row and nonchalantly gaze down to see her? Or maybe, I should just lay still and wait for her to come to me? My Israeli nature would not allow me to do either.

Putting my infantry training to use, I began to crawl on the ground making movement only with my elbows. Like a giant sea turtle I slowly progressed towards the enemy. As I approached the trees before her, I stopped. Motionless only a few meters away, I reached a tragic flaw in my strategy. In my haste to sneak up on her, I never completed my plan. What on earth should I do next?

Retreat was in order. Unnoticed, I felt like backing up and that's just what I did. Slowly I began sliding back slithering like a snake in the grass. Who was I scared of? A good Israeli soldier never retreats under fire. That ever present element of discipline had long since been become a part of me. My retreat to the rear was halted. Charge!

Crawling to within a meter of her I had to maneuver a few degrees to the south. While I was deep in planning my attack, she steadily worked. Only centimeters away, without warning, she mounted an aerial bombardment. In front of my field of vision I could see, as if in slow motion, her pruning shears fall to the ground.

She had fired the first shot mounting her counter offensive. With the swiftness of computer logic, I began planning my next course of action. In seconds, I knew she would bend down to pick up her shears. I had nowhere to hide . . . nowhere to run. Seconds falling fast, I braced for the frontal attack.

I saw her legs bend slightly. Next her arms drifted toward the ground, her movements lightning fast. I had relatively little time left; her knee hit the ground and my heart beating ever so fast. Below the bottom of the tree line I saw her hair drifting down. I braced myself . . .

Contact! Her face . . . I could see . . . I saw her . . . old wrinkled face. Not my leprechaun, that woman looked like the Wicked Witch of the West. What trick of nature was that? She may have been startled to see me, but I was totally devastated. We both rose together on opposite sides of the row of trees. Of course, she had to be Selah's mother.

Laughter echoed in area six as I sought a release from the intensity of the previous moments. His mother indeed! I just stood smiling at her. Judging from her look, she did not know how to react, scared and amazed written clearly on the lines of her face. After a brief moment of eye contact, she returned to pruning.

I, on the other hand, returned to my bucket of water line connectors and water pipes a few rows back and just kept smiling that it was Selah's mother.

Not paying any attention, I walked to the end of the row and resumed repairing broken drip lines and then I saw her.

THIRTEEN

Standing there she was more beautiful than I had remembered, but just the way I had hoped. She didn't see me at first. Time was on my side and I planned its advantage well sizing up my thoughts of the past days. Yes, I was ready for her to enter my life even though she was Selah's sister. Instead of oil and water, I saw only a woman and a man.

Contemplating the moment at hand, I vowed she would not escape me again. If she started to disappear, I was determined to run after her having spent so much time in anguish and inner turmoil to see her again.

Slowly I began walking toward her, careful not to make any distracting noises, closer and closer I came. Inside I was prepared to leap at an instant to pursue her escape, fear long since abating. My eyes fixed on the position of her head, like a photo journalist, wanting to capture, in my mind's eye, her first reactions when she turned.

About ten meters away a rather silly thought entered my mind. I felt like a kid at play. Surfacing within me was a strong desire to sneak up from behind and yell boo. With that thought uncontrollable laughter overcame me and I began laughing out loud. As the first laugh slipped away, I realized I'd broken the silence.

Before I knew it, she turned toward me. I couldn't put that laugh back, but she had to turn sooner or later anyway. I never, for the life of me, expected her reaction to be what it was. She smiled at me, neither flight nor fright, she just smiled. Make no mistake; her smiling face belonged to my leprechaun. I finally had found my pot of gold and its keeper at the end of the rainbow. Searching desperately for a measured response, I came up totally blank. What should I do? Doing what came naturally, I smiled back.

Suspended in time, we just stood there fixed on each other. I so wanted to know what her thoughts were, however, I couldn't muster anything within the realm of telepathy. Slowly her eyes revealed her thoughts. I felt calmness in her look or was it more a feeling of a relief. For a fleeting moment, I thought she had spent the last days wanting to see me again. A mutuality of presence began to develop. Her look was calling to me . . . calling me to . . .

Without warning she began to move. My arches tensed to sprint after her. Her movement was not toward the opposite direction, but rather she slowly walked toward me, each step separate unto itself. I began to count them as if I was the starter of a big race. Two . . . three . . . four . . . how many more steps? Twenty or thirty? . . . eight . . . nine. Had it all been worthwhile?

A few more steps . . . eighteen . . . nineteen . . . twenty . . . I fantasized and I would spontaneously embrace at the completion of the last counted step . . . thirty . . . thirty-one . . .

She stopped and looked at me; or rather it seemed through me. Gone too was her smile replaced by a look of shame. Slowly even my smile eluded my face. Why the sudden change? What on earth did I . . . could I have done? Like Lot's wife, she stood there motionless while I moved toward her.

From behind I heard a strange sound, a high pitched shrill voice. Quickly turning, I saw at the end row Selah's mother. Matriarchal in her stance, she exuded a force of strength. I understood seeing my leprechaun had resumed her pruning.

Our second encounter had concluded prematurely. I wanted to remain in the row to watch her every move. Having a guard posted now, I knew to stay would only complicate matters. At least I sought refuge in knowing her smile was genuine. Deep inside I felt she was glad to see me again, appearing almost happy about it. So was I.

Rainbows

Bending down to pick up my bucket of pipe connectors, I thought of how to plan my retreat. Crouching over, I tilted my head toward the row's end and saw her mother was still there. I stood up and look towards the heavens, but no answers fell. The mere thought of walking towards Selah's mother didn't thrill me and it would be compromising on future possibilities to go past his sister. I looked at her mother then toward his sister.

Oh! What the hell, I grabbed my bucket and headed in the direction of my leprechaun. Her mother wouldn't like it, but who cared. Walking toward her, I noticed she had not moved a centimeter. Exactly opposite her, she ever so slowly turned her head, her stillborn face mechanically stopping when it was parallel to mine. Suddenly, the corners of her frozen lips began to thaw. I saw the birth of a smile extending from one end of her face to the other.

Running, my spirits lifted, I leaped into the air and clicking my heels together, an echo in the vineyard as I yelled for joy. Nothing could possibly end my happiness.

Rounding the end of the row, I sank up to my ankles in mud. Speeding back to reality, I had stumbled upon a break in a main line, water gushing at least two meters into the air. Within seconds I was covered from head to toe in water. All thoughts of my previous precious few moments escaped me. That wasn't going to be an easy to repair, I sighed. For the life of me I couldn't understand how it could have broken.

Maybe someone did it deliberately. The pipe's depth was well beneath the reach of a plow's point. I was utterly confused about where to start first. It would still take at least a few hours to finish giving water in the areas six and seven. After thinking about it, I was sure someone dug below the ground level to break the pipe on purpose. Trouble of that kind was all we needed. I started back to the pump house to turn the booster off as Chaim drove up.

"I saw water gushing up over the tree tops from the bottom of the area," Chaim said. "Mainline?"

97

"Yep! I think some Intifadanik did it on purpose."

"I don't think so, Ari, remember when you were the moshav manager we had the mains on this side replaced?"

"That proves my point, Chaim, the pipes aren't that old."

"That's true except for one fact. This is the second time we had one break. Shortly after they were installed, the water company discovered a problem with the pipe's manufacture. I'm not quite sure, but I think it was a flaw in the casting or the mold itself."

"How do we get it fixed, Chaim?" I asked still dripping from head to toe.

"I'll call the water company immediately. They have some kind pressure boot they place around the pipe which will hold at least until the end of the season when they will replace the pipe at no charge to us."

"Good, Chaim, I was beginning to wonder if . . ."

"To save time, I'll get Selah to send you someone to help you dig around the pipe. Enjoy the mud bath, Ari," Chaim laughed as he drove away.

By the time the water company finished the repairs, it was almost four o'clock in the afternoon. I wandered back to the shed to wait for Chaim to surface. Boy was I tired. Approaching the shed, I remembered what had transpired earlier. Would I see . . . ? Yes, I would. She sat with her mother and Selah under the tree. Someone had started a small fire to make coffee.

She didn't even raise her head as I walked by. Like a flash of lightning Selah handed me a cup of coffee. By the end wall of the shed facing the quiet oak, I sat on the ground. My knees up, I leaned painfully against the shed. As it always did, the coffee hit the spot. Sipping on the cup I sat staring at her.

And she knew I was watching her and I was sure her mother also knew. Contently I was prepared to sit all night by the shed, but then I got a great idea. Why not join Selah and the others around the fire? I could do with another cup, quickly drinking the remaining thick coffee. Soon I was sitting next to Selah with my legs crossed under me. He leaned over and poured me a second cup.

"Meet my mother and sister, Ari."

"Pleased to meet you," I said.

"They don't understand Hebrew, Ari," Selah said. "I'll tell them what you said."

"Thanks, Selah."

I didn't know what to do. How was I ever going to communicate with her? Smiles were good for a short encounter, but my Arabic was only at best basic. All my years in the vineyard allowed me to pick up a few words and phrases. How do you say 'I love you' in Arabic? I couldn't ask Selah for a crash course in passionate Arabic. Some fine relationship we would have only being able to tell her 'get in the truck,' 'fix the leaks,' 'get the bucket' and the most romantic of all 'stop the tractor.' Some romance indeed!

Being that her mother was already suspicious; I couldn't just come out and ask Selah her name. How to find out? Suddenly an idea came to me.

"Selah, I need to see their identity cards."

"Why only theirs, Ari?"

"And the others as well," I answered. "Because of the recent troubles in the area, the army wants all workers from the territories checked out."

"Ari, take my word that everyone here is okay."

"It's not me Selah. Moshe said I had to bring the list back today."

While Selah got up to get their identity cards, I took pride at my slick idea. Once I had written all their names and identity numbers down, I'd also have hers and no one would be the wiser. After thinking about it, I decided it probably wouldn't be a bad idea to actually have the army check them out. When we got back to the moshav, I would give the list to Moshe and have him run a check.

Selah returned with a stack of orange identity cards in his hand, hers fourth from the top. Glancing at the picture, I began reading her name . . . Aisha. Over and over I said it to myself. Aisha . . .

Aisha . . . Aisha. The sound of her name played music on my very soul. Completing the list I realized there were identity cards missing.

"I'm missing two cards."

"I know, Ari, they left them back in the village. Midweek I'll send them home to get them, okay?"

"Sure," I said knowing full well they would not return once they returned to their village. I was certain they had something to hide. If so, my charade had the additional benefit of getting rid of two potential trouble makers. Selah would have to be more selective in who he brought to work in the vineyard. Maybe we limited our Intifada problems as a result of their leaving. I was sure it had to have been those two who cut the water lines.

"What about your card, Selah, it wasn't in the group you gave me?"

"Do you really need mine too, Ari?"

Once again I sensed in Selah a feeling that I was betraying a confidence by asking. To him, I was saying he was no different than the rest, his years of loyal service meaning nothing. What should I do? After all, it wasn't really something the army wanted me to do. I only made it up to find out his sister's name.

Yet, why didn't he want to give me his identity card? Was there something he didn't want me to find out? Then again, what if he was just testing me on how I felt about him? Could it be he just wanted me to say 'okay Selah, you are different . . . one of the family.' What to do?

"No, Selah, I don't need your identity card," I said in the end.

"You can have it if you want, Ari, no problem."

Should I see if he was bluffing and take it? No, I trusted him. After all, I laughed to myself; he was going to be my brother-in-law, wasn't he? To show him I did indeed have trust in him, I decided to offer him a gesture of good faith.

"Come to think of it, I really don't need your mother's or sister's either."

100

Going down the list with my pencil, I drew a faint line through their names and identity numbers as not to totally cross them out.

"Thanks, Ari," Selah said in relief that I still regarded him as an equal to Chaim and I.

To be honest, I was a little bit suspicious of his behavior. Call it paranoia or just a feeling, but when I got back to the moshav I was going to get his identity number from accounting and add it to the list. On his payment stub would be his number. Also, I was going to add his mother's. But Aisha's name I would strike totally from the list. If she had been in trouble with the authorities, I didn't want to know.

Folding the list and squirming to put it in the back pocket of my jeans, I glimpsed, from the corner of my eye, Aisha looking at me. Within her eye was a twinkle which to me said it all.

"Are you and your sister the only children in your family, Selah?"

"Why no, Ari, we have two more brothers. Well, I mean two, one of my brothers died."

"I'm sorry . . ."

"That's okay, Ari, death is a friend that we all have."

"Right you are Selah," I said wanting to shift the discussion, "are they older or younger than you?"

"In order of our family, I'm the oldest, then was my brother Ibrahim, next brother my Nassir, and lastly my sister. And you, Ari?"

"I'm an only child, Selah, so is Chaim."

"I think the world is safer with no more like you two," laughed Selah.

I also broke into laughter. Guessing it was the spontaneity of it all, soon even Selah's mother began to laugh. The sudden upswing of the lines of her face must have signaled approval because Aisha too began to laugh. Soon all of the other workers became infected and joined in. No one really knew what was so funny in the first place, but everyone was seized by uncontrollable laughter.

"What's so funny?" Chaim asked as he drove up to the shed.

Everyone stopped momentarily as he spoke. The puzzled look on his face was more than I could bear. Laughing so hard at Chaim, I fell to my right side against Selah causing him to fall against the next person like dominoes.

"One big happy family, Ari," Chaim said, "I'll buy you a traditional black and white *keffiyeh* so you can fit in properly. I'm sure you would like that."

"If you only knew, Chaim, if you only knew," I muttered.

"Let's go, Ari, it's been a long day," Chaim said, "but I'll leave you here if you want."

For the next few minutes we unloaded our equipment from the truck and placed it in the shed. Looking around the room I thought of something which required a sacrifice on our part. Chaim's going to kill me for bringing it up.

"Selah, why don't you combine all of our junk from the end room into one of the others so your mother and sister can have a bit of privacy? You know, like you had it fixed up before the robbery."

"Are you sure, Ari?" asked Selah. "I thought Chaim said you needed . . ."

"It's okay," Chaim said, "besides the way all of you snore, they'd never get any sleep on the tree house. I've even heard the animals complaining."

"We'll bring a couple of cots from the moshav tomorrow," I added.

"No, you don't have to do that, the grass mats will be fine for them," Selah said not wanting to make more of an imposition than he already had.

"Nonsense, I insist," I finally said.

About thirty meters from the shed I turned around and looked back. With gracefulness of motion she lifted her head for one last look before I was out of sight. She smiled at me just before we went down the hill. Her smile again said it all.

FOURTEEN

Chaim sternly looked at me. "You can tell me, Ari."

"Tell you what?" I asked as we approached the vineyard.

"All week you have been acting, well, not yourself. One might say you have been even pleasant . . ."

"Oh! Yeah!" I interrupted. "What's that suppose to mean, Chaim?"

"Don't get me wrong," Chaim defended, "but ever since you came back from reserve duty in Gaza, you have appeared to be always preoccupied with what, I have no idea. Since the first of this week, I began seeing the old Ari."

"The old Ari?" I asked. "I'm only forty-one Chaim, how old have I been acting anyway . . . fifty . . . sixty?"

"No, Ari, not in years. You have been the Ari I knew all along or should I say the Ari you were until Vickie and you separated. I've seen you this week smile, be polite, notice flowers and birds . . . you know like you used to do."

Not knowing how to react, I just sat there with a dumb look on my face. What Chaim said I guess was true. Ever since my meeting Aisha face to face I had a different outlook on life. I'd been . . .

"Is it Vickie, Ari?" Chaim sheepishly asked. "Is there something going on between you two? Ari, you can tell me . . ."

"Chaim, there is nothing happening between Vickie and I. In a lot of respects I wished for so many years there would . . . could be something, but now it well might be too late for us."

"Ari, I don't think it will ever be too late for you and Vickie to get back together. Well, if it's not Vickie, then it's got to be someone else!"

"Let's just say for the time being it might be someone," I answered trying to stop the conversation.

"Aviva was right," Chaim said, "we talked about it last night. You know how she can be. She kept insisting you had to be in love."

"I wouldn't go that far, Chaim. It's just that I've met someone I find appealing and that is all!"

How could I lie to Chaim like that? I made it sound like a casual affair, yet it was anything but casual. During the past week I spent an endless amount of time trying to catch glimpses of Aisha. So much so I was sure Selah had become self-conscious about his work; my always popping up in whatever area they were working. At least I made him more productive.

Most times, Aisha didn't know I was there. I felt like a voyeur intruding on her privacy, but then there were times we would see each other and her face would light up. With each smile my heart was set ablaze. Almost always, though, her mother would appear having an uncanny way of heaving water on my flaming heart.

Aisha didn't always work among the rows with the others. Some days she spent under the friendly oak by the shed giving me ample opportunities. On those days, endlessly I needed water line parts, diesel fuel for the tractor, tools, etc. Any excuse was sufficient to go back to the shed. Those were the times Aisha played the voyeur watching my every move as I loaded and unloaded the truck. When I caught her staring, I would be rewarded with a smile.

So it was until yesterday by the carob trees near area two. At the time I was in a great hurry to find Selah. A valve burst near area five and I needed him to help me close the water, I drove over to Aisha to ask if she had seen him. As I pulled up under the trees, she stood and came close.

Innocently, I asked if she had seen her brother or knew where he was, Aisha staring at me like I was from outer space. Repeatedly I asked, but received no reply. All of a sudden I began to laugh. Of course she didn't answer, Aisha spoke no Hebrew. I might as well have been from outer space. Then I just said 'Selah' without any other accompanying words and Aisha seemed to understand what I wanted, pointing to area seven.

I started the truck in order to drive to area seven. Aisha approached my window before I put the truck in gear. Standing next to the truck, she placed her hand on my left forearm as it rested on the outside mirror. Her touch stopped my every motion. Oh! How I longed to feel that touch.

All thoughts of broken valves dissipated. Aisha mumbled something to me in Arabic as if she expected me to understand. While she spoke, she lifted her other hand which held a bag of chocolate wafers offering me something to eat. Apparently even Palestinian women knew the quickest way to a man's heart was through his stomach.

As I ate two wafers, I couldn't remove my eyes from hers. Although not a meal prepared for a king, those wafers had a taste beyond compare, however, in the heat the chocolate had melted, oozing onto my finger. Slowly Aisha began removing more wafers.

To her surprise I said thank you in Arabic. As she heard that word, her ever smile turned to a blush. Rosy red, her cheeks glistened. More chocolaty, oozing wafers were handed to me. As I feasted, I remembered the geyser of water from the broken valve. I held up my hand to signal no more. How to tell Aisha, without offending her, that I had to go?

"Selah," I just said, "Selah." Aisha lifted her hand and again pointed to area seven, understandably nodding her head. Oh! I didn't want to leave. Driving off, I kept licking my fingers vowing like a school boy never to wash her touch from my arm.

"You had better come back tonight and start spraying, Ari," Chaim said as we stopped to look at the first row.

"Wait a minute; we are not scheduled to start the next round for at least four days."

"I'm sorry, Ari, it looks like the last round of spraying Selah did wasn't effective. You'll have to start tonight."

Yesterday Aisha touched my arm. With each new day unfolded an expansion of our relationship and Chaim had to put a damper on my week. If I sprayed all night, I wouldn't be able to see Aisha during the day because I'd be sleeping on the moshav while she worked in the vineyard. Chaim was condemning me. Oh, Chaim, if you only knew.

"Maybe you should drop me off and go back to the moshav and get some rest," Chaim said.

"That's okay, Chaim. I'll just sleep by the shed in the tree house."

"Oh! Good gosh, Ari," Chaim screamed, "please, no more rainbows!"

Chaim dropped me by the shed and left to find Selah. For most of the morning I busied myself preparing the tractor and sprayer for the evening. The rest of the morning was spent hoping Aisha would return to the shed. She never came. I lay down under the towering oak and soon fell asleep. At least, I thought I would see Aisha in the early afternoon when our cousins finished work.

"Honk! Honk!"

I almost fell out of the tree house, Chaim honking feverishly below. Looking at my watch, only 11:30, I couldn't figure out why he woke me up.

"Ari, let's go," Chaim called out.

"Where?" I asked lifting my head barely enough to see him.

"Moshe just called on the radio. The tractor parts for the power take off just arrived in Tel Aviv. I'll drop you back at the moshav."

"Chaim, you don't have to go out of your way. I'll just stay here," I said not wanting to miss my opportunity to see Aisha.

"Don't flatter yourself, Ari, the parts arrived C.O.D. I have to go back to the moshav to pick up a check. It seems that our credit rating isn't so good," Chaim laughed, "probably a leftover from your days as moshav manager."

Climbing down I didn't want to even reply. Slanderous indeed were Chaim's comments, but more than likely true. Driving past the last rows onto the main road out of the vineyard, my heart sank. One thing I never could endure was separation.

Rainbows

Many times when I first started dating Vickie, I would physically feel ill if I didn't see her every day. After we were married, I had an opportunity for a special officer's course. At the time I had been contemplating a military career or I should say a first career. Since in the Israeli army you can become a senior officer at a young age, there was plenty of time left to pursue another career; army retirement benefits being nothing to write home about.

All hopes of an army life were abandoned during those few months of the course. We simply couldn't bear the separation. Even though in the Israeli army frequent leave was the rule rather than the exception, it wasn't enough. Our lives had become so close we both realized that we couldn't part from each other. Even now, to a certain degree, I'm sure Vickie would agree the separation still hurts.

But this time it was not seeing Aisha for a few days. If she hadn't touched my arm yesterday it might have been better. Maybe I could delay each morning going back to the moshav. At least, I would see her for a few moments before they went to work. No, I couldn't do that. Chaim needed the truck to come into the vineyard. What to do? Oh! What could I do?

Back on the moshav I made lunch. The vegetables in the salad looked so unappetizing; I opened a can of tuna fish and threw it on top instead of making a sandwich. At least the potato chips were crunchy.

After I finished cleaning up, I laid down on the couch. Soon I was dreaming about being the moshav's business manager. One of our banks had just called to say the winery check bounced. The bank apologized, but they were returning our checks.

"Chaim! Let go of my arm!"

"I didn't mean to scare you, Ari, but I knocked on the door. When you didn't answer, I assumed you were sleeping. Thinking about your you know who?"

"My you know what?"

"You know; the somebody you told me about."

"No, Chaim, I was explaining to the bank."

"Ari, bank? . . . Never mind," Chaim said. "I want you to start spraying the back areas tonight. Selah has already filled the sprayer and the tractor will be by area sixteen so you don't even have to waste time by the shed."

"Thanks a lot, Chaim," I said, disappointed.

"And since it was really late notice," Chaim continued, "Selah's agreed to finish spraying if you need him too. He'll be asleep in the tree house. You'll have to wake him if you want him to spray. Otherwise, if you feel you can last the night, let him sleep. I've got a full day for him tomorrow."

"I'll make it okay, Chaim," I said staring out the window.

"Oh! One other thing," Chaim said matter-of-factly, "his mother's going back to their village tomorrow morning. Can you believe it; Selah is married and has a little boy."

"What's that got to do with his mother leaving?" I asked happy to be rid of my chaperone.

"Since his mother is staying in the vineyard he asked if his son could come for a couple of weeks. I told him it would be okay," Chaim said, "any problems?"

"By herself?"

"By who's self, Ari?"

"Is his mother going back to the village by herself?"

"No," Chaim answered, "his sister's going too. They'll be back by the end of next week before Ramadan begins. It's funny, Ari, since they've been here the shed area always looks clean. Selah and the others don't go off joyriding at night as much on the tractor either. I'm even going to miss them. What about you Ari?" Chaim asked.

"Me too, Chaim, me too," I said as my heart slowly slid to the ground.

"They might even have gone by now," Chaim added, "if Selah could arrange a ride. Better hurry to the vineyard, there's a lot to do tonight. Spraying is critical, Ari."

"You're so right, Chaim," I said, "there's a lot I need to do tonight.

FIFTEEN

Finally it began to cool off. One good thing about the Israeli sun, when it leaves the sky for the night everything becomes cooler. It was very comfortable driving in the valley. Spraying should be uneventful, I thought, since I'd be using our tractor. Borrowing a tractor was okay for an emergency, but the one we were using wasn't as powerful as ours nor did it take corners as well. My only real problem was not seeing Aisha.

I spoke too soon. About a hundred meters in front of me in the middle of the road was a large pile of rocks. Menacing as those road blocks were, you still had to be careful. First, the builders were probably hiding in the trees or rocks above waiting for an opportunity to throw stones at you. Second, in some cases, innocent piles of rocks have been booby trapped. Prior to their removal, each rock had to come under close scrutinization. And last, but not least, it was surely a sign of ninjas. Many a smart person tried to go around the rocks only to sit on the road side with multiple tire punctures.

Getting out of the truck, I withdrew my revolver from my belt. Approaching the mass of rocks, I heard whistling. Immediately, I loaded a round into my gun's chamber and started shooting in the air. Once, twice, by the third shot the whistling stopped. In the distance, I could make out maybe three teenagers running as fast as they could up the hillside to their village.

Whistling signaled trouble was about to start. During the outset of the Intifada, it was used to convey simple commands such as attack or retreat. I learned during my reserve duties in Gaza, it had been developed into a bona fide method of communication among the young Palestinians. Various rising and falling notes gave one command while high pitched shrills another.

Usually a couple of shots in the air sent them packing. Most youths didn't want a martyr's death. Couple that with Israelis really not wanting to harm anyone meant in most cases no one got hurt. Unfortunately, it had become like a sick game. When deadly weapons were involved, there always existed a chance of severe damage to person and property. Maybe Vickie was right about guns after all. But a rock in the hand of a kid was definitely as deadly a weapon as my gun.

As I began removing the rocks from the road, an army patrol came by. I explained what had transpired to their satisfaction. The young lieutenant in charge gave me a stern lecture about discharging my revolver. We both took it in stride given the circumstances. He also informed me ahead were the remains of burning tires, probably from the same group.

In my truck I had a large bag of cookies I brought to munch on while spraying. Walking back I decided, to give the soldiers the cookies. I got the bag and approached their jeep, forcefully insisting they take the cookies. Unfortunately, I told the group of young soldiers, I knew all too well what night patrols were like. I was sure that their night would prove more eventful than mine. They capitulated.

True to Selah's efficiency, I found the tractor fueled and the sprayer ready to begin. The wind was still too strong to start so I sat on a group of rocks to wait. Of course all I could think of was Aisha. Should I or shouldn't I make up some kind of excuse to go to the shed? Before I could make up my mind, the wind died down. Chaim's insistence the night's spraying was critical still rang in my ears. Within moments the sound of the tractor echoed among the hills.

Every precaution was taken during spraying. All of the chemicals we used were highly toxic. Certain ones were prohibited for use at least a month prior to harvest. As a kid I remember my mother always nagging that I wash fruit before I ate it. For the life of me I never understood why. To me the fruit never looked dirty. Since I

110

know how deadly the sprays could be, I'm extremely careful about washing fruit.

I dressed in extensively protective gear, wearing a heavy plastic rain jacket and pants. On my head was a rather expensive looking space helmet fully equipped with a blower; a pleasure to wear during the hot summer months. Air forcing itself from the inside to the outside through a filter kept contaminated air from entering the helmet. It worked under the same principle as an active filtration gas mask.

Until finishing the nights spraying, you never took the protective gear off. One night I ran out of pesticide, so I walked back to the shed to get another three liters. On the way, I evidently passed one of the new kids Selah brought to work squatting among the trees answering nature's call.

Under the light of the full moon, I must have reflected quite an image. All of a sudden I heard a blood curdling scream. Turning toward its direction, I saw a kid running back to the shed with his pants down around his knees screaming as he went. I must have laughed for a good fifteen minutes.

About midnight I had finished about a third of what I needed to spray. Already getting tired, I pulled the tractor near a group of rocks by the top of the area. Planning only to take a short break, I left the tractor idling under some trees while I sat on the ground and made myself comfortable. Sipping the coffee Aviva made for me, I wished I'd kept a couple of the cookies I gave the soldiers for myself.

Looking at the sky I realized in the next few days there would be a new moon. Ramadan was to start soon, a major holy month for our cousins. I never really understood all of its meanings except their not eating during the day. When evening came, however, they feasted. How they survived working all day without food or water was beyond me. Certainly they had more religious dedication than I did. We allowed them to begin work at four o'clock in the morning during Ramadan. By the time it got blistering hot, their work day was finished.

Moonlight always had a way of relaxing me. Against the white sands between the rows of trees, the moonbeams seemed to bounce back toward the sky. The crisp, cool evening air made me feel sleepy. So, I decided I'd better drink another cup of coffee. Besides, it gave me more time to think about Aisha.

Suddenly from behind hearing a noise, I sat motionless trying to determine if it was an animal, a person or just my imagination. Nothing. Silence can sometimes be so loud your ears would ring from it. There it was, this time I was sure it was a person stepping on twigs. Army training had always taught me to remain calm and think before acting, however, time was of the essence. I had to react quickly before I was attacked, my every movement being watched. Slowly I slid my hand under my rain pants to withdraw my loaded revolver.

My plan of action was to quickly slide my gun out as I rolled on the ground making one complete turn to the left. Reaching my stomach, I would aim in the direction of the noise assured my rolling would commit whoever it was to action; my choice to shoot or not only being made after I stopped rolling and saw who it was. That would give me at least a split second to make my decision.

Inhaling very deeply, I yelled . . . "Now!" I rolled to the left as if I had hit ground after falling from a plane during a parachute drop, my right leg hitting a sharply pointed rock. The pain was intense, but I had no time to worry about it, adrenalin pumping throughout my entire body. Landing fully on my stomach, I saw the image of a person to the side of a large pine tree about twenty meters ahead.

Appearing as if he chose not to commit himself, he crouched next to the tree. If he was friendly he would have shouted out when I rolled and pulled out my revolver. Surely if his intent was on harming me, he'd maneuver to the best vantage point. The tree was perfect in that respect.

My mind made up, I pulled back on the hammer of my revolver. Pinpointing the gun's barrel I readied my arm to shoot, a cold sweat bursting from my pores. Suddenly I was back in the Sinai Desert twenty years earlier with gunfire all around. Yigal had just been killed and I smelled the smoke from his half track as it blazed against the sands. Steadily my finger slid over the trigger. My life or his held in balance on the next second. I began squeezing the . . .

"Aisha!" I yelled as I threw my revolver down. All I could think about was going to her. Running, I felt blood oozing from my leg, but surprisingly there was no pain. The few meters till I reached Aisha seemed so distant, each step an eternity.

Staring at her I didn't know what to do unable to turn my eyes away from her. Against the moonlight glittering through the trees, she never looked more beautiful. Slowly my faculties returned, but composing my thoughts wasn't easy. Still in front of me was the image of myself squeezing the trigger of my gun. How could I have reacted so quickly . . . so rashly . . . ?

Dropping to one knee in front of her, I knew what to do. As the wind blew my hair, I began saying a prayer for the first time in over twenty years. Yet at that moment, my soul cried out to be heard. I begged for strength never to aim a gun at another person as long as I lived. Vickie had been right all along.

Lowering my head, I felt a serenity of purpose realizing how in the past I only appreciated someone after it was too late. Looking at Aisha, I vowed never to make that mistake again. If only I knew some Arabic or she spoke some Hebrew. Then maybe . . .

"You're hurt," Aisha said to me in accented English.

"You speak English?" I excitedly asked, "Are you okay?"

"Why, yes I am, thank you," she smiled. "Did you think I was a snake?"

"Did I think you were a what?" I asked trying to understand. Maybe she made a mistake in her choice of words.

"My brother told me you carry a gun because you are afraid of snakes," Aisha giggled.

I gazed at my little leprechaun embellishing laughter from the deep recesses of her soul. For weeks I'd imagined what it would be like just to talk to Aisha spending literally hours trying to decide what would our first conversation entail. I had become frustrated in my growing attraction to her because neither of us spoke the other's language. English! Imagine that. I was glad Vickie had spent so much time improving my English.

"I'm very sorry," I said, "I could have . . . are you sure you are okay? Why didn't you let me know it was you when I started rolling? You could have been . . ."

"I did not know what you were trying to do. When I saw you with your gun, I became frightened. In my village when someone has a gun, death is always in the shadows. Your leg!" Aisha continued, "Sit here and let me see it."

Aisha took a light, blue scarf from her neck. With my knife she slit my jeans and rain suit past the cut and began wiping the blood from the wound. All of a sudden she got up and began looking for something in the brush. Returning, she had pulled some leaves from a plant. Placing them on the wound, she tied her scarf around my leg to hold the leaves in place.

"These will help stop the bleeding and keep the cut from becoming too painful," Aisha said.

"I am called Ari."

"I know. I am Aisha, the sister of Selah."

"Does Selah know that you are here?"

"I should say not. I am leaving tomorrow and I just wanted . . . I mean, I could . . ."

"You don't have to say anything, Aisha, I think I know," I smiled. "Now that I can talk to you using English there is so much I want to ask."

"Ari, don't you need to continue spraying?" Aisha asked as she got up. "I know I had better return before my mother wakes and discovers I am not next to her."

"Wait!" I said grasping her right hand as she turned to walk away, "please only a few more moments."

Silently Aisha sat down beside me, still holding my hand. We talked, only moments earlier my almost killing her. Before we could only look at each other from different worlds, now we spoke to each other so naturally. Wasn't it fitting, I thought, we had to communicate in a language foreign to both of us, a bridge between our two worlds.

"Tell me, please, how is it that you understand English well, but not a word of Hebrew?"

"Hebrew is not taught in our schools, only Arabic and English. We lived in Jordon, Ari, not Israel," Aisha answered.

"Where do people like your brother learn Hebrew if it is not taught in schools?"

"Hebrew to us is only a language for work. Among the Israelis one needs to know your language. Since women are prohibited from working, I never had an opportunity to learn."

"Aisha, I have one very hard question to ask. Why on earth do you have any interest in getting to know me? I am at least old enough to be your father. In these times to speak to an Israeli, let alone be here with one, places you at risk among your own people. Yet, you steal away in the middle of the night to . . ."

"Ari, why do you sit here to talk to me?" Aisha asked. "I believe that may well be my answer to you."

"Aisha, it's just that . . ."

"Let's not ask too many questions now, Ari, you need to continue spraying and I must return to the shed before I'm noticed."

"Aisha, let me walk you part of the way back," I begged.

"Okay, Ari, but not too close to the shed."

We got up and walked down a narrow goat path through the woods. Going only about ten meters, my leg began to burn inside with pain. About five meters ahead was a clearing. When we reached it, I laid down on the soft grass. Aisha took my knife and completely cut my jeans off just above the wound. Shredding them to make a fresh bandage, she discarded her scarf.

"Please, let me have your scarf. I'll clean it on the moshav and return it to you," I said.

"You will never be able to clean the blood stains. It's not important to me."

"Just the same, I'd like to try." I put the scarf in my left back pocket.

"Ari, I do not think you will be able to continue spraying. Maybe you should wake my brother and ask him to finish. He is half expecting it anyway."

Aisha was right. My leg had started to swell. Selah would probably have to finish, but later. I wanted to spend as much time with Aisha as possible. Oh, how I didn't want the night to end.

Looking at Aisha, I realized how deeply in love I had become. Under the moonlight she appeared to be a vision, not real. Yet, more than ever, I knew she was very real indeed. There we sat Israeli and Palestinian together with nothing mattering to each of us except the other. I prayed the night would be more than ephemeral.

"I'm leaving the vineyard tomorrow. My mother does not want me to return with her when she brings my nephew. She feels not being married; I shouldn't be around so many young men," Aisha began, "which is why many times she had me stay by the shed instead of work in the rows."

"I don't think you have to worry. I've seen Selah handle people who speak badly of you. Recently a red haired, blue eyed kid . . ."

"I know," interrupted Aisha, "a couple of years ago I was supposed to marry his brother."

"That explains a lot," I mumbled under my breath.

"What did you say, Ari?"

"You said you were going to be married. Why didn't you go through with it?" cautiously I asked.

"My father gave me permission a long time ago that I didn't have to marry a man unless I wanted to. Several times I thought I did, but in the end I realized how shallow those men were. If he didn't support me in my decisions, I would have been forced to get married," Aisha explained.

"Getting married is the easy part," I said, "staying married is where it gets complicated."

"My brother told me that you once were married. He said your wife seemed to be a special woman, yet now you two are not together. Why?"

"Let's just say the same people who got married didn't live together," I answered not wanting to ruin the moment at hand by thoughts of Vickie.

"Ari, you are the first Israeli I have ever talked to, but I feel that you are not like the rest," Aisha said in a serious tone. "The first time I saw you by the shed I sensed you were different."

"Then why did you run from me that day? What did I do?" I finally asked after weeks of wanting to know.

"You were naked from the waist up. It is not proper for a girl to be alone with a man like that. I didn't know if you were going to take the rest of your clothes off."

"Is it also not proper for you to be here with me now, Aisha?"

"Ari, please don't question my actions. I am here and that tells a story unto itself."

"You remember the first time I saw you. Well, I had just seen a rainbow when suddenly an image . . ." And with that I told Aisha how I first saw her at the end of my rainbow. We spent the next moments in simple conversation. So natural it was to speak to each other, talking as if we had been friends for ages. Together, however, for the first time I began to explore feelings I'd never known existed.

"Ari, I really must go back," begged Aisha.

"I'll walk with you then. You are right, Selah will have to finish spraying; I can't."

Approaching the shed, I saw Selah coming down from the tree house. What to do? I couldn't let him see us together because that would compromise more than just Aisha. I wanted to wait and let Aisha go in by herself. She could tell Selah she had gone for a walk or needed the toilet. Aisha, on the other hand, said she knew her brother well. He would never suspect anything except the best of her.

"Selah," I said before he had noticed us, "you'd better tell your sister the vineyard is not a safe place to stroll around late at night. You see, she even ran into me and I'm probably as bad as anything out here."

Selah at first showed no emotion. Then slowly the right corner of his mouth cracked into a smile.

"What's happened to your leg, Ari?"

"I stopped to take a break and while I was walking, lost my balance on a rock. I think you're going to have to finish spraying. My leg's beginning to really hurt."

"You do have a problem, Ari," agreed Selah.

By the time Selah answered, Aisha had already sneaked back into the shed without waking her mother. Through the shadows, I could see her looking at me.

"Ari, thank you for watching out for my little sister; I agree the vineyard's no place for her. Maybe when she goes back to the village tomorrow she'll remain."

"I thought you wanted," I interrupted, "her to care for your son? How old did you say he was?"

"Maybe you are right, Ari, we'll see," Selah answered.

Walking back to the tractor with Selah, I wanted to plead with him to allow Aisha to return to the vineyard. At one point my leg hurt so much Selah had to help me walk. Inside the truck was a small first aid kit which contained codeine tablets and I couldn't wait to take them.

As we approached, the tractor was still running. Selah asked where I left off spraying. Seeing how much was left to do, he asked that I leave Chaim a note in the truck not to wake him. Selah would get the others started working early. About the same time a taxi was suppose to come pick up his mother and sister to take them back to Deir El-Salam. He'd wake up about noon and help Chaim then.

Back on the moshav, I thought of waking the nurse to attend to my leg, but decided whatever Aisha had done would suffice until morning. I crashed into bed without taking off my clothes. Tomorrow I'd have to wash them and my bedding because of the chemicals from the sprays. The codeine began to work very well. Soon I escaped into my dreams . . . of Aisha.

SIXTEEN

Staring at the clock in utter disbelief, I laid in my bed contemplating how could it possibly be almost five o'clock in the afternoon? Then I realized I'd lost track of taking those codeine pills. Riding home, the pain grew so intense; I kept eating them like candy. I tried lifting my head pounding something awful like a hangover only from the codeine.

Rolling out of bed, I could hardly walk on my leg. I hobbled over to the moshav nurse's house knowing she was going to yell at me for not coming during clinic hours. Removing the bloody, rag bandage, she was amazed that the wound hadn't become infected. She wanted to know what kind of plant it was and could I bring her home some of it. Pleading ignorance, I told her one of the Palestinians in the vineyard gave it to me. Well, that part was true.

With a clean, new bandage on my leg the nurse told me not to work for a couple of days. Under her breath I heard her say, "Fat chance he will!" My reputation as a workaholic haunted me on the moshav. One thing I didn't look forward to was taking a shower with a plastic garbage bag taped around my knee to keep the wound dry for three days. I knew I should have taken a shower before I went to the nurse.

Back home I made myself something to eat, a breakfast, lunch and supper special consisting of scrambled eggs, a tuna fish sandwich and four day old fried chicken. The crowning touch was an ice cold two liter bottle of cola. For desert I devoured a box of chocolate sandwich cookies. Laughingly, I thought of sending my menu to a gourmet food magazine.

Searching the whole house, I was hard pressed to find another pair of jeans. Usually I wore the same pair every day for three or four months or until the jeans literally died. Last night Aisha had destroyed my jeans making bandages. Pity, they were only three months old. Instead, I had to settle for a pair of my army trousers.

Putting my hand in the back pocket of my trousers, I found a piece of paper left over from my reserve duty in Gaza. Unfolding the paper, I recognized it was a leaflet from the leadership of the uprising. Just the thought of that name made me laugh. Almost weekly the competing factions of the Intifada released those leaflets. Their purpose was a cross between a newsletter and a hate mail usually condemning what had occurred during the week toward advancing the peace process. Most importantly, they contained the scheduled days of general strikes.

General strikes were called as a protest or for just about any reason. Calling a strike was a very serious political game. On the Palestinian side, by ordering a strike, it made them feel in control. The army had the power to close a village down by curfew, but when a strike was called, the army was impotent to have life go on as normal. Palestinian popular committees were used to force merchants to close their stores on strike days, with few exceptions such as pharmacies.

Not wanting the Palestinians to be in control, the army spent endless amounts of time in vain forcing Palestinian store owners to stay open, rarely succeeding. I would say the majority of Palestinians enjoyed general strike days at the beginning of the Intifada. Time off was welcome after almost never being allowed an annual vacation from work. Lately every week a strike was being called by some petty, political group. Often the leaflets revealed the internal bickering of one group calling a strike while a second group urged the people to disregard the other's strike.

If Palestinian day laborers didn't work, they didn't get paid. While the strikes cost the Israeli gross national product untold losses, they also harmed the individual Palestinian. At the end of the month his pay packet was thinner because the more strike days the fewer days he worked.

To help support from other Arab countries money was smuggled in. Most villages received sums of money to partially assist the individual worker. Each person was eligible to receive a nominal payment from those funds.

Curiously enough, Selah and the others always worked on strike days. Once I asked him about it, thinking he didn't care for the politics of strikes. He explained, however, it was all economics. In his village the person in charge of their fund had no scruples. Most of the monies he received from outside went into his pocket. Therefore, the amount Selah and the others would receive was so paltry they decided it was better to work for full wage than strike.

"Ari, are you awake yet?" Chaim asked as he bolted through the door of my house.

"Just barely," I answered, "just barely."

"Relax," he said, "Selah's going to spray tonight. He told me you seriously cut your leg last night. I just came from the nurse. Very impressive, Ari, you actually went to see her before your leg had to be amputated."

"Funny, Chaim!"

"Go ahead and take a couple of days off. You are no use to me lame," Chaim laughed. "You must have had some night partner." Chaim reached into his haversack and pulled out my revolver.

"Oh! My God!"

"That's right, Ari, it's your gun. Bet you didn't even miss it, did you?" Chaim continued. "I guess when you fell on the rocks, it must have dislodged from your holster."

"Where on earth did you get it, Chaim?"

"Believe it or not Abu Ali brought it by the shed. One of his boys was grazing sheep around where you fell and found it."

"You know what would have happened if I had lost my revolver?"

"Just be glad it was your personal gun," Chaim lectured, "if it was your army gun, I'd be visiting you in jail for the next seven years."

"Can you believe Abu Ali?" I asked in amazement. "Any Palestinian who finds a gun these days becomes an instant hero. Think of it."

"I'm not surprised," Chaim said, "most of our older cousins don't have a taste for the Intifada or its politics. They've been around too long and seen too much to be duped by another political tide rolling in. Most really just want to live out their remaining years in peace and quiet."

"I guess you're right, Chaim."

"Say, Ari, what's that hanging from your jeans pocket on the floor," Chaim asked as he bent down to my jeans before I could pull them away.

"Some nice bandage you got here. Your blood or someone else's on the scarf?"

"Let me have it back, Chaim," I demanded.

"Could it have belonged to miss you know who?" Chaim said as he dangled it in front of me just out of my reach.

"Chaim, give me the damn scarf—*Now!*"

"Okay! Okay!" Chaim said as he threw the blood soaked piece of material at my feet. "Oh, Ari, one other thing," Chaim said as he stood in the doorway to leave," Selah said we can take the beds back to the moshav. His mother and sister are not returning to the vineyard."

Chaim's bombshell left a rather large crater in my heart. All I could do was just to stare at the walls. Sill numb, trying not to think about what it would mean to my life if Aisha didn't return I went into the kitchen with Aisha's scarf in hand. Try as I did the bloodstains wouldn't come out. It was clean, but stained nonetheless. That was okay since I never had intention of returning it to her. Now it could very well be all I would have left. I held it so tightly in my hands water began to drip onto the floor.

While I was still staring into space, the telephone rang. At first I wasn't going to answer it. I knew it was Vickie, slowly picking up the receiver. I could always tell when Vickie was trying to contact me.

"Chaim told me."

"My leg is fine. Chaim told me you were in Eilat with someone?"

"Ari, I know Chaim didn't say it was someone. Stop always fishing. You might not like what's at the end of the line one day," Vickie curtly said.

"Well, what is it then?" I asked out of curiosity more than anything else.

Vickie said it was the society of something or other. I never really paid much attention to all of her organizations. She got that from her father to be sure. The pair of them were always off crusading on white horses somewhere together; never in my opinion for the right causes. Or as Vickie was fond of saying, she championed the left causes while I caused the right.

I remember once, before we were married, I had a strong difference of opinion with Vickie over a policy of our government. The issue dealt with the introduction into the coalition agreement of religious parties or something of that nature. My Dad happened to be in Jerusalem at the time for one of his very rare sojourning away from the kibbutz.

He sensed immediately I was a little down about something. We walked to a small park to talk. At a street side vendor I bought a falafel while he ate something from a brown paper bag my mother had made. As we sat down to eat, I poured my heart out to him. Then my Dad put his strong hand on my shoulder saying maybe I was the one who had the problem understanding Vickie's view. He added, of course, Vickie's views were so left of center they might fall off the edge. Nonetheless, I should see where she was coming from. I said to him that if he agreed with my assessment of her views, how could he advocate such a thing? Finishing his food, he gave me one of those rare jewels only he could find.

"Ari, do you love her or not?" he asked. "If you are serious about her, then you must agree to what I'm about to say. Never and I mean never talk to her about politics or religion."

"But Dad," I said, "ours is a relationship built on trust and commitment."

Try as I could to dissuade my Dad, he remained unaltered in his statement, insisting the greatest virtues in a marriage were peace and harmony. That was, he said, more important than being each other's evening news broadcast and added I should never listen to Vickie's father at all on either subject.

"Just hearing his views could warp my sense of right and wrong," he said.

Later that night I had a date with Vickie. Keeping to heart his advice, I told her maybe we needed to establish a few ground rules to our relationship. She laughed at my suggestion to keep political and religious discussions from our lives. Realizing I was very serious, she agreed. Telling Vickie it was my Dad's suggestion made it more palatable.

When she laughingly told her father later about it, wholeheartedly he endorsed the idea. Given my extremely rightist views, he felt Vickie would be safer. We accepted that doctrine as our way of life together and for a long time it worked. Our sages of old praised children who honored their father's wishes. That was the only thing our two fathers ever agreed upon. Vickie and I did talk about current trends in Israel. You can't be an Israeli and not be political, but we knew when our discussion reached the proper limits. Unfortunately, the times in which we lived knew no limits.

SEVENTEEN

To me there is little difference between urban and bane. Most people who live in the metropolitan Tel Aviv area aren't aware there exists another dimension to Israel; another world entirely. Once, while visiting Vickie's parents in their Ramat Aviv home, a neighbor came over to me and asked if I was on reserve duty at the moment. Puzzled, I asked why.

"Because you are carrying a gun," he replied. I began explaining to him where I lived. He admitted he never knew that anyone really lived in the occupied territories as he called them. What ensued was a rather heated debate with extremely differing opinions on the affairs of state. Vickie's father ended the discussion by commenting on whom I voted for in the last election.

"Oh! One of them," the neighbor smirked.

I used to joke with Vickie about having to travel through the tunnel to get to Tel Aviv—tunnel vision. She never saw the humor of it.

Mevo Ayalon to some was indeed very remote. Surrounded by a dozen or so Palestinian villages, people fostered the idea the land was theirs not ours, however, the opposite was true. It was the residents of Tel Aviv, Haifa and the Ramat Gan that lived in isolated areas, not us. Pristine in its natural beauty, Mevo Ayalon and other Jewish settlements represented the true epitome of living the land of Israel. Our Sages of old called upon us to dwell in the land, not as many believed in an artificial world bereft our people's values.

To that end I decided I would spend some time touring the city of gold, Jerusalem. As I approached the capital after driving up the steep hills of the forest lined highway, I remembered learning in school that in the days of old our people sojourned on foot to the Holy Temple in Jerusalem during the three pilgrimage festivals. Funny, even until today we referred to a person's going up to Jerusalem; a city of the highest levels; a holy city where a person elevated even his soul.

Jerusalem is holy not only to our people, but to others as well; how true that was. Sadly, access to her holy places was severely restricted until Jerusalem returned to our hands. Given the varied opinions in Israel on how to achieve peace, one thing was almost unanimously agreed upon. Jerusalem would remain forever the united capital of our country, her return the most glorious triumph of the Six Day War. Today anyone could freely worship their chosen way within her holy confines.

Of all the places in Jerusalem I liked to visit the most was naturally the Old City where I first met Vickie. During the past few years, massive excavations of the Cardo, the main north-south street in the Ancient Roman city, the sight of the Roman era markets had revealed much more of her splendor. Since the intifada, however, sections of the Old City were not readily visited by Israelis anymore; once frequented cafes of the Arab quarter becoming taboo.

A visit to the Old City was never complete without going to the Western Wall, the last vestige of the Holy Temple built by King Solomon. To construct the Temple the king drafted 3,300 people to oversee over 150,000 Jewish workers, taking seven years to complete. Two thousand years ago the Temple, with all its beauty and national, religion and social significance, was totally destroyed by the Roman Legions.

Since reunification in 1967, it had become once again the focal point for the whole country. Frequent visitors often were treated to the latest group of young Israelis being sworn in as members of our Defense Forces by the Western Wall. Pledging their lives to defend our country, the young men and women vowed Jerusalem would forever remain united.

Sitting on the back of the plaza, I watched as multitudes tried to squeeze notes in between the wall's cracks. A time honored custom, in the cracks of its massive stones have been stuffed scraps of parchment, cloth and paper containing the prayers and longing of countless Jews. The wall has ears, Jews say; it hears the prayers of its children, it absorbs the tremulously written prayers they place in its crevices.

Caustically, I once teased Vickie for putting a note in the cracks of the woman's section. "Of all people Vickie, you went to the separated sexist area to talk to a stone wall?" I mocked.

"I placed a note asking that you will always love me as I love you," she chided.

Suddenly the air was filled with the call to prayer from the mosque on the Temple Mount. The muezzin's cry echoed throughout the surrounding valley. A big question entered my mind. How could the world demand the de-unification of the holy city?

Below were flocks of black garbed Jewish people at prayer. Directly in front of me were dozens of Christian tourists from an Italian cruise ship listening to their guide. To the side a small group from Japan. On top, Palestinians assembled for prayer. Jew, Arab and Christian observed their separate beliefs in harmony. Merely two decades ago, that scene would have been impossible to observe, free access denied. Why did the world insist on turning a blind eye to that fact?

For me, the Western Wall held a more personal meaning and of late my rarely visiting there on purpose. Each time I sat and stared at the ancient wall, I was reminded of my meeting Vickie, relishing unto today those precious moments. I could still see Vickie by her menorah lighting her ninth candle.

"Do you believe someone really reads and answers the prayers people place in the cracks of the wall?" a solider asked me.

Not being religious, the question was tantamount to asking if fairy tale characters were real. I've always insisted on honesty in return for curiosity. Were giants real?

"I'm not really sure," I answered, "look below. What do you see?"

"A lot of people," he replied.

"Not only our people, but Christians and Arabs as well pouring their hearts out. It's not easy for a person to reveal his innermost needs and pains. Do you," I continued, "think that they would do it if they believed no one would answer?"

"I guess not," he said.

"Then I suppose the answer to your question is yes. Whatever you asked for will be answered." I then thought again about what Vickie had inserted in the cracks.

"Good!" the solider sighed. "I am going to Gaza next week." I stood, hugging him with all my might. "Yes," I said emphatically, "Notes and prayers are definitely answered. Do not worry!" I assured him.

Turning for a moment to capture one last look of the wall, I noticed the very old, bent frame of a man dressed in long black coat approaching the wall. Laboriously he lifted his right arm barely high enough to place a folded piece of paper into a crack. His face revealed all the hope he could muster that his plea should be heard. Was it possible his request really would be answered? What about the other notes, they also? I just wonder.

Walking around the Old City gave me a tremendous appetite. Nothing less than a whole pizza pie would do. I decided one more stop was in order. With my pizza and cold soda begging to be consumed, I drove to Ammunition Hill. Under the shade of an olive tree I feasted like royalty.

Ammunition Hill was a favorite spot for Vickie and me. Webbing the landscape was a maze of trenches left from the Six Day War. As the sun slowly descended, the cool winds began to blow. I just stood with the expansive view before me. Ammunition Hill, prior to the Six Day War, was Jordan's most fortified stronghold in Jerusalem. On that hill the Jordanian Army blocked our approach to Mount Scopus and the Old City thereafter. In a desperate, bloody battle, we were successful in its capture literally hand to hand combat the order of the day. And when the fighting was all over, thirty-six brave Israeli paratroopers, two Chaim and I knew from jump school, were added to the martyred defenders of our people.

A memorial museum stands where once the Jordanian command bunker was. Olive trees were planted on Ammunition Hill as a living representation of each of the one hundred and eighty three who perished during the battle for Jerusalem.

Rapidly the sun descending into evening, I knew where I wanted to cap the day. Quickly I got into my car and sped back in the direction of the Old City. Staring at the memorial olive trees had reminded me of a place Vickie and I frequented often, but now many years since I'd been there.

Travelling through East Jerusalem, I arrived at the foot of the Mount of Olives. Famous for its legendary happenings in the Christian world, it held an even deeper and sadder place in our people's hearts. Surrounding the hill was probably the largest and oldest continuous Jewish cemetery in existence. The truly and the not so truly religious died wishing that spot would be their eternal resting place; a little earth from there always finding its place into the coffins of Jews the world over.

Approaching the Intercontinental Hotel, I was stopped by an army roadblock. The sergeant in charge explained that some youths had stoned a bus of Christian tourists so they were sealing off the area. I pleaded that all I wanted was to view the sunset over the Old City. His insistent advice directed at my welfare was to no avail; I out ranked him.

Parking the car in the lot in front of the hotel, how beautiful the setting sun was. I sat on the hood of the car, watching in utter amazement at the light show before me, the city line a remarkable contrast. Against the Old City's wall rising in the background was the newer, more modern Jerusalem.

Within minutes the rather large, red ball of light appeared literally to rest on the city wall. Then, as it began to disappear, her colors spread in all directions. As the top of the disc slid below the wall itself, the sky exploded with one of the most beautiful sunsets I had ever seen.

Clearly, Jerusalem was held above all else by those who lived within her confines; be they Israeli, Arab or Christian. Yet, she had always been targeted for terrorist activity. The city cried out in pain with each occurrence. Seeing her so beautiful before me, I was full of rage at anyone who could dare break her peacefulness.

The Jewish sages of old said that ten measures of beauty were given to the world. Nine measures were given to Jerusalem and one to the rest of the world. Watching the sunset, it was easy to see they were correct.

During the entire day I realized I had virtually no thoughts of Aisha, Jerusalem the exclusive domain of Vickie, an unsettling thought. All I could think about for weeks was Aisha. Now, she escaped me. Why?

Getting back into the car, I took one last look at Jerusalem; a day I would cherish for a long time to come. In many respects, I wished Vickie had been there to share it with me; in some respects she had.

As I drove one last time though the city, I was reminded of the immortal words of King David. Truly he said it best in his Psalm:

> *"If I forget thee O' Jerusalem, let my right hand lose its cunning.*
> *Let my tongue stick to my palate if I remember you not.*
> *If I set not Jerusalem above my greatest joy."*

EIGHTEEN

In order to reach the moshav from Jerusalem, I had to trek an old Jordanian road which wound its way through two Palestinian villages. Plans were drawn up several years ago by the government to build a new road bypassing the villages. The road, however, was a political causality in the last election, its backers losing out in the coalition. Mercifully the Intifada had placed the road once again on the agenda.

Approaching the village of El-Azrear, the smaller of the two villages I needed to pass, about fifty meters ahead I saw the flashing amber light of an army jeep and sped to follow them through the village. Five minutes later I was out. Slowly the jeep pulled to the right side of the road, stopped, honked and waved as I passed.

Both villages had been the scene during the last couple of weeks of increased stoning incidences. Instituting a new policy, the army dealt more severely with stone throwers. In other areas, the next day, after an incident, giant bulldozers unearthed groups of trees along the roadside that had given protection to the rock throwers. That policy was beginning to have effective results.

Nearing the village of Beit HaTarr, I looked ahead to see if there was an army presence. Seeing none, I decided caution was in order. I stopped, rolled up the windows and loaded a round into the chamber of my revolver, released the safety and laid my revolver beside my right leg on the seat.

Entering the village, I slowed to less than half the posted speed limit. To minimize the impact of a thrown stone, speed reduction was in order. Most people mistakenly speed through a Palestinian village. Unfortunately, a rock hitting a speeding car shatters the glass brutally attacking the passengers inside.

I proceeded with my headlights off, the moon giving plenty of light to maneuver down the narrow streets. Hopefully if there were any stone throwers around, they might not see my coming. Sheer surprise and luck might vanguard my escaping unharmed.

Ahead on the top of a two story house, I saw two teenagers looking down, but further on the street appeared deserted. Since it was still early evening, I took it as a bad omen. If there was a crowd of people walking or children playing, no trouble would be in sight. The situation was not looking good.

Rounding the last corner of the village, only two more houses till I was out. The road began a sharp decline toward the valley below. Between the last two houses I thought I spotted silhouettes. Nothing! I began to think all my worry had been for naught. Only a few meters to the last house at the apex of the road remained to be passed.

Whistling began.

As I approached the end of the last house, I felt safe when suddenly . . . *bam*! . . . *bam*! . . . pelted from all sides. *Crash*! The back window shattered into a thousand pieces. I looked up and saw Palestinians . . . kids . . . throwing large rocks from the roof. I decided to stop the car and shoot in the air.

Without warning, all of a sudden I lost control and slid down the road until the car had turned 180 degrees, the brakes useless. *Crunch*! The car slammed backward into a stone wall about twenty-five meters down the road. Overcome with hate, I immediately jumped out of the car.

Still on the roof I saw the three Palestinians, mere children, jumping with joy in the fact I was almost killed. Gathered around the front door were at least half dozen others. I aimed my gun squarely in the middle at a dark haired boy about sixteen years old. Pulling back on the trigger, my arm went limp as I holstered my revolver and leaned against the car.

Abruptly the silence was pierced by a series of gunshots. Looking back toward the house, I saw the jeep that had given me escort through the last village. All the soldiers had jumped from the jeep and were in pursuit of the stone throwers while the driver sped in my direction.

I feverishly ran up the hill screaming and waving my hands for the jeep to stop. Luckily the driver understood and immediately applied his breaks. As he got out of the jeep, he saw why I was warning him. Our cousins had poured oil on a ten meter area of the road just where it began its descent. Glistening in the moonlight were handfuls of Ninjas, the deadly combination which made me lose control.

I was lucky because the other side of the road opposite the wall dropped at least a hundred meters. What had happened was not a demonstration of frustrations by a stateless people, rather an attempt at premeditated murder, lest anyone think otherwise he'd be the world's biggest fool. Any person, even a child, who would throw stones at the driver of a moving vehicle, commits attempted murder, but to lace a hillside road with oil and nails would be murder in the first degree.

The driver in the jeep gave me something to drink. I was fine I said. In the end the army caught no one who they suspected of committing the crime; the kids seemingly vanished among a thousand hiding places in their village.

However, instead the soldiers returned with eight able bodied Arab men and shovels. One began picking up the ninjas while the other seven dug sand and gravel from the roadside to cover the oil. Two large trucks of soldiers arrived to place the village under curfew.

I knew the officer in charge. He lived in one of the settlements north of Mevo Ayalon. As he put it, I was "damn lucky" to be alive. On its way from the military headquarters in Ramallah was a large bulldozer. By morning, he said, the grove would be a memory.

Upset was the young sergeant in command of the jeep. He apologized profusely for not giving escort through the second village. They had driven through Beit HaTarr only a half hour earlier, the streets full of children playing.

While driving through El-Azrear they had seen a group of teenagers painting slogans on building walls, but they wanted to get me through the village safely before quickly turning around to go back. By the time they returned, the slogans were up with the authors nowhere in sight.

Only my right driver's side tire had gone flat. The soldiers changed it for me over my protests that I could manage alone. Tomorrow I'd have to drive to Ramallah to make a police report. Hopefully the government would pay for the damages. The officer said he also would file a report on the incident.

A few weeks ago, I read in the newspaper that the government was thinking of subsidizing the purchase of protective replacement windows for cars. That night I decided to draft a letter to our Knesset representative urging its adoption.

Approaching the gate, I passed Amos on guard duty shaking his head as I passed. I was sure he'd heard it all on the army radio he held in his right hand. I decided to park by the office on the top. Walking down the path to my house I could see Vickie and Aviva were sitting together on the lawn in front of Chaim's house. I never understood what Vickie incessantly kept coming back to the moshav after out divorce. Yet, seemingly, she appeared always at the most inopportune time, in my opinion.

Ever since Chaim and I were born, he also had an extremely well developed ability to be in either the wrong place at the wrong time or say the wrong thing at the wrong time. We were forced to be best friends because our fathers had survived the Holocaust together and were also first cousins because our mothers were sisters. Whenever he put his foot in my mouth, I wished they had never met.

"Are you okay, Ari? I just saw the car by the office. You are lucky to be alive. Did you see the car, Vickie?" Chaim yelled as he made his grand entrance on the scene.

For about twenty minutes I explained my brush with fate. Try as I could to minimize the actual danger, Vickie grew whiter and whiter with each word until I reached the part about drawing my revolver and aiming at the crowd of Palestinian youth.

"Why didn't you shoot, Ari? They almost killed you . . . I can't believe you of all people didn't shoot . . . why didn't you shoot . . . why didn't you shoot . . . ," hysterically Vickie kept shouting.

"Calm down, Vickie," Aviva said, "let's go inside."

"No! I want to see the car."

"I don't think that's such a good idea," Chaim said.

"Okay, come with me, Vickie," I said.

As we walked to the car together, I tried to understand. Looking at Vickie, I was more confused than ever. There was my leftist ex-wife mad at me because I didn't shoot at a group of Palestinian youth, a lioness protecting her mate, I guess, and me Mister Gung-Ho trying to explain to her why I didn't shoot. Vickie kept saying she couldn't believe it happened, things like that always happening to someone else, she kept repeating. Yet, that one incident seemed to return our worlds upside down.

"Oh! My . . . Ari . . . you could have been killed." Vickie burst into tears as she saw the car.

Maybe it was the spontaneity of it all, I pulled Vickie over to me and gave her a hug, my arms wrapping around her small waist as her head lay on my right shoulder. She continued to cry while I patted the back of her head with my left hand. I held her closer and that's how we spent the next few moments or should I say many moments.

Probably they were the longest four days of my life. I'd returned to work in the vineyard and still no sign of Aisha and her mother. Each day it was all I could do to keep from asking Selah when they were returning. Driving to work I wondered each day if she'd be there waiting. Tomorrow, would it be day five? And the next day six? How long could I continue to simply count the passing days?

Near the back of area eight was a special place for Chaim and me. During our first years of clearing land, laying water lines and planting trees, we camped out there. It was high enough to see the majority of the vineyard below. Abu Ali in fact was the one who suggested it to us.

Chaim and I spent many a night passing out from sheer exhaustion under the stars. One large rock, flat on two sides and peaked in the middle appearing to be two chairs back to back, had special meaning. There we sat on our rocky throne and solved the world's problems together. I left the endless job of checking water leaks and sought out the throne of refuge.

Lying on the rock, I began reliving the events of past couple of months over and over again until all I saw Gaza, Aisha, mildew, Vickie, stoning, my parents, churning before me like an old time kaleidoscope. The more it turned, the more jumbled the mosaic became.

"Dad," I said loudly, "you never understood when I said it was all a matter of confusion."

Within each events image, I sought to uncover a key, a sliver, that would help me understand why things happened as they did, accepting it easier to uncover the workings of the universe. Desperately I needed help to understand my life as it stood.

In the same week I held the hand of a Palestinian maiden I loved and comforted my ex-wife after a near tragedy accident. I couldn't bear it alone anyone. What I needed was an angel of mercy to help me sort it all out.

"Thought you could hide from me up here, did you?" Chaim said as he walked in from out of nowhere.

Poor Chaim. Innocently he sat on his side of the rock to relax for a few moments. What I did to him, I guess, paid him back for a lifetime for any wrongs he might have caused me. I unloaded everything that had been weighing me down. Starting with the real story of the rainbow, I continued until Vickie tearfully fell into my arms. All he could do when I finished was just to stare into the pale blue cloudless sky.

". . . and you have to swear not to tell a living soul, especially Aviva," I begged.

"Even for you, Ari, this takes the cake. I think it's all going to be academic anyway. There's probably no chance she, what did you say her name was?" Chaim asked.

"Aisha."

"Oh! Right, Aisha's not going to return."

"What if she does?"

"Then I'll speak to Moshe and have you transferred to work with chickens back on the moshav."

"Chaim, I never asked a lot from you."

"Ari, cut the bull . . ."

"Okay, I don't want you to try to help me unless I ask you to, please? I need to play each act until the end by myself. All I want from you is to know you'll be there if I need you."

"Short of coming to your wedding in Deir El-Salam," Chaim said with a smile, "but I will have to tell Aviva something."

"Why?"

"She made plans for all of us to meet Vickie by the beach in Tel Aviv. Aviva thought that you and Vickie might be . . ."

"Okay, I'll go. Tell her what you have to, but not a word about what we spoke about today."

"Ari, just one thing. Be careful your father doesn't get wind. I don't think his heart can handle the shock."

"Don't you think I've considered that, Chaim?"

Chaim, after all, was my best friend in the world. It's rare to find a person, let alone a relative, that you can call a true friend. So what if he wouldn't be my best man at my wedding, he'd already done it once before. If it got that far . . .

"Ari, what will you do if she doesn't come back?"

"You'll be a lot happier."

"No, I don't care she's a Palestinian . . . that much. I just want you to get on with your life . . ."

"To answer your question, Chaim, I don't have to worry. Aisha will come back and I'm sure of that."

We spent the remainder of the day inspecting the vineyard together. I drove while Chaim jotted down an endless amount of notes, noticing an innumerable of broken wires, infested root stock and a host of other problems. Before the season got too busy was the best time to make repairs.

Just before returning to the moshav, Chaim said he needed to go back to the shed. I insisted we didn't have time. The last thing I wanted was to go to the shed and not see Aisha.

"I really need to get those catalogues," Chaim said. "Tonight's the only time I'll have this week to order parts."

"Okay." I capitulated.

Selah and the others were sitting under the spreading oak as usual. Chaim said it would only take a few minutes to get what he needed. When we cleaned the end room of the shed for Aisha and her mother, we threw everything together in the middle room. Boy! What a mess.

"Come sit and have a cup of coffee, Ari," Selah called out.

"No, we are not going to be long. I'll just lay here in the truck and rest. Thanks anyway."

Leaning back, I heard contrasting sounds. Chaim was cursing because he couldn't find what he wanted while Selah and the others enjoyed a well deserved rest after a hard day. My feet hung out the passenger's side window as I quickly nodded off.

Asleep, I didn't hear the late model, white taxi pull up next to the hiding oak. Opening my eyes, I realized I'd dozed, wondering what was taking Chaim so long. Suddenly, I heard screaming. Jumping up I hit my nose on the steering wheel. I looked out the front window while my nose dripped blood.

"Hey, look whose back, Ari," Chaim said as he came to the truck lugging a stack of books from the shed, "guess you were right after all."

Selah's mother was screaming at him from the top of her lungs while Aisha walked with a little boy. She didn't look back as she entered the shed. I doubted if she had seen me.

"What's all the fuss, Selah?" I asked as I approached.

"It's my sister, Ari."

"Is she alright?"

"It's nothing like that, you're lucky you don't know her. My sister's stubborn . . ."

"Sounds like you, Ari," Chaim butted in.

"What did she do?"

"It's more like what she didn't do. My mother wanted her to stay in the village."

"But, she's here," Chaim said pointing out the obvious.

"I know. This afternoon when the taxi pulled up, she jumped in and refused to get out."

"So, that's what your mother's carrying on about?" I asked.

"Not exactly, she's giving me an earful about my father."

"Your father? How did he get into this?" Chaim asked.

"Well, you see while my mother was screaming at my sister, he came out and told my mother Aisha could go back to the vineyard," Selah continued, "his word is law. Understand?"

"I guess I do," I said, "at least it will be good for her to look after Ali."

"How did you know my son's name, Ari?"

"You told us last week," Chaim lied.

"I don't remember saying . . . maybe I did," Selah said under his breath.

"Good thing we didn't take back the beds, huh Selah?" Chaim said.

"Chaim, I have a small favor to ask. Could you possibly find another cot for my son?"

"Don't you think he'll want to sleep in the tree house with you and the others?" I asked.

"That's what I'm afraid of," Selah answered.

"I know what you mean," I said, "all he has to do is roll out of bed and . . ."

"I have a kid's bed at my house I'll bring tomorrow."

"Thanks, Chaim."

"One other thing," Selah added. "Tomorrow starts the holy month of Ramadan. No need to pick us up food till the end of the day."

"No problem," Chaim said, "anything special you want to eat?"

"Just add a couple of extra bottles of cola for the next month."

"I'll have them frozen overnight so by the time you sit down to eat, they'll still be cool."

"I'd appreciate that."

"How 'bout we throw in some cookies for your son?" Chaim added.

"Please, if you don't mind," Selah said, "he likes chocolate sandwich cookies."

By now Aisha had come out of the shed. She sat on the ground to the left of the door with her legs folded in front of her, Ali, Selah's son, sitting on her lap, so natural her holding a child. Selah's mother carried the rest of their things into the shed; ostracizing glances at Aisha. Boy was she mad.

"She's looking at you mighty hard," Chaim said as he got into the truck, "I don't think their mother likes you, Ari."

"Maybe so . . . maybe so." I wondered if she suspected anything between us.

"You never get along with mothers-in-law, do you, Ari?"

"Funny, Chaim, even hysterical."

Aisha waited until we had turned the truck around to look in my direction. Her mother had gone back inside the shed while Selah rejoined the others and engaged in a conversation with the taxi driver from Hebron. Motioning her hands, Aisha was trying to tell me something. *Charades*, I nodded I understood that she wanted me to come back at night.

Meanwhile, Chaim had already begun to pull out of sight. Aisha was trying to signal me something else. What could it be? Place? Time? I'd have to wait till later to find out, thanks to Chaim, now he was in a hurry!

Normally I dreaded the thirty-five minute drive back to the moshav from the vineyard. Today I wished it would take longer, wanting to talk to Chaim to see how he really felt about what I told him earlier. Somehow the confines of the truck weren't the right place I decided

"Ari or Chaim! This is Moshe, over."

"Yes, Moshe," I said, "the transmission is a little weak. What can we do for you, over?"

"Guess what? Over."

"Oh! No," Chaim said to me, "don't tell me the bread truck didn't come again today?"

"Bread? Over," I asked.

"You got it, Ari, over."

"What do you need, over?"

"Twenty white, eighteen rye and one French loaf, over."

"We're not going to waste time looking for one lousy French bread in Ramle, over," Chaim screamed taking the transmitter from my hand.

"It's for your wife, Chaim, over."

"Oh!"

"Hey, Chaim, I got a great idea . . ."

"You? A great idea?"

"Seriously, why not stop while in Ramle and buy a couple of ice cold beers?"

"For once, Ari, you've come up with something."

Luckily it only took three stops to find a French bread. Although someone had taken a small bite from one end, Chaim said he didn't care and broke off the rest of the lipstick stained edges.

Who would think buying a beer would be political? In Israel everything's political, even beer. My Dad never told me not to start up with bartenders, but he should have. As we sat under the yellow and white umbrellas of the sidewalk cafe, I ordered two imported beers.

"What's the matter with you guys? Can't buy blue and white beer?" a burly figure behind the counter blurted out.

"I've had white beer," I said, "but what's blue beer taste like?"

"Wise guy, huh?"

"Buy blue and white . . . buy blue and white," a small man with a moustache two tables over yelled.

"Fine, give me a blue beer and a white for my friend."

"You think you're pretty smart," said the man behind the counter, "products made in Israel. Buy blue and white . . . like our flag."

"Oh!" I said. "Why didn't you say so?"

"Too many people are losing their jobs because this country's gone import crazy. The more of those products we consume, the higher our trade deficit goes. Local products sit," continued the small man, "and people get laid off."

"Please forgive me," I said, "make those four Israeli beers."

"That-a-boy," the burly guy behind the counter said.

"To carry out though, we'll drink them in our truck," I said as we started walking away, "our Japanese truck."

"Prefer a Palestinian beer?" Chaim asked as we got into the truck.

"What?"

"I couldn't believe you back there, Ari."

"I was just having a little fun, Chaim . . ."

"Ari, if you want to have a fling with a Palestinian, that's your business, but don't let her turn your head around. You've almost unscrewed it by yourself."

"Go ahead and say it Chaim. Don't be afraid . . . spit it out."

"Just don't discard all your values to win her over. Back there you were joking about something very serious."

"I hear."

"If you have to change to win her over, maybe it's not worth it. Not, at least, at the expense of yourself."

"Thanks, Chaim."

"For what?"

"Understanding . . . and lying."

"Lying?"

"Yeah, when you lied to Selah about him telling us his son's name last week."

"It's just a habit I've gotten into, Ari. Bailing you out has become second nature for me."

With that Chaim poured his bottle of beer on the top of my head. In turn I shook my bottle and squirted him all over. There we sat soaking and stinking of beer. Chaim picked up the drenched French loaf and broke it in half.

"Here, Ari, have half a beer sandwich."

Boy did we laugh. I've described Chaim in my lifetime by many adjectives. Friend . . . cousin . . . pain in the . . . idiot. Yet, I never called him what he really was to me . . . my big brother which has made all the difference in my life.

NINETEEN

Looking at my watch, I couldn't believe it was only 8:30 p.m. The past hour waiting in the bushes passed by ever so slowly; watching mosquitoes get caught in a spider web my only excitement.

I started to wonder what Aisha was trying to tell me at the end. The shed, in full view, I saw everyone sitting around a fire except Aisha, Ali and her mother. Surely, I thought she would use some ruse to leave the shed area. But how long would I have to wait?

All of a sudden, I saw Aisha walk past the shed with a towel over her shoulder toward the top of area twelve. Smart girl, I thought. Near area twelve we had constructed one of our three water filtration systems. The water in the vineyard had to be filtered before it entered our elaborate irrigation system. As such, it passed through six filter tanks filled with special black gravel. When water came out of the filter it was potable enough to drink.

Beside the filtration system, Selah and the others had constructed a makeshift shower. Lying in the sun all day, the water in the pipes became very warm providing a nice hot shower. Since area twelve was opposite the shed, I also showered there after I finished spraying. Although the filtration system area was set back from the road into the trees, there was still little privacy.

I waited to make sure no one followed Aisha like her mother before I going after her. When I reached the shower, she was just sliding her jeans off from under her dress.

"Aisha!" I whispered.

"Ari! What are you doing here?" she asked blushing from ear to ear.

"I'm not here with bad intentions, I promise you," I said somewhat embarrassed.

"Why did you follow me to the shower?"

"I thought you were using taking a shower as an excuse just to leave the shed area."

"Oh! Ari! I really came to shower. My brother told me to come first before the others."

"I'm sorry; I thought . . . well, when can we be together?"

"You didn't understand me. I tried to motion to you."

"Chaim was pulling away too fast."

"I meant after midnight when everyone was asleep," Aisha said. "Ari, you must leave now. I have to shower."

"Can't I stay . . .?"

"Ari, please don't ask that of me. What kind of woman do you take me for?" Aisha said looking hurt.

"No, Aisha, I didn't mean what you think. I'll just sit over there on the rocks with my back to you. Please, we'll talk while you shower. Okay?"

"I know I can trust you. Just don't give me reason not to."

Aisha began, after I was situated about ten meters away behind some rocks, to remove the rest of her clothes and shower. Needless to say, I had a really strong desire to turn my head slightly to the right, but didn't.

She was very religious and I understood what that meant. Orthodox Jews also held the ideal of modesty highly. Surely it could be no different among the religious of our cousins. After all, Aisha vanished from my rainbow just because I was bare from the waist up. Feeling the way I did about her, I could do no less than give her my utmost respect.

"Okay, Ari, you can turn around now," Aisha called out.

As I turned and walked toward her, I could see little beads of water still clinging to her cheeks and nose. Aisha looked so pure standing there. I walked toward her not removing my eyes from hers. Standing directly in front of her, I took the towel from her left hand. Rolling one end into a ball, I raised my arm to dry the little beads from her face.

"Stop, Ari, that tickles," Aisha giggled.

I couldn't stop. With precision, I blotted each drop feeling an intimacy I had never known even with Vickie. Yet, I knew that would be as close as Aisha and I would come, no more touching. I had already compromised her modesty enough.

"Ari, I must go back now. The others are waiting to shower also. I'll meet you at the corner of area two by the cluster of pine trees. Be there in about four hours. Okay?"

"Yes, but Aisha . . ."

"We have no more time now, Ari, I must go."

Aisha walked away in a rather hasty gait. I knew she felt uncomfortable about my being so close while she showered. After she had gone a few meters, she turned to look in my direction. Not paying attention, she stumbled on a rock in the road. I ran to help her up. Our eyes caught each other's and then she broke away and ran toward the shed.

With nothing else to do but wait, I walked down each row inspecting the development of the grapes. All indications were we'd have a better than average yield at season's end. That thought, the end of the season, gave me despair. What would I do after the last grape was harvested?

We didn't need Selah and the others after the harvest. He always returned to his village until about January when we started pruning the trees. Only this year he wouldn't be returning alone. During the past weeks I'd never given a thought to the fact one day Aisha would return to Deir El Salam. What would I do . . . could I do then?

Reaching the pine trees near area two, it was still so much before time Aisha would arrive. The growing realization, in a few months it all might be over weighed heavily upon me, neither could I show up in Deir El-Salam to visit Aisha, nor could she come to the moshav. The only thing I could do under the circumstances was fall asleep. I awoke after what seemed hours. I sat up to look at my watch.

"Aisha! How long have you been here?" startled I asked.

149

"Not long, I've just been watching you. Ari, you make a lot of noise when you sleep," Aisha laughed.

"How long can you stay?"

"As long as I need to," Aisha answered. "I came to an understanding with my brother. I told him there is much in my life at the moment I need to think about."

"I can understand that."

"And I told him that I couldn't think clearly with he and my mother around," Aisha continued. "I needed time alone at night if only to sit under the stars and seek their help."

"What did he say?"

"My brother just told me to be careful. If I left the shed not to go too far and always stay within screaming distance, as he put it."

"You have a good brother, Aisha."

"Ari, I told you before he only thinks the best of me and always will. In that respect he's like my father."

"Selah told me," I said, "about your mother being mad at him today."

"It's not just today," Aisha said. "Haven't you wondered why my mother and I came to live in the vineyard?"

"If I remember correctly, Aisha, Selah said something about circumstances preventing your mother from remaining home."

"I'll tell you those circumstances, Ari, my father got married again!"

"You mean your parents are divorced?"

"You don't understand Ari, in our belief, according to the Holy Koran, a man may have more than one wife. Up to four wives are permitted to a man under one roof," Aisha explained.

"At the same time?"

"Yes, but usually a man if he wants another wife will wait till he's older and take a much younger one."

"Oh!"

"Ari, that's what he did six months ago. My mother loyally has spent her life since she was sixteen with him. She couldn't understand his wanting another wife."

"That explains a lot, Aisha, why doesn't she divorce him?"

"No, Ari, my mother loves him very much. Besides she has always been faithful to the teachings of our prophet in the Holy Koran. Her name is even Fatima after our prophet's daughter. She'll always stay true to my father."

"I don't understand, Aisha, why did she leave her house?"

"It's the woman he married, Ari, she's my age. We were in the same class!" Aisha said with a tear escaping from her right eye.

"But you just told me that men often take younger women . . ."

"This woman, Ari, tried from the very beginning to drive my mother away . . . and she succeeded. She's caused a rift between my parents."

"How can that be, Aisha, they were married a long time?"

"At night she can give my father what my mother because of her years cannot and that's what she has used to turn my father."

"I see." I wished I could have comforted Aisha more. "I'm sorry your father is that kind of man."

"Ari, he is not at fault. He's a terrific man and my brother Selah's just like him; both have had it hard all their lives."

"I didn't mean anything."

"My mother's intention for coming to the vineyard was to give him enough time to see the bad choice he made in a second wife. And he will; I'm sure of that."

For the next hour or so Aisha told me the story of her family. I was fascinated as she revealed to me a side of our cousins I'd never known.

"I have to return to the shed now, Ari," Aisha said after what seemed like an eternity together.

"What about tomorrow night?"

"No, I don't think so. Ramadan starts tomorrow; I'll be too tired from not eating. I'm sure I'll fall asleep during the meal. The first few days are the toughest. After that we get used to not eating or drinking during the day."

"We must find time to be together," I begged.

"Tomorrow, mid morning, I'll take Ali for a walk. Come to area fifteen. We'll be there."

"Yes, that's a good idea. Everyone will be working in area four on the other side of the vineyard. Aisha . . ."

"Ari, let me say the last words tonight."

"Okay."

"What I told my brother was true. I have a lot to think about now and I do need some time to sort it all out . . ."

"Aisha, please don't . . ."

"Ari, do not worry. You are the center of my thoughts." Aisha smiled and walked away into the darkness.

Driving back to the moshav, all I could think about was Aisha's father. Sharing with me her family's story brought us one step closer to each other giving me the feeling I'd known Aisha and her family all my life.

Originally her family didn't live in Deir El-Salam. Her grandfather and his father before him were born in Old Jaffe, once the main seaport of Palestine. In fact, recent archeological discoveries dated Jaffe as one of the oldest ports in the world. From Jaffe, Jonah boarded the ship would take him on his ill fated journey, his voyage ending in the belly of a whale.

In both Hebrew and Arabic, the city's name meant "beautiful." Over the centuries the many invading armies agreed to her splendor. After a succession of conquerors encompassing King David, Saladin, the Crusaders and Richard the Lion Hearted, Jaffa returned to Arab hands in the middle of the thirteenth century.

Aisha's grandfather owned large land holdings in the Jaffe area, apparently earning a rather successful living from orchards of oranges and almonds. Their home was in the Old City itself adjacent to the seawall. When Aisha's father became old enough, he helped her grandfather manage his affairs. During the times of the British occupation of Palestine they prospered well.

When the partition plan was announced by the United Nations like many other Palestinian residents her family was gravely disheartened by the thought of living within a Jewish state. Closely her grandfather watched the political tides as they rolled in.

Some Palestinian residents of Jaffa voiced their desire to remain; however, they were the minority, most feeling impotent to reverse the process. After listening to the neighboring Arab states talk of the impending annihilation of the Jewish inhabitants, they decided to seek safety temporarily elsewhere.

On Passover day, 1948, almost all of the Arab residents of Jaffa felt their backs against the wall. In one single, mass exodus seventy thousand men, women and children literally dropped everything and fled, most assuming it only a temporary move confident they soon would return to live in a Palestinian state of their own.

Aisha's grandfather fled with a substantial amount of wealth. He had realized for some time that the situation would get worse before it got better. In the village of Deir El-Salam he had a relative. Aisha never really knew the exact relationship. It was very hard, she said, to relocate in those days. A newcomer to a village was always regarded as an outsider. Her grandfather hoped being related to someone would make his ultimate acceptance possible.

Quickly he began to purchase land. A small plot here, a larger parcel there and several were near the village itself until he'd secured a respectable amount of land. Most were purchased from absentee landowners who lived as far away as Beirut. Being satisfied with his dealings, he began again his livelihood from the earth.

Meanwhile, Aisha's father, almost twenty at the time of the move, decided to try his fortune in the City of Amman, one of the many who fled to Jordan. At the time, Amman was just a cut above the surrounding villages. However, the onslaught of refugees almost doubled the city population in a matter of weeks.

Luckily he was able to find employment apprenticing himself to a dentist. For nearly two years he worked for only food and a corner to sleep in order to learn a craft. At the end he became a dental technician. With no formal education, Aisha's father thought he would be set for life in his newly chosen profession.

Shortly before his apprenticeship ended, he met Aisha's mother, a Palestinian refugee from Nablus, now called Shechem, the traditional burial place of Joseph. The Israelites during their exodus from Egypt carried his remains until they were laid to rest there. Aisha's maternal grandparents decided at the beginning of 1948 for the sake of their children it would be safer for a few months to live in Jordan proper; they never returned to Nablus.

After only three years in Amman, Aisha's father realized although he had a good career, he couldn't continue to make ends meet. As the city grew so did its cost of residency. Each day after paying for food and housing, little else remained. Aisha's mother suggested they move back to Nablus. All was quiet then and from what she had heard the city was growing rapidly. Living in Nablus only six months both realized the move had been a mistake.

As a last resort, they returned to Deir El-Salam, Aisha's grandfather welcoming them with open arms. Her father happily resumed his old job of caring for his father's land. Soon he became as familiar with olives, wheat and corn as he had been with oranges and almonds. In a short time he built a house adjacent to her grandfather's.

Since the village had no dentist, her father was forced to fill the role. Reluctantly he accepted the anguished pleas for mercy from his neighbors. A simple tooth extraction was a lifesaving operation to the pained. Yet, he never would accept payment. Always he told them he wasn't really a dentist, only an assistant.

Many times he told Aisha that the Holy Koran praised those who gave alms to the poor. That was his way of fulfilling the wishes of the prophet and would gladly wait to receive his payment in the next world. Aisha added until this day the older ones of the village still go to her father with their toothaches.

Only Selah of all the children was born in Amman, Jordan. Aisha and the rest entered this world in the same room of her father's house. As time passed, her family prospered in comfort and size. Her mother and father together worked her grandfather's land wisely. Their whole world was closed to the outside revolving solely around Deir El-Salam, rarely journeying to neighboring Hebron.

Even the outbreak of the Six Day War caught them completely by surprise. Aisha said her father always talked about the fact one moment there was peace and the next there was war. While working one day in their olive grove, he encountered the war. About midmorning he heard the sound of a truck approaching. Looking up, he recognized an army jeep, but it wasn't Jordanian. Quickly he hid in the bushes.

Driving toward his direction, the jeep stopped literally next to the bushes where he was hiding. Six men with Uzis leaped from the jeep and began searching the area. Scared and not knowing what to do, he crawled under the jeep. Soon he was surrounded by a dozen trucks and jeeps full of Israeli soldiers while he lay motionless on his back under the jeep.

About an hour later, the soldiers began to get back into their respective vehicles. Engines roared while one by one they drove away in the direction of Deir El-Salam. The last to leave was the jeep over her father pulling in tandem with the others. Only a few meters away it stopped. Immediately the soldiers jumped from the jeep and ran toward Aisha's father, lying perfectly still on his back with his eyes closed as they approached with cocked guns. Eight days lapsed before he returned home.

Today they still had the land except a grove of olive trees the government confiscated in order to build a new road linking Jewish settlements. Until a few weeks ago Aisha and her mother tilled the soil of those fields.

To survive nowadays her father had to supplement their income by working odd jobs as a day laborer, for his age a very difficult task. Aisha said soon she and her mother would have to return to harvest the wheat. During the fall it was Selah's responsibility to manage the olive harvest for his father.

Aisha said all Selah really wanted to do was follow in his father's footsteps and care for their land. As her father always told them, she said, land was more valuable than money. With a smile he added because they're never going to make any more of it.

Even though Selah could never earn enough to support his family, he would have to assume its responsibility after their father died. Selfishly I wished Aisha's father a long and healthy life. I couldn't bear to run the vineyard without Selah's help.

I asked Aisha about her other brothers. Oddly Aisha allowed very little about them. When I asked how her brother died, she politely said we had talked enough about her family. Maybe some other time, she said, but not then.

Listening to Aisha reveal her story and thoughts about her family, I realized many similarities. Her father sounded so much like my own. Hard working and easily made happy, both were cut from the same fabric. Simple men, they were trying to live out simple lives during a not so simple time.

Naively I realize I had so much hidden prejudice toward our cousins. That night for the first time I was confronted with the fact they were living specimens of the human race with a past, present and hope for a future the same as my people. How could I have been so nearsighted my whole life not to see that? Like Chaim said, we'd worked with Selah for almost five years and never bothered to ask one question about his life. Yet, now I felt I knew him as well as I did Chaim. Even his son Ali loved chocolate sandwich cookies the same as me.

Within the confines of our great land, our fathers, mine, Chaim's, Aisha's and even Vickie's sought to find peace and solitude. Why wasn't it possible we could all live in harmony together? The land had known only strife and conflict since time began. When would it stop? The saga of Aisha's family only further complicated the confusion reigning in my mind.

Thankfully all was quiet driving through Beit El-Safa. In the middle of the village I felt Aisha's presence watching over me. She wasn't the only one who needed time to sort out their life. I was as much in need as she. And like Aisha said to me, she was definitely the center of my thoughts.

TWENTY

"I'm sorry, Ari, but I can't hold back any longer!"

"What on earth are you talking about Chaim?" I asked as we rode home at the end of a typically rough day.

"Three weeks . . . I've been quiet for three weeks. Now, I feel I have to say something."

"Chaim, if you have something to say . . . say it. Okay?"

"It's been three weeks since Aisha came back to the vineyard . . ."

"We've established that fact already."

"Let me speak, Ari!"

"Okay! Okay!"

"Ari, you are not dealing with reality, acting like you and Aisha are married and Selah's son, Ali, is your child."

"Don't be silly. I've just gotten attached to him and that's all, Chaim."

"Attached, my foot."

"Chaim, I enjoy being with him. Aisha and I . . ."

"That's just the point, Ari; there can't be an Aisha and you. It would be easier if you fell in love with someone else's wife. You've been divorced from Vickie too long. The first little girl who dances your way . . ."

"Enough, Chaim! That's not what is going on."

"Enlighten me then, Ari, what is going on?" Chaim pulled the truck to the roadside and switched off the engine.

"Chaim, you said that I might as well fall in love with someone else's wife."

"Yeah, doing that is an easy way out of reality. You can fantasize all you want, but you know you'll never get hurt because the woman you love is already married. The unreachable Palestinian maiden is the same . . ."

"Imagine, Chaim, for a minute you were in love with a married woman. Every time you were around her you felt terrific, but you hurt deeply inside because you knew, just as you said, she was married and in love with another man. All you had were affairs of the mind."

"See! I'm right. Nothing can come of it."

"Wait, Chaim, just suppose also one day you are innocently alone with her. To your surprise she shares her innermost secret thoughts with you. Your distant love also feels the same way about you."

"So?"

"Now you're given hope and in the end it all works out. She and her husband separate; enabling you two to live happily ever after. Chaim, when Aisha smiled at me that first time, I knew our feelings were mutual."

"Ari, Aisha would have to divorce herself from everything she holds dear for you."

"So would I, Chaim, so would I."

"And you're prepared to do that?"

"Sometimes, most times, I think maybe I am."

"Not while your father is alive you won't. That much I know for sure, Ari!"

"Chaim, honestly I'm as happy now as I've ever been. That's important to me. And yes, I've changed . . . changed for the better I think."

"Time will be the judge of that, Ari, only time will tell."

I guess in some respects Chaim was right. In the vineyard, Aisha, Ali, and I were becoming inseparable. Selah assumed I had taken a liking to his son since I never had children of my own, which for the most part was true. Not to draw suspicion to Aisha and me, Ali spent a lot of time with us. I think even Aisha's mother, Fatima, approved of me with Ali although I'm sure she'd never admit it.

Two weeks ago I wanted to bring Ali a toy to play with other than the scraps of wood and steel scattered around the vineyard. I went to a toy store in Ramle and all I found were guns, swords, bows and arrows. I couldn't believe it. Everything had a quality of death and destruction. War toys they were. I wasn't going to give Ali a weapon. Vickie after all was right about guns!

In the end I bought him a kite and boy was he happy. I never flew it with him leaving that for his real father to do. All over the vineyard the kite with its colorful, two meter tail could be seen flying above. Honestly, I thought Selah enjoyed the kite more than Ali, always the little kid in all of us.

Riding the last few kilometers to the moshav, I could feel Chaim and me distancing ourselves, nothing really to put my finger on. Since he said his peace he didn't look at me the same old way.

"Chaim . . ."

"What Ari?"

"If I told you . . . never mind."

Sometimes saying nothing says more than anything you could say. I didn't want to tell Chaim tomorrow night I'd been invited by Selah to have supper with them. Selah came up to me early in the morning and asked if I would join them for the evening meal after the fast ended. Try as I could, no excuse I gave would suffice. Finally I said Chaim needed to return early. Tomorrow Selah knew I was starting another round of spraying.

"You'll come back early and eat with us," Selah insisted.

"Selah, I really can't . . ."

"Ali will be disappointed,"

"Okay, Selah." It was flawless, many nights dreaming of sitting down with Aisha and her family. Now her brother was the one who had done the inviting.

As I lay in my bed on the moshav, I tried in vain to sleep. The thought of having supper with Aisha reminded me too much of the first time I met Vickie's parents. I came in jeans, sandals, and a slightly torn sweater. Her father sat down to eat in a three-piece suit complete with paisley tie. I don't think even the president of our country ever attired himself so formally.

More and more I began to think of Vickie and was driven by a strong urge to call her. I stretched to look at my watch on the nightstand . . . 1:15 a.m. Was it too late to call?

"Hello, Vickie, I hope I didn't wake you?"

"Ari, I'll give you the benefit of the doubt that wasn't your intention. Is there anything I can possibly do for you at one in the morning?"

"I just wanted you to know I've been seeing someone . . ."

"Ari, if it's not a psychiatrist, can't it wait until the morning? Aviva already told me a few weeks ago. I'm really glad for you, Ari, but it's late and I'm very tired. Maybe tomorrow . . ."

"She's a Palestinian, Vickie . . . I've been dating a Palestinian woman," I blurted out.

Silence always says it best, but sometimes a person wants more of a direct response.

"Vickie . . . Vickie . . . . are you still there . . . Vickie . . . say something . . ."

Try as I could, Vickie said nothing. Was she laughing or what? I couldn't tell, Vickie depriving me of her reaction. Then after an eternal pause . . .

"Ari, does your Dad know?"

"That's all you can say, Vickie?" angrily I yelled.

"Ari, I was only thinking of his heart. 'Cause if he knew . . . well, the shock was almost more than I could bear."

"Give me a break, Vickie; I just met a girl I liked . . ."

"Ari, you can't give me that line; you of all people to date a Palestinian. Listen, this isn't the time or way for us to discuss this. I truly want to hear about her and I am happy for you. Aviva says you've been a changed person since you met her. Does Aviva know she's a Palestinian?"

"No, only Chaim."

"Come to Tel Aviv tomorrow night and we'll walk on the beach and talk about it," Vickie suggested.

"I can't tomorrow, Vickie."

"Got a date, Ari?"

"Something resembling that; I'm having supper with her mother and brother."

"You must be serious, Ari, are you going to her village?"

"Let's make it the end of the week," I said. "I'll let you know what night's good for me."

"I want you to know I'm really happy you are interested in someone and I know she must be special if you like her."

"Sorry I woke you, Vickie."

"Ari, you can always call if you need someone to talk with, that much hasn't changed between us."

"Thanks, Vickie."

From my bedroom window, I saw a sky filled with stars overhead. Mesmerized by their twinkling, I couldn't help but think of Vickie.

Why on earth did I call her? Was it just to let her know I could love someone other than her? How awful of me if that had been my sole motivation. What was it I really sought? Maybe deep down I'd hoped she would protest and beg to return to my side. Why did I have to call?

Suddenly I realized why. Despite the past few years, Vickie still remained my truest friend. Chaim had been more of a brother to me. Vickie, on the other hand, had befriended me in ways that made her almost approach being my alter ego. What's more important, it's been a mutual friendship in that respect.

What must she think of me now? I wouldn't be surprised if she were laying in bed awake at this moment thinking about what I said. I could almost hear her say to herself.

"Ari . . . a Palestinian girl . . . Ari? No, not my Ari. It must be someone else's Ari who called."

Clouds blew in from out of nowhere hiding my mosaic of comforting lights. Even without starlight some things were becoming crystal clear. Feeling so ashamed for having called, I was certain she perceived it as a grandstanding technique intended to jolt her back to me. Surely, she thought, my seeing a Palestinian girl was my way of obtaining instant credibility as a liberal.

"Ring! Ring!"

"Ari, are you still awake?"

"As a matter of fact I've found it difficult to fall back asleep."

"Me too!"

"Something you need, Vickie?"

"I just remembered I'm going to be in Jerusalem Thursday night. Maybe we can meet there?"

"I can come to Tel Aviv, Vickie, it's no problem."

"Ari, I haven't been in Jerusalem at night in ages. I guess I'd forgotten how special a city she really is."

"Where will you be?"

"I'll be visiting a friend near the windmill. Meet me there about seven. Okay?"

"Fine," I said, "I'll be there."

"Good night again, Ari."

Jerusalem . . . our Jerusalem. Vickie and I in Jerusalem again together. Oh! How I'd wished so long for that. It was going to be a night . . .

"Allah . . . Allah!"

Looking at my watch it was unmistakably four in the morning. The mosque near the moshav was calling people to arise for prayers. As the sound echoed among the hills and valleys, my heart began to heed its call.

"Aisha . . . Aisha!" the muezzin seemed to chant. That feeling of her watching over me began to reappear as if she sensed my drifting back to Vickie. The call to prayer was no coincidence; so strange.

TWENTY-ONE

I could think of many ways to be woken up from a sound sleep. Noises from a garbage truck outside, however, would definitely not be on the list. Reaching for my watch on the night stand, I got an awakening shock. Just as I touched the band, I saw a scorpion next to the watch, impulsively withdrawing my hand. My second look revealed its disappearance.

Slowly easing out of bed, I saw the scorpion scurry into my clothes closet. Totally naked, I quickly ran into the kitchen to get a broom. Bending down on "all fours," I saw my friend in the right corner. Aiming the broom head in its direction, I heaved it with all my might.

Pulling the broom back, I saw my successful efforts splattered against the wall. Some of its pieces were stuck to the broom itself, the deadly tail still vibrating intact. In Israel there are basically two types of scorpions, black and gold. The black were not as deadly as the gold except to small children and infants. Gold scorpions, on the other hand, could even make a large man seriously ill or worse. My little visitor was twenty-four carat gold.

Picking up my jeans from the floor, I began thoroughly shaking them out, not wanting anymore uninvited guests. Checking lastly my shoes, I began to get dressed. It was almost noon. At least I had slept late and after last night I needed the rest. I just hoped it was enough to complete the night of spraying that lay ahead.

Chaim had graciously given me the task of entering information about our operations on the office computer. I guess it was only poetic justice. When I was the moshav business manager, I talked Chaim into buying a special computer package designed to help a vineyard manager save time on his record keeping.

Up front the salesman said, "For only a few moments a week complete up to date information could be instantly available." His words still rung in my ears; I only had maybe four hours left until I had all of the manpower utilization data entered for last year's season. Working with the ultra simplified program was like falling in a bottomless pit. The further you fell, the farther you had to go.

I reached the office just as an army supply truck was approaching. Luckily I was the first one they saw.

"Which building is the office?" asked the sergeant in the front seat.

"That depends on which office you are looking for," I said.

"I have a report for the vineyard manager. It's a list of names he supplied and wanted checked."

"I wanted checked," I said.

"You're the vineyard manager? . . . Just sign and we'll be out of here. Oh! Yea! There's a copy for the moshav business manager, Moshe. See he gets it too. Okay?"

"No problem." I signed the army form in triplicate. All they needed was my name, army identity number, citizenship number, date of birth, father's first name, place of birth . . ."

"Blue," I continued.

"Blue what?" the sergeant asked.

"My eye color! You didn't ask for that."

Sitting in the accounting office I fumbled as I turned the computer on, finally our program appearing. Unmistakably, it was ours with its two clusters of grapes centered among lines of computerese.

My curiosity began to get the best of me; I kicked the door closed so I could have a little privacy. Typical of army procedure, all that was in the sealed envelope was a computer printout. A carbon printout was stapled to the inside of the envelope, some clerks' idea of a joke.

Each name was listed in numerical order according to their respective identity numbers. Following the family name was the first name, father's name, mother's name, place of birth, etc. To the left was a column headed "File" under which was entered either a yes or no indicating whether the person had a file with the authorities.

Having a file didn't mean a person necessarily had been in trouble, however, most indicated if not actual incidences implied complicity. To the extreme left was a detailed breakdown of the files contents.

Surprisingly quite a few of the names I provided were listed, all for minor things such as just being in a crowd when the army was rounding up people after an incident. If someone had been detained, he was recorded. One kid by age fourteen had been questioned about four different incidences.

I began to breathe a little bit easier. Apparently we employed kids in the vineyard that followed a crowd. Selah, I trusted, would keep them in line. I wished I had a report on the two kids who went back to the village and never returned to the vineyard.

The list revealed Selah had no file, no surprise. His family, I was sure, stayed as far away from the Intifada as they could. Skimming to the bottom of the list was Aisha's mother, Fatima. Even though I read it with my own eyes, I couldn't believe what the computer had typed next to Fatima's name.

"SON . . . IBRAHIM . . . AGE 32 . . . KILLED HEBRON JANUARY 14, 1988 . . . RESISTING ARREST . . . SON . . . NASSIR . . . AGE 29 . . . SUSPECTED LEADER POPULAR COMMITTEE DEIR EL SALAM . . . ALSO SUSPECTED COMPLICITY MURDER OF DR. JAMYEL SALIM . . . AGE 46 . . . DEIR EL SALAM . . ."

Instinctively, I crumbled the army printout in my hands, shaking my head in disbelief. Shock? Shame? Anger? No feelings at all like I had fallen through a black hole in space. Within me such a vacuum was created that I almost imploded. Even the computer began to stare at me.

"This year or last?" Moshe asked as he stepped into my black hole.

"What's that, Moshe?"

"Are you entering this year's or last year's vineyard information?"

"Neither! I was just trying to watch cartoons, but I couldn't figure out how to change the channel."

"Funny, Ari," Moshe said as he walked out slamming the door behind him.

Chaim was the beneficiary of my distress. To take my mind away from the army report, I entered information with lightening speed. Not only did I finish last year, but I made a breakthrough in the current year as well. The last program was manpower utilization. Completing name after name, all thoughts of the army report slipped away until I reached Aisha's name. At that point I fell back through my black hole.

"Selah wanted me to remind you not to be late," Chaim said as he stood in the office doorway.

"Good grief!" I yelled as I looked at my watch.

"Late for what, Ari?"

"Nothing . . . it's nothing . . ."

"Expect me to believe that, Ari? Besides," Chaim continued, "Selah has to spray tonight."

"What did you say?" I asked as I logged out of the computer.

"On the way home, I hit a rather large rock placed in the turn by Beit El-Safa. The connecting rod to the front wheel is bent completely out of shape," Chaim said. "I'll ask Amos if he can straighten it out tonight."

"Chaim, it's not fair to Selah," I argued.

"Since when have you ever complained about *not* spraying. Oh! I get it, Ari, now I understand what Selah meant . . ."

"Moshe!"

"What, Ari?"

"Do you think I can take the van to the vineyard? Our truck has a bent tire rod and I have to spray tonight. Right, Chaim?"

"Spraying must be done, that's a fact," Chaim said standing just over the edge of a white lie.

"Not even if the governing board of the moshav gave permission would I let the van go near the vineyard."

"But, Moshe . . ." I pleaded.

"After five minutes on those roads it would be in the garage for a week," Moshe said as he stepped into the accounting office.

"Spraying has to be done by someone, Moshe," Chaim chirped.

"What if I parked it at the end of the paved road and walked in?"

"Ari, if you bring it back with so much as a speck of dirt on it I'll have your rear end!"

"I promise," I said holding both my hands up toward the sky.

"Thanks, Chaim," I said after Moshe left shaking his head in utter disbelief that he'd given in to me.

"For what?"

"Just for being the old Chaim."

"Try and stay the old Ari. I don't know what you are planning out there tonight. Please at least try to spray a little, okay?"

Having lost track of all time, I quickly ran home to change clothes. It would be dark in about an hour and I needed to move fast. At tops, it would take me thirty-five minutes to drive to the gate of the vineyard. Add to that the twenty minutes I would need to walk to the shed. If I left immediately, I could make it. It was one date I wasn't going to stand up.

As I opened the door to leave my house, in walked Aviva. The entire time since Vickie and I had gotten divorced, Aviva only set foot into my house on one other occasion. She was the one who brought me news of my Dad's first heart attack. By the look on her face, I was expecting something equally as traumatic.

"Ari, may I come in?" Aviva asked as she passed me by walking directly into the kitchen.

"Aviva, I'm very late. I have to begin spraying before dark. Unless it's really critical . . ."

"Late for a date, Ari?"

"As a matter of fact, Aviva, yes," I answered as I picked up my rucksack and made for the front door.

"Not so fast, mister!" Aviva yelled in hot pursuit of me.

"Aviva . . ."

"Ari, I demand you tell me what's with you and Vickie."

"Nothing, I promise."

"Going out now to have a date with you know who and later in the week a date with Vickie."

"Aviva, Vickie and I don't have a date Thursday night. We're just meeting because we have something to discuss and that's all, honest."

"Ari, Vickie wouldn't call me at two in the morning just to tell me you two had things to discuss."

"She what . . . two in the morning?" I asked as I fell on the couch.

"You know, Ari, you two are confusing the hell out of me."

"I'll be . . . ," I said. "Aviva, I really have to go."

"Ari, are you planning to get back together with Vickie?" shyly Aviva asked.

"Aviva, I promise if we do you'll be the first to know. Just don't grow grey waiting."

"Funny, Ari."

I jetted out of the kitchen door. Running up to the office, I couldn't get over it. Vickie must have phoned Aviva immediately after she hung up from me. Why did she call? Was it because I told her I was dating a Palestinian? Was she genuinely excited I called?

Reaching the van, I realized I was way behind schedule, at best making the shed by dessert. Sailing past the soldier at the front gate, I sat low in the driver's seat. Once on the main road, I hoisted the jibe and put three sheets into the wind. Almost bottoming out in the valley, the van glided effortlessly down the road.

Approaching Beit El-Safa, I saw a familiar sight in the road . . . tires not yet ablaze. Placed only moments earlier on the road, I was certain if I hadn't arrived they would have already been ignited. I looked at my watch and had no choice but to push the accelerator to the floor and drive through.

Eighty . . . eighty-five . . . ninety . . . ninety-five . . . one hundred kilometers per hour and climbing. I figured to zip through the tires before any trouble could begin, looking in all directions before I reached the second group of tires, all except one.

"Crash! . . . Bang! . . . Ping! . . . Bang!"

Struck first was the front window with its thousand pieces covering the front seat. The next volley made a waffle out of the van's right side. Looking down at the speedometer, I was cruising at one hundred ten. Because I was going so fast, I was literally in and out of the trouble zone in an instant.

With my right hand, I pushed the remaining glass out of the front window. The wind pierced my face so hard I had to wear my sunglasses just to see. I was lucky; however, the moshav's van wasn't as fortunate. Then I realized my injury would come later when I confronted Moshe.

Reaching the end of the paved road, I knew I'd never make it on time, having no strength left to walk in. Although Moshe gave me implicit orders not to take the van in, I had nothing to lose. What further damage could possibly happen? Ever so slowly I drove toward the shed. From a distance I could see Selah and the others were just sitting down. Capriciously I began speeding toward the shed. I didn't notice . . .

171

TWENTY-TWO

By all accounts, I must have been in a dream state approaching the shed, oblivious to everything while the van kept accelerating. When I topped the hill just before the shed, the front of the van left the ground. Touching down in the soft dirt of the road, I came crashing back to the present.

Focusing on the shed, I barely comprehended what I saw, Selah and the others running for dear life; moments before they sat quietly under the peaceful oak beginning their evening meal. Last to leave the shed area were Aisha and her mother who was holding Ali tightly in her arms. I wondered what it could have been that frightened them.

Speeding the last remaining meters to the shed, I reached the overlooking oak and slammed on the brakes finally stopping about ten meters later. Bolting from the van, I ran after them, but I saw no one as if they had vanished into thin air. Not unlike, I thought, the first time I saw Aisha through the rainbow.

"Aisha! . . . Selah! . . . It's me . . . Ari." I screamed to no avail at the top of my lungs.

Quiet . . . deathly quiet was all that prevailed. Whatever had scared them did a good job. For several more moments I kept calling out in the vain. Slowly I turned and headed toward the shed. About five meters from the shed it hit me.

Of course, how stupid could I have been? At first I cracked a smile and then burst out with laughter. Our van was painted blue. In Israel all police vehicles were painted the same blue. I would have run too if I had been them. Seeing the sight of a blue van speeding up the hill I was sure scared the pure living hell out of them.

Sitting under the thoughtful oak, I debated whether I should stay until they came back or return to the moshav. Eventually Selah would sneak back to see if all was okay. A sudden sick feeling in my stomach made me realize I really didn't want to be around when they returned. How does one apologize for wreaking havoc on a group of people, friends?

Everything was all set for a feast. Plates were laid on top of straw mats on the ground, enough for all to partake. And what a spread it was too. Sticking my finger in a bowl of something that looked like pudding, I felt great empathy with Goldilocks when she invaded the three bear's domain as I began to eat.

Fire! It was like drinking molten lava. My mouth began to burn so badly my eyes watered like a crying baby. Boy was I in pain. Seeing nothing set before me that would extinguish the flame in my mouth, I ran to the water wagon. There I connected my lips directly to the faucet as if I were filling up the sprayer.

"You must be very thirsty, Ari?" Selah said as he came up from behind the water wagon.

"Selah, I'm really sorry about scaring everybody," I apologized. "I realized only after you had run away that you must have thought I was the police."

"We really didn't know who it was, Ari, but seeing a strange van fly up the hill did make us a little bit apprehensive I must admit." Selah cracked a broad smile as he too bent down to take a drink.

"But I don't understand, Selah, none of you have been in trouble with the authorities. Why did you run?"

"That's why we've never been in trouble. We're too fast to get caught!" Selah laughed slapping me on the back.

I too began to laugh, but inside I questioned whether it really was a joke or the truth. Remembering the army report, I wondered if they were really clean or just fleet of foot as Selah said.

And what of Selah? The report was explicit about his two brothers. Could it be the only reason his name didn't follow

Fatima's was he was fast? Were his two brothers just bad apples in a barrel? Or was it true the apple doesn't fall far from the tree?

"Selah, can you spray tonight?"

"If you want, Ari."

"I have to be back on the moshav early tonight. Something came up the last minute." I lied through my teeth. All I could think of was my Dad being right about my having been duped and felt I needed some more time to sort things out. Sitting down to supper with my cousins would just further confuse me. I bet they even called Selah "speedy" in Deir El-Salam.

"You will stay for supper won't you? Everyone will be returning soon. We'll eat then."

"I don't know; it's getting late."

"Aisha and Ali have been preparing all afternoon. Ari, you know this banquet is in your honor. Ali will be very disappointed."

"Aisha," I thought to myself, my little leprechaun.

Maybe I was jumping to conclusions again. After all Selah had always before proven his reliability and worth, trust becoming a bond between us. Surely, his two brothers were the exception. In these days of Intifada families splitting allegiances was certainly plausible. Yet, not having any siblings of my own, I couldn't really get a gut feeling either way.

About fifteen minutes later the rest started drifting back a few at a time. I guess a life "on the other side" as Vickie always called it had taught them to be cautious. And did they ever give me dirty looks. Fasting all day and then I show up like something out of a "B" movie script. Graciously, I accepted their glares as highly justified.

"Ari! Ari!" Ali screamed as he ran from Fatima's arms.

"Ali," I said as I picked him up, catching a glimpse of Aisha walking toward the shed. She appeared not to have any direct eye contact with me and I couldn't understand why. Hopefully, it was nothing more than my imagination.

"Come, let's eat," Selah said as he lit the fire in the middle of the circle of plates, its blaze illuminating the darkness surrounding the shed. On it he placed the *cezve* to make Turkish coffee. Our cousins, I think, couldn't work without one. It was used for cooking coffee, tea or just to boil water. I've heard it said among the Bedouins of the desert that whenever a group set out to work one remained by the fire to keep the *cezve* cooking at all times.

"Selah, since I don't see a printed menu, would you mind explaining what I'm about to eat?"

"No problem, Ari, I wouldn't want to start a fire inside of you again," Selah laughed as he proceeded to describe in full the feast before us.

There were dishes of eggplant, rice, tomatoes, eggs and potatoes, fresh vegetables and fruit in abundance everywhere. Upon each dish was poured a generous amount of olive oil. Instead of utensils, we rolled pita bread, using it like a spoon.

Partaking of each delicacy, I thought of my diet staple, pizza, tuna fish and French fried potatoes. For the first time I was eating exactly what my doctor had been prescribing for years to reduce the cholesterol level in my blood. No wonder our cousins always looked healthy and we looked fat.

One dish, to me at least, was very tasty. Aisha last year had cured some green olives in a mixture of lemon juice, pepper and water. Boy, were they good. I kept popping them into my mouth like candy. Suddenly, my stomach began to feel the cumulative effect of all the spice and pepper. Selah kept pouring tea glass after glass. Or should I say tea flavored sugar. Soon the tea's medicinal effect worked.

During the meal, I noticed something out of order, but just couldn't put my finger on it when all of a sudden I realized what it was. The entire time while we ate till our heart's content, Aisha and her mother kept serving our needs. Never did they stop to eat. Only later after we finished did they finally sit down to eat alone.

I found that very strange and it made me remember an incident a few days earlier when Selah and the others had finished working in area four. I drove up as they got ready to return to the shed. Selah started the tractor with two or three kids hanging from any place they could. Yet, his mother was literally bringing up the dust by walking alone behind the tractor.

At the time I thought it disjointed. If it were my mother, she would have ridden on the seat next to me. Other times, I'd noticed similar behavior. There I sat, Mr. Chauvinist, advocating women's rights among Palestinians. I just hated to think any man would treat Aisha that way.

Fully satisfied with our supper, we stretched out to relax. Aisha sat to the right of the shed door with her legs folded under her, Ali almost asleep on her lap. Fatima had already gone inside for the evening. To my surprise, a few of the younger kids brought out a hand carved pipe and began smoking hashish. Surprised not that they were smoking it, but that they had no fear in front of me.

Observing that motley group gave me a great sense of satisfaction. My confidence in Selah and the others appeared to be justified. Sitting around the fire reminded me of an old American Western movie I saw as a child. After a hard day on horseback herding cattle, the group of cowboys gathered around the campfire to relax. A really rustic scene not unlike the one I participated in by the shed. I was even sure that a similar scene was repeated many times among the early Jewish pioneers who settled our land.

"I guess I'd better get started spraying," Selah said breaking the bond of comradely that existed. "Don't you have to go also, Ari?"

"Oh, thanks Selah," I said, "I completely lost track of time."

"What was it you had to do back on the moshav?"

"I have to be standing by the main gate at ten o'clock," I yelled looking directly at Aisha, not in Hebrew, but in English so Aisha could understand the message.

"What did you say, Ari? It sounded like English."

177

I repeated to Selah exactly what I had said in Hebrew. Aisha nodded to me as she got up holding Ali in her arms. With a smile, she turned to go into the shed.

In the flickering shadows of the fire, I saw Aisha raise her hands slightly crossing over her heart. Then she lifted them away from her body like the wings of a butterfly. Her movements, I guessed were some form of endearment, or at least I hoped.

As I boarded what was left of the moshav's van, Selah began to approach.

"Ari, just a minute, okay?"

"Sure, Selah," I said as I got out of the van.

"When you came flying up the road earlier . . ."

"I'm still very sorry . . . ,"

"We . . . well… I don't want you to think we ran because we had done something that would make the police come after us."

"Selah, I'm sure you were just plain scared," I said, "and who wouldn't be the way I topped the hill."

"Ari, remember the two kids I said left their identity cards back in the village."

"I remember, Selah."

"Well . . . that wasn't exactly the truth. Both had been in trouble with the army . . ."

"Why did you bring them to the vineyard if they were troublemakers, Selah? I'm surprised at you."

"Ari, I thought long and hard before I did. But what you don't see or know about any of us is the hardships we face because of the Intifada."

"You're right. I only know we're the ones who get stoned, fire bombed and have had our fields burned."

"Their mother begged me, Ari, she begged me to give them an opportunity to work."

"She begged you?"

"Those two kids were her oldest boys among six children. Since her husband died four years ago, they've been the sole support for the family."

"But you said they had been in trouble with the army."

"Ari, I'm not going to underplay those who cause trouble. They are a menace to both our people, but some kids have gotten caught up in the fever of the times . . ."

"Fever of the times?"

"After years of occupation, the Intifada has brought hope to our people. A hope that in the end things can be different."

"I know you don't want to return to Jordanian control, correct?"

"Our parents, most of them anyway, have lived through it all like my father has. He remembers hearing of the Turkish occupation as a boy. Then it was the British. Next he lived under Jordanian rule by a monarch from Saudi Arabia. Finally in 1967 his life turned to Israel occupation."

"Be honest, Selah, hasn't it been better under our government economically for you than the others?"

"Until the Intifada that might have been true, Ari. We are Palestinians. Never have we been Turks, English, Jordanian and surely not Israeli."

"You're right; we lived together, maybe not always as perfect as it could have been. Only after the Intifada began did Palestinian nationalism surface."

"Don't get me wrong, Ari, but you Israelis have been so naive. Years of rule over us haven't taught you the most important lesson," Selah said somewhat angrily.

"And what lesson is that?" I snapped back.

"We were Palestinians before the Intifada not as a result of the Intifada. During the 1960's in the United States, the riots didn't teach the black people they were black . . ."

"Selah, before the Intifada began in December, 1987, the so called voice of Palestinian nationalism wasn't heard."

179

"That's another lesson you must learn, Ari. The Intifada for my generation began the day after the 1967 war ended and has grown steadily ever since beneath two decades of Israeli rule. Ari, do you realize almost everyone throwing stones in the street was born after that war!"

"So what!"

"Those kids," Selah continued, "have only known what it's like to live under Israeli rule. And their entire lives they've heard the voice of Palestinian nationalism ringing in their ears.

"Well, I guess I've been deaf all these years to it," I admitted.

"Even if you haven't heard it yourself, it's been singing out loud and clear. To them it's a dream of a life being master of their own destiny. The same dream your people dreamt for many years, Ari."

"Selah, do you think this is all going to end with a country of your own?" I asked with a sharp tone.

"Ari, I honestly don't know what to think anymore. I've never been more confused in my life."

"I share the feeling, Selah, believe me I know exactly what you mean."

"Maybe we won't have a country of our own. It would be a nice thought. You have a country and a flag you can stand up for. What do we Palestinians have I ask you?"

"If tomorrow our government agreed to capitulate and created a Palestinian state say in Gaza, would you leave Deir El-Salam and move there? How many Palestinians do you honestly think would uproot from Hebron?"

"You're right to a certain extent. My father's generation somewhat fear a state of our own. They'd rather live out their years in whatever comforts they have left. The young unmarried would move, however, to be sure."

"What about you, Selah, would you move?"

"No, probably not. I think most of us that are married with families and have never been in trouble with the authorities would stay where we live."

"So, I'm right," I grinned.

"Ari, the issues at hand are not for our generation to decide. The young Palestinian and Israeli kids of today will determine the future. They will be the leadership five, ten, fifteen years from now and not those who fled long ago to live in comfort outside our land who have lost touch with our people's needs."

"How long do you think it will all last, Selah?"

"Ari, the Intifada is something that will never end. This stage, however, probably has at best three to five years to run."

"Then peace will be possible?"

"I only fear the next phase will be a violent one."

"Don't worry about that, our army . . ."

". . . is totally impotent against the Intifada," Selah interrupted, "the streets are controlled by kids. They will make something happen by force if they have to. Our parents have lost control of their sons and daughters."

"I thought in a Palestinian family whatever the father said was law?"

"It used to be that way, but I've seen it change in my own family."

"You mean Aisha's rebellion?"

"No, I have a brother who would laugh at my father and call him old fashioned. To him the Intifada was a challenge. One night he told him if our people gave up, we'd get our heads bashed in or worse even killed. But if we held on long enough, we might get back Jaffa, Tel Aviv and Haifa."

"In a war of attrition like that you'd have so much to lose."

"I would, Ari, that's a fact, but the kids in the streets have nothing to lose and everything to gain. Like I said, the future of it all doesn't rest with any of us. It will depend on those kids throwing rocks. Their voices will ultimately have to be heard."

With Selah's last comment a strange silence prevailed. We had never before discussed the weather. Yet, he and I had one of the most provocative discussions I'd ever had. I felt like I'd met him for the first time. Funny how you can be around someone for years and never know what makes him tick.

"Those two kids," I said breaking the silence.

"What kids, Ari?"

"The ones that left because they were in trouble."

"What about them?"

"If you give me your word they'll cause no trouble here, you can bring them back next week. But understand, Selah, they'll get blamed for anything that happens and you have to be responsible, okay?"

Getting back into the van, I started the engine and looked down at the dashboard clock. There was enough time for me to go to Ramle before I met Aisha. After my dialogue with Selah I needed a beer, a nice cold Israeli blue and white.

Backing out, I saw Selah turn and head toward the van again. The thought of another endless debate ran through my mind as he stood by the door. Selah extended his hand to me and I clasped his with both of mine.

"Thanks, Ari."

And with that Selah turned and walked away into the darkness of the night.

TWENTY-THREE

"Ten thirty!" Where could she be? Aisha's nod led me to believe she understood my message. Rather than worry, I decided to sing in order to distract myself. At first they were quiet songs, however, I got progressively louder and louder. In my repertoire was everything from Israeli folk music to modern pop. Finally reaching the ultimate, I began making up my own opera out of plain old gibberish, my bass voice echoing among the trees.

"Clap . . . clap . . . clap!"

I turned around to see Aisha sitting on a rock by the rear of the van clapping and laughing hysterically. All I could do was smile from embarrassment. On that rock she looked so alive . . . so happy. I could almost see the essence of her spirit within. Every time I was near Aisha I felt good all over.

"You didn't know I could sing, did you?"

"I still don't, Ari," Aisha said as she continued to laugh uncontrollably.

"Come get in the van," I said, "there's a place I want to show you."

"Ari, I don't think I should go too far," Aisha protested.

"It's near Abu Ali's encampment."

I opened the door and helped her up to the front seat. Once she was seated, I began to let go of her hand. As I did she tightly held onto mine. Not knowing what to do, I leaned over and kissed her hand. Immediately Aisha snatched it back. I guess once again I had crossed over the line of permitted and forbidden.

We reached our destination, an old lookout post left by the Turkish army around the turn of the century. Built high on a hill above the Ayalon Valley, the view was simply breathtaking. When we arrived, the moon was already overhead lighting up the ground

183

below. Looking toward the left, we could see the fires burning brightly at Abu Ali's.

I motioned for Aisha to follow me to the lookout. The Turks had fashioned the main level on the hilltop. Steep steps lead, however, to a tier below carved out of the cliff face itself. To be hidden far away from everyone totally alone with my little leprechaun was all I desired.

"Aisha, first let me say I'm sorry I scared all of you like I did."

"It's okay, but what of you? How did the van get so damaged? Were you in an accident?"

". . . something like an accident. Near our moshav is a village called Beit El-Safa. I was driving . . ."

"You don't have to say anymore, Ari, I know all too well what happened next."

"Aisha," I said, "someone has been upsetting me the past few weeks."

"Who, Ari? I hope it wasn't me."

"Well, to a certain extent it is you."

"I'm sorry for whatever I've done to upset you."

"Aisha, don't worry, directly you've done nothing."

"Please tell me then, Ari, what's upset you?" Aisha asked with a sorrowful look.

"I've spent the last several weeks trying to spend every minute I could with you . . ."

"And I with you," Aisha interrupted.

"That's exactly the problem, Aisha, I've grown deeply in love with you, not that it's a problem in itself."

"Ari, I don't understand," Aisha said, her eyes puzzled.

"Aisha, I don't even know how you feel about me. I think what we have for each other's mutual, but you've said nothing . . ."

"Ari, I don't know what love is supposed to be. I don't think anyone does at the outset of a relationship."

"I've been married before, as you know. With my wife it started with love from the first day and never stopped."

184

"My mother and father never really knew each other before they married, Ari. In fact they only met once or twice prior to their marriage. Her parents felt that my father would provide a good life for my mother. Love never entered into it."

"You told me once your mother loved your father very much despite his taking a second wife."

"Ari, that's what I know of love. My parents, after years of sharing a life together, developed their love."

"What of us, Aisha? I love you. Whether you can define your feelings in those terms or not you must admit that they exist."

"It's true I have feelings for you, Ari. Feelings, well, feelings I've never known before. When you surprised me that day while I was starting to take a shower, I admit I crossed a threshold in those feelings. Otherwise I'd never have chanced that you remain while I was vulnerable to your desires."

"Aisha, I honestly don't understand what you are trying to say."

"Do you have any idea what it took for me to let you stay?"

". . . but, I said I wouldn't compromise your modesty and I didn't."

"No, I even wished, to a certain extent, you had turned around to see me. You stayed because I wanted you there. I agreed freely because I felt a bond between us that never existed within me before."

"You love me then, Aisha, admit it!"

"I can't, Ari, not because I don't feel for you. I'm just scared."

"Scared? Of what?"

"That there can never be an *us*," Aisha said as tears trickled from her blue eyes.

The moon shone brightly at the top of the sky, its beams lighting our little alcove like a torch giving not only light, but warmth as well. I looked away from the tears cascading from Aisha's face toward the valley below.

185

Among the rocks I saw see a pair of rabbits at play. Each was jumping to a higher rock stopping only to look at the other, prancing together to and fro in their coats of brown and white.

"It's only natural for two people to love each other, Aisha," I said, "just like the two rabbits below. Who says we can't stay together forever?"

"In my village there are several Israeli women who have married men of my people."

"See, it's possible then."

"But," Aisha continued, "I've never heard of a single case where a Palestinian woman married an Israeli man. There must be something within our Holy Koran forbidding it. If so, we can never be together."

"By your own admission, Aisha, Palestinian women are prohibited from working or doing most anything outside of their home. Even going to a neighboring village is never done alone. You and the other women live dreadfully protected lives."

"True, but what's that got to do with us?"

"Don't you see? Palestinian men marry Israeli women because they are around them. Every day they leave their villages to work in hotels, restaurants, construction jobs, stores, etc. All these places are in Israel proper and all among other Israeli workers. That's why they know Hebrew and you don't."

"I think I understand," Aisha said wiping the remaining tears from her eyes.

"If a Palestinian man can marry an Israeli woman then I'm sure the opposite must be true," I argued.

"Ari, what you say makes sense, but you left out one very important part. All of the Israeli women I'm familiar with became Moslem. Are you willing to do that for me?" Aisha asked deeply peering into my eyes.

In all my life I was never one to believe in fairytales, ghosts or witches. However, immediately after Aisha asked me that most provocative question, I sensed the presence of Chaim looking over my shoulder.

Chaim told me at the outset having a fling with a Palestinian maiden was one thing. To reject all of my life's beliefs was a totally different story. Deep down inside I was glad Chaim's ghost was present. However, I wished he was really next to me. I desperately needed someone to talk with fast.

"Aisha," I said after an endless silence, "would you leave your faith for me?"

"I don't think I could, Ari. No matter how much I feel for you I think that would be impossible."

"Now you can understand my reservations about becoming Moslem. It's not because I don't love you."

"Ari, I think now I have an answer to my feelings for you. If in your terms it's called love then that's what it must be. Even though the impossibility of our growing old together exists, I feel I couldn't live another day without you."

"It is love, Aisha, true love," I said as her eyes regained their sparkle.

"Maybe it is not so impossible after all, Ari."

"What do you mean?"

"In our Holy Koran it is written whatever is permitted to the Jewish people to eat, we are also allowed to eat. Ari, if you really love me as you say, then you'd be willing to do almost anything for me."

"Aisha, I think I've proven that already. Just ask," I said as my heart began to lift itself up.

"You would have to respect my way of life and I yours. Food would have to be restricted to only our peoples. My modesty in dress will certainly continue. You can't expect me to expose myself to others like those women in Hebron. Days holy to both of us must be kept. Agreed?"

"In other words at my age after shunning attempts to convince me to adhere more closely to my people's religious laws failed, now

I'm going to keep the laws of two faiths. It's only poetic justice, Aisha. With all my love and conviction I promise to never let you down."

"I feel it was Allah himself deemed we meet. Despite what anyone might say, we were meant to be together."

"Only one thing, Aisha, who will marry us?"

"How do your people get married, Ari?"

"Basically we go to a rabbi. He's the one responsible for our religious affairs."

"Like our Qadi," Aisha interrupted.

"He prepares the marriage contract," I continued, "then in front of two witnesses the man announces his intentions by declaring he wants to live with the woman under the laws of our people. That's about it except for the dancing and eating."

"In our village, after a man sees a woman he wishes to marry, he goes to his parents first. They in turn go to her parents to discuss the proposal. If both sides are in agreement, they contact the Qadi."

"Then you get married?"

"No, the Qadi undertakes an investigation of his own to see if the man and woman are of good character."

"And if they are?"

"Usually the Qadi will come to the house of the woman. First he talks to the woman alone to see if she has any objections to the man. I've been at that stage before."

"What did you tell the Qadi, Aisha?"

"Simply I had no desire to spend the rest of my life with the man. The Qadi from there went to tell him, for good reasons he couldn't say, he felt the marriage shouldn't take place."

"And if you had said yes?"

"The Qadi would have proceeded to talk to the man in the same way. If we both were in agreement, he would enter our names in his registry and give each of us a paper stating the entry occurred."

"That's all?"

"From that moment we are permitted to each other, but we usually wait a week or so to consummate after a big feast for our families and friends."

"Somewhere we will be joined together. I'm sure of that, Aisha."

"Ari, I want so much to stay with you always. The times make it difficult, but not impossible. When it's right, we'll know."

"Aisha, I've never felt happier in my life than I do now."

For the next hour Aisha and I walked around the groves of pomegranates, figs and almonds surrounding the outlook. Ever so natural were the words we spoke as we talked of our lives together.

Several meters from the van were the ruins of a very old house. Left somewhat intact was the courtyard wall completely surrounding the house. We ventured into the compound and sat opposite the main gate. Aisha said she was getting a little too cool so I built a fire from some wood scraps nearby. Watching the flames dance around the embers created a very relaxing mood.

"Ari, back by the shed earlier tonight, what were you and my brother arguing about?"

"Selah and I were just talking about current events."

"You mean the Intifada, don't you?"

"Aisha, your brother opened my eyes to a lot tonight. Some things he was right about one hundred percent. I never for a moment have given a thought to there being another side."

"We really suffer too, Ari. Most of us don't want any part of troubles. If there is a benefit at the end, of course we'll enjoy its fruits."

"From what Selah said, most young people are very much in favor of the whole uprising."

"In our village the women usually are the last to become involved, but that doesn't mean we don't understand what it's all about."

"I suppose it's hardest during a curfew."

"A village under curfew, Ari, is like a castle under siege by an invading army," Aisha responded in a slightly raised tone.

"Aisha, curfews are placed on a village only after it has been decided the situation is potentially explosive. It's done to protect people, not harm them," I explained.

"In some cases that might be true. From my vantage point, I see a single stone being thrown and the army clamps a whole village under curfew."

"And if a curfew wasn't called, then I'm sure many would get hurt or even killed . . . on both sides."

"What of the extended curfews? Who do they protect? We run out of food and water after a day or two. It may give the army peace, but for us it's worse than a few hours of confrontation. Ari, please don't try to defend an action that's totally wrong. I've even heard some of your leaders have said curfews are a good tool. Since the Palestinian people won't let your people live normal lives anymore, curfews are imposed to insure that we won't either."

"You must understand our frustrations," I said, "if we are to understand yours. We've been stoned, firebombed and even shot at until we've had enough. Remember, I was almost killed a few weeks ago, Aisha. Our lives, because of the Intifada, have been anything but normal."

"We've had to become accustomed to a routine of abnormality, Ari. Strikes, fights with the army and settlers, curfews and perpetual school closings haven't made our lives enjoyable either."

"You must admit for both our peoples the Intifada has had devastating effects. It should never have started," I said.

"Ari, the uprising started by momentum, not by people," Aisha said looking sorrowful about the shift in conversation away from things pleasant.

"Does Intifada mean uprising in Arabic?"

"It comes from the word *nafada* which means many things. Depending how it's used, it can mean trembling, shaking, shivering, etc. How we use it today means to shake off, or better, the act of shaking off."

"And Israeli occupation is what's to be shaken off. I got the message from your brother Selah."

"Let's not quarrel over matters bigger than us both, Ari. I love you. I say that with all the conviction of my heart. No uprising or worse will ever drive us apart," Aisha said regaining her composure about her.

"I love you, too," I said, "more than you realize Aisha."

"Understand for my sake, Ari, how I see and feel the Intifada. Not as a diehard in the street. I've never been with the others throwing rocks although my brother, Nassir, has tried to force me."

"I'm glad you haven't participated in the Intifada."

"Oh, but I have, Ari. I've stood with my mother outside army camps for detainees waiting in the cold rain for a glimpse of my brother."

"I didn't know," I apologized.

"My family has been torn apart because of the Intifada. My brother Ibrahim was killed by the army near the Beit Oman mosque in the northern part of Hebron."

"What did he do to get shot?"

"His only crime was trying to stop my brother Nassir from destroying our family. It's Nassir's Intifada, not mine. Nassir was involved with killing a doctor in our village. Ibrahim was only trying to persuade him to flee to Kuwait and live with my cousin Mahmud who works at an oil refinery there when the army caught them. Nassir tried to grab a rifle away from one of the soldiers. The gun went off and Ibrahim collapsed. My mother sent him because she didn't want to live to see her son killed."

"So instead, she saw another son killed," I said seeing how difficult it was for Aisha to continue.

"And every day she waits to hear of Nassir's death," Aisha cried.

"I'm sorry, Aisha, for my arrogance earlier."

"Ari, do you know why I came to the vineyard with my mother?"

"To keep her company I guess."

"No, I couldn't bear to walk down the streets of Deir El-Salam anymore and look into the faces of the children."

"Why?"

"I'd look into the faces of the children who used to play with footballs and with dolls and cry. Now all they talk about are demonstrations, strikes, throwing rocks, and being arrested. Sometimes they even throw stones at each other as practice."

"I've seen the same behavior on my moshav, Aisha."

"Ari, the saddest part of the horrible time in which we live is that the little children are being taught to hate even before they understand why if there is any reason at all worth giving them." Aisha leaned her head on my shoulder and began to cry.

TWENTY-FOUR

"A . . . R . . . I!"

"Quick, Chaim, let's get out of here fast," I yelled as I slammed the passenger door to our truck.

"A . . . R . . . I!"

"Why is Moshe screaming your name into the moshav's public address system, Ari?" Chaim asked as he started the truck. "Don't you think you should see what he wants with you?"

"I had a little accident last night with the van. Not wanting to wake him, I left him a note that the van was parked in front of the garage."

"I . . . F . . . I . . . G . . . E . . . T . . . M . . . Y . . . !"

Leaving the moshav, we could still hear Moshe's voice at the front gate. Surely when we returned I'd have to face him. On the way home I figured we'd detour to Ramallah in order to file a report on the incident last night. That, I hoped, would at least settle Moshe down a little. Luckily, the government was quick about repairing Intifada damage. Only property damage, however, the other damages could never be repaired.

Last night was some experience for me. Not only did I really meet Selah for the first time, but I got closer to Aisha than I had ever dreamt possible. For the first time, in a very long time, I honestly looked forward to being alive. Since separating from Vickie, I'd lost that feeling.

Driving to the vineyard gave me ample time to reflect on all that had transpired in my life since I returned from reserve duty in Gaza. Ironic, how confusion instead of clarity reigned in my life. Being exposed to the other side last night caused a gnawing away in my life long belief system. Try as I did to sort things out, I kept hearing my Dad's voice warning me not to follow my emotions. "Time proven facts direct one's life better than feelings of the heart." His words still rung in my ears.

"Tell me again why it was Selah sprayed last night instead of you, Ari?" asked Chaim.

"Never mind about it now, Chaim," I snapped back. Once again, like hundreds of times before, his ill timed interruption had broken my train of thought.

Nearing the shed, we saw Abu Ali approaching on a small, grey donkey. Sitting atop his beast of burden, he looked like a Middle Eastern poster child. As he rode, his long white robe and *keffiyeh* fluttered in the breeze. A knife hung from a rope snuggly tied to his waist and on his feet were fastened well worn, brown sandals.

"Ari, I think we should start calling him Ali Baba," Chaim chuckled.

"Maybe we should," I agreed. "I'm sure instead of forty thieves he's had at least forty wives.

Dismounting, Abu Ali motioned for me to come join him under the revealing oak. Chaim proceeded to check on Selah and the others in area ten while I sat opposite Abu Ali on the ground. He lit the fire to make coffee taking the *cezve* from my hand and filling it with rich, black coffee. While the water was heating up, Abu Ali broke the silence.

"A taxi came early today for Fatima, Ali and Aisha," he said in almost a whisper, "to help with the spring wheat harvest."

"Selah didn't say anything about it to me yesterday," I said in shock.

"He didn't know himself. His father just came with a driver to take them back."

"I don't understand. Was his new wife with him?"

"No, he was alone," Abu Ali said.

"Did he say when they would be coming back?"

"That's an interesting question." Abu Ali took a long sip of coffee while he leaned against the trunk of the supportive oak.

"I would appreciate an answer," I demanded as thoughts of Aisha ran through my head.

"It appears," Abu Ali continued, "that his father threw the second wife out of the house. Fatima persevered after all."

"But will they return?"

"Certainly Ali will stay back in the village with his mother. Selah said she's missed him too much. Now I wouldn't think that Fatima's likely to abandon her regained husband too quickly. That leaves us with Aisha," Abu Ali said with a weird smile on his face.

"Well, is she or isn't she coming back?"

"Maybe it will be best for everyone if she didn't return."

"What's that supposed to mean?"

"Ari, at the beginning of time it was decided that all people would be different. Some were to be white, black, brown, yellow, etc. Many different types make up a world and it's the same with traditions. You are Israeli, I am a Palestinian and your father and mother were from Europe. I think it's best to leave the natural order of the world alone."

"Abu Ali, I have no earthly idea what you are talking about."

"I've lived among these hills and valleys all my life, Ari. When the land speaks to me, I listen. From my tent last night I saw a fire. A fire burning out here any night is always of interest to me, but what I saw in last night's fire was of even more interest."

"You didn't tell Selah, I mean that Aisha was with me," I said feeling like a child who'd gotten caught with his hand in the cookie jar.

"My years, Ari, have taught me to be a man of peace. Water away from where I swim causes me no concern. Only if its waves approach me do I worry." Abu Ali raised his lips to finish his coffee.

"You needn't worry, Abu Ali, I have only the most honorable intentions where Aisha is concerned," I said trying to dispel any fears he might have.

"Last night wasn't the first time you were together. Maybe it should be the last before you lose more than your gun next time."

"You don't understand . . . how could you?" I pleaded.

"Once, Ari, I had a wife who was Moroccan. I loved her more than any I've had since. She was my very first wife," Abu Ali confided.

"It's not the same Abu Ali . . ."

"She wasn't a Palestinian," Abu Ali interrupted, "she was a Jew. Her family had only been in this land a few months. She found it very difficult to live among the European Jews here, her whole life steeped in Arab culture; not one word of Hebrew could she speak, only Arabic."

"You see, you married a Jewish woman and by your own admission she was loved by you more than any other."

"Ari, we parted because of our love for each other. Despite the fact that the Jews who settled the land had customs unfamiliar to her, nonetheless, they were her people. It was one thing to live as a Jew among Arabs in Morocco. Yet, it was a totally different thing to be a Jew living among Arabs as an Arab," Abu Ali said as a mist filled his eyes.

"Where is she now?"

"We parted and she returned to her people. I was told she died during your war for independence. She wanted to live among her people and in the end she died with them."

"I'm sorry, Abu Ali."

"Just remember this, Ari; it's important for a person to live among his people in order for him to die with them. When it's all over, that's the only thing that really counts."

With those words, Abu Ali unfolded his legs and painstakingly stood up. Reaching around my back placing his right arm across my shoulder, he compelled me to walk with him to his donkey. As he mounted, he turned toward me.

"Don't despair, Ari, Aisha will return to the vineyard. I can see that written in the heavens. What will happen in the end between you two, however, is written on the sands by the sea. Try to read it before the tide washes it away. Once that happens, you'll never know what the end could have been," Abu Ali said as he sat taller on his donkey riding away.

Lying flat on my back under the lofty oak I watched as the sun's rays peaked behind the leaves. My old friend the sun; it was his brightness that gave me the rainbow at whose end I found Aisha, my little pot of gold. So much had happened in my life in such a short period of time. I guess life always happens that way. Oh, why is life ever so short.

"Are you dead, Ari?" Chaim yelled as he drove up, "you are lying like a corpse. That'll be good practice for when you return to the moshav."

"Why is it I never know what you are talking about Chaim?"

"I spoke to Moshe on the radio."

"Oh!" I sighed.

"Don't worry I reassured him down by telling him what happened to the van. He was somewhat relieved when I told him we'd file a report in Ramallah today."

"Thanks again, Chaim," I said to my trusty knight in shining armor.

"But there is one little thing he is confused about. He wanted to know if you got stoned in Beit El-Safa, how did grape vines get caught in the exhaust pipe." Chaim said as we both burst into laughter.

TWENTY-FIVE

Sir Moses Montefiore, my old friend Sir Moses. I can still remember the last time you and I talked. We spent many nights together contemplating where Vickie and I should live after we got married. Sir Moses, can you help me now?

Looking at my watch, I realized Vickie was due to arrive in another twenty minutes. Given her punctuality you could set your watch that when she showed up it would be seven o'clock exactly. This time I would surprise her by being early.

I felt a slight chill as a cool breeze passed. Montefiore's Windmill was one of the Jerusalem skyline's most prominent sights. Built in 1857 by Sir Moses, he hoped it would provide an industrial base as an effort to entice residents Old City to dwell outside its protective walls. In the 1850's no one dared venture beyond the security of the locked Zion Gate.

To alleviate the serious overcrowding in the Old City, Sir Moses helped build the settlement of Mishkenot Sha'ananim, dwellings of serenity. An isolated fortress just beyond the city walls, in the beginning he had to pay people to take up residence. However, even the first occupants scurried back to the safety of the Old City at night.

Thirty years later, the third settlement outside the city, Yemin Moshe, was constructed adjacent to the Mishkenot. During that period, living outside the wall was not so unheard of. The houses atop the hill overlooking the Old City originally comprising Yemin Moshe have stood until today.

Yemin Moshe was where I first met my old friend Sir Moses. At the beginning of the new state, the neighborhood was occupied mainly by poor immigrants from Turkey and Iran who could afford nothing more. At the time Yemin Moshe was neatly placed on the no man's land between Israel and Jordan. Once Jerusalem was reunited after the 1967 war, the municipality decided to redevelop the area.

Homes in Yemin Moshe were sold by the city to the wealthy that would be able to undertake the massive reconstruction required. Vickie's father, sensing always a good deal, bought the rights to one of the cottages. Since then, Yemin Moshe has been one of Israel's prime neighborhoods. When we first got married, he wanted us to live in his cottage there. During the same week Chaim brought us the news of Mevo Ayalon starting. Vickie and I spent an endless night sitting on the ground by the windmill trying to decide what to do.

By dawn, we had reached a compromise. Her father still had at least a year left before the house would be completed to his satisfaction. We agreed to try the moshav for that year. If things didn't work out there, we'd move to Yemin Moshe. In the end Vickie yielded to my desires. She knew I'd never be happy living the affluent life in the city. I knew she'd never adjust to the lifestyle of a farm. Some compromise!

Waiting with trepidation for Vickie to come, I walked past a sign the City of Jerusalem had placed near the entrance to the windmill plaza. The sign, divided into four panels, each depicted a specific era of the city's history. 1840 was the beginning of Turkish rule. In 1870 construction of the new city outside the wall began. 1917 saw the British soldiers march into Jerusalem. And 1948 brought division of the eternal city along armistice lines.

Written on each panel were the total populations of Jerusalem and the component figures of Jews, Arabs and Christians. I was simply astounded that over the one hundred year period the Jewish population was always the clear majority group in the city. But then there also was the ever-present Palestinian minority. History seems never to let us forget

"You're late, Vickie, its seven-o-one."

"Funny, Ari," Vickie said as she sat down next to me on the ground beside the windmill.

"Well, what do we do now?"

"I don't understand, Ari."

"You're the one who wanted to talk to me, remember?"

"Stop playing games, Ari. You call me in the middle of the night, tell me you're in love with a Palestinian woman, say goodnight and expect that's it." Vickie had set the ground rules.

"Where do you want to go?"

"We can sit here, Ari that is unless the memories are too difficult?"

"Not at all; I've just been spending the past hour thinking precisely about those times."

"So did I, driving up," Vickie admitted.

As Vickie and I talked, I realized the magic spell was working again. I was in Jerusalem with Vickie. Mustering any thoughts of Aisha were difficult. Why was it every time I was around her I felt nothing had changed between us? In all the time since our divorce she had never shown any remorse at all. It was her idea, not mine, for the separation.

"Ari, did you ever wonder why we parted?"

"Why all of a sudden are you of all people asking that question?" angrily I asked.

"When you called the other night . . ."

"Oh! That's it. Now I see through you, Vickie. You've realized that your life isn't what you'd thought it was going to be when we separated. When I called and said I was in love with someone else that threw a red flag in your face. You always had me at the end of a string. Now the string broke . . ."

"Good-bye, Ari!" Vickie said jumping up to leave.

Without turning back, Vickie started walking toward Yemin Moshe. I watched as she disappeared into the evening. What a fool I'd been. I don't know why, but I always up front tried to destroy my moments with her. Maybe it's always been a self-fulfilling prophecy. I never could take Vickie's rejection of me. Falling back against the windmill, I gave a look toward the sky. What do I do now Sir Moses?

"Vickie . . . Vickie . . . Vickie . . ." I yelled as I ran through the narrow streets of Yemin Moshe looking for her.

Of course! That's where she'd be, I thought to myself. Yemin Moshe was built on a sloping hill facing the Old City in four levels further subdivided in quadrants with each house opening into a little lane for security.

Vickie's father had purchased his cottage in the middle of the complex. Approaching, I saw Vickie sitting opposite her dream house as she called it. She didn't see me as I sat beside her.

"You startled me," Vickie said as she moved a little closer.

"Vickie, you know I've never even been back to this house since we decided to move to the moshav."

"I've been here often, Ari," Vickie said. "Before we separated, I would sit here and stare at its walls wondering if we'd ever live here. After our divorce, I've never been back until tonight."

"I remember you saying if we didn't move to the moshav we'd probably end up apart from each other. Now I wonder if we'd lived here instead of the moshav would we still be together."

"I was wondering exactly that when you sat next to me, Ari. Isn't it funny how our lives have unfolded."

"Vickie, I've never stopped loving you. I want you to know that," I said choking on each word.

"Nor I, you, Ari, but you already know that I'm sure."

"No, I don't Vickie. I don't know that. Ever since the night I walked into our house and found your note saying you had moved to Tel-Aviv to live with your parents, I've never known what to think of your feelings."

"I left because I love you," Vickie said in her defense.

"You know, Vickie, that's the second time in as many days I've heard of separating from someone because you love them. I guess I've had it backwards all my life. I thought if two people loved each other, they would stay together forever. Now this week I find out that if you really love someone you're supposed to leave them."

"Oh, stop it Ari! That's been your problem all along. You see things only through your eyes. You've never tried to focus on a situation from anyone else's position. Look at the world from 'another side' once," Vickie said raising her voice.

"Vickie, please calm down. Just tell me honestly how you can love someone so dearly that you can't live without them and then let them go?"

"Ari, I still love you now," Vickie said, "yet, if we didn't part when we did, I felt I would have grown to hate you. That's why we broke up; it was purely selfish. I didn't want to stop loving you and I never wanted to feel that you stopped loving me either."

"Why then in all these years didn't you agree to attempt reconciliation?"

"Because I never saw in you any changes that lead me to believe we could work out our difficulties."

"I never knew I needed to change. All I ever heard from you was I was married to the moshav. So, I thought all I needed to do was leave the moshav and I wasn't prepared to do that."

"Ari, I couldn't care where we lived. I think I proved that to you from the start. Your narrow minded attitude did me in. Everything is always so black and white with you," Vickie said on a roll.

"Black and white?"

"Look beyond for a change, Ari, the world is full of color. It's been a rainbow of colors that has kept us apart."

"Rainbows!" I sighed.

Deep in concentration, we started walking not paying attention to where we were going. Jerusalem was always our city and she would watch over us as we walked. I started to tell Vickie all about Aisha, complete with rainbows. Ever since I first met Aisha I needed to talk to someone about her. My parents would never have understood. Chaim was perfect to a point, but it was Vickie's ear I needed to bend the most.

203

"I never would have believed any of this possible for you, Ari," Vickie said as we walked through the darkness.

"You see, my eyes have been opened to the rainbow a little," I said. "Vickie, do you think Aisha and I will make it together?"

"Ari, I think it matters little that she's a Palestinian and you're an Israeli. You two love each other and that's very important, but sometimes love's not enough. Haven't we seen that?"

"What do you mean, not enough?"

"You're too settled a person, Ari, how are you going to uproot from the vineyard and leave your precious moshav? Oh! You never for a moment thought you'd have to do that. Did you?"

"I sought clarity from you, Vickie, not more confusion."

"I'm sorry, Ari, but now maybe you'll understand what I meant earlier. Love brings people together, but it can also tear people apart. It did in our case. Be careful it doesn't with you and Aisha."

"I have to get back to the moshav," I said looking at my watch.

"Please don't think in the least bit I'm trying to discourage you. Just beware, Ari, you can neither listen to the logic of a situation nor the palpitations of your heart. Look somewhere in between the two. Okay?"

"I'll try Vickie, and thanks for talking so openly. I'm glad we had this time together."

"Tell Aisha I wish you both the best," Vickie said as she got into her car.

"I will."

"Ari, one other thing. No matter what happens, I always will love you." Vickie pulled off, driving down King George Street.

"And I you," I said watching her go, "and I you.

Israel has always been a land of many contrasts. Modern and old peacefully exist side by side, each seemingly the base for the other. Sometimes a person has difficulty distinguishing their beginnings and endings. Archeological excavations have vividly revealed this problem. Many were the times an archeological team labored at restoring an ancient wall only to return the next day not knowing what they had done and what existed beforehand.

However, not every aspect of our society has yielded the harmonious development. For the past weeks I had witnessed one of the most obvious of contrasts. On the journey to the vineyard, I had watched myriads of women and children leaving Beit El-Safa to harvest their spring wheat crop. The burden fell on their shoulders because the men had to pursue full time jobs. As we drove by each day, I studied their tired, worn faces, hoping to see an Aisha among them.

At that time of the season, the hills were covered with a patchwork of amber stitched with threads of green. Our cousins laborious worked their small, private parcels from sun up to sun down; bending, cutting, shaking were all set in motion to an ancient ballet. Searching for words to describe their appearance while they harvested, Chaim came up with a most appropriate answer simply calling it biblical.

By contrast our moshav owned one thousand dunams of land neighboring the patch work parcels. Our land, unlike our cousins yielded more than just wheat. When the winter, rain soaked land began to dry and parch before summer, we would have cotton sprouting because of our massive investment in modern irrigation. Our cousins' land lay fallow, however, until fall when the rains came once more.

One day the contrast became more than obvious to me. After passing the children and women cutting their wheat using but a simple scythe, we passed Amos riding atop our giant, yellow European combine. Each effortless pass by him made a mockery of our cousin's honest labor, finishing in a few moments what would take them more than a day to complete. Modern and old suddenly lost its harmonious serenity of time.

"You know, Ari, each year it appears to me that our cousins have more land under cultivation," Chaim said.

I just nodded not wanting to respond. Since Aisha returned to Deir El-Salam, the Intifada had heated up a bit. All around Israel related incidents were on the rise. For us it was impossible to escape Beit El-Safa without being stoned. To alleviate the problem, we pioneered a new path around the village along our wheat fields. Soon others followed our trail until it had become a well worn road. Our cousins even began placing the new trail with menacing *ninjas*.

I had taken notice that Deir El-Salam was on the news a couple of times. Once was to report a sixteen year old had been shot in the leg by a rubber bullet after a jeep had come under an attack of stones and steel pipes. The second was announcing the lifting of a two day curfew in the village. Upon hearing that report, all I could think of was Aisha and her family living under "siege."

Daily I wondered if Aisha would return, stopping short many times of asking Selah. Yesterday I was given renewed hope. Selah told Chaim over the weekend he would be going home, the first time since Ali left. I knew he was looking forward to seeing him. Chaim said that he was bringing back the two kids who had troubles with the army and was he furious with me for agreeing.

To top everything, the day after Aisha left my Dad was rushed to the hospital. His doctor's diagnosis was simply another warning. Despite his frail heart, he had survived his third warning, anyone of which would have laid another man to rest.

I was only able to visit him once during his week's confinement. Try as I could, while I was there, I just couldn't look directly at my him lying in bed with all of those tubes and monitors attached. The thought of my Dad being merely mortal was more than I could accept. My mother understood and explained to him I was swamped with work in the vineyard. I guess he also understood.

"Tomorrow night's going to be fantastic," Chaim said from out of nowhere.

"Tomorrow?"

"Independence Day, Ari, we are all going to Jerusalem and . . ."

"Oh! I guess I really forgot all about it."

Aviva had arranged for Vickie and me to join them in celebration of our countries modern birthday. During a much younger time in our lives, we four looked forward to the Independence Day celebrations. Why not? It also was my birthday.

Celebrations then were highlighted by a large military parade; once even Chaim and I found ourselves uniformed and marching to beat of the band. Since nowadays, there was no military parade, most of the activities centered on Har Herzl for the official ceremony. The fun, however, was the gathering of thousands upon thousands in the heart of Jerusalem.

Normally, I never had any problems sleeping. Yet, the thought of tomorrow night with Vickie caused me to toss and turn endlessly. If Aisha was still in the vineyard it wouldn't have been so bad, not wanting to feel the pains of separation any longer. Besides, Vickie was giving me difficulty, my inability to handle her changing mood toward me. This time even counting grapes didn't help, I was up the entire night.

"Ari!" Chaim screamed as he burst into my house.

"Good grief, Chaim, it's only four o'clock. What's so urgent at this hour?"

"Moshe told me late last night the Ministry of Agriculture is having a demonstration in Tel Aviv of a new machine made in France that automatically ties branches."

"Sounds interesting," I said. "What time do we have to be there?"

"Seven thirty."

"Nothing in this country ever starts on time. Relax and let me at least get another hour of sleep."

"I want to get there on time because we have to be back on the moshav before one o'clock."

"Why so early?"

"The army asked for a meeting with the moshav to discuss security arrangements. Some new regulations I think," Chaim laughed, "that are suppose to end the Intifada before the week is out."

"What kind of regulations do you suppose?"

"Moshe said they want us to run security checks on our cousins that work for us."

"I already ran a check on Selah and the others."

"You did? When?"

"Don't you remember? There was even a copy for Moshe."

"Ari, you must have dreamt about running a check. Moshe asked me yesterday, in advance of the meeting, to obtain all the identity card information so he could run a check."

"Oh!" I quickly said, "I was thinking of some other report I guess."

Could it be possible, I thought, that I really dreamed the army report about Aisha's family? In the space of a few weeks not only had I fallen in love with a Palestinian woman, but her brother Nassir was an Intifada cell leader. No, the report was very real indeed. My only worry was Moshe finding out I received the army report and kept his copy.

Luckily the day went fast. Just as I thought, the demonstration started an hour late, but it was well worth the wait. What we saw was a phenomenal machine that rode over the rows of trees picking the branches up while simultaneously tying them in something like a basket. The technology evidently has existed for years.

In Israel because of the Intifada the machine had specific implications. Billed as a labor saving device, its use could dramatically decrease our dependence on Palestinian labor. With the myriad of strikes occurring weekly that itself would be a desired goal. All in all it was a most productive morning.

I only wish I could say the same for the afternoon. Unlike the agricultural show, the army meeting started exactly on time. Chaim and I stopped on the way back from Tel Aviv in Ramle for beer and lunch. Moshe was livid when we were the only two who came late.

The young lieutenant had briefed everyone, prior to our arrival, on new security measures as we walked in.

"First," he said, "I need a list of all your Palestinian workers except those in the vineyard."

"Why not the vineyard?" asked Moshe.

"Well, it seems you already ran a security check on the workers there," he replied.

"I remember sending it in, but I never got an answer," Moshe said.

"According to our records," the lieutenant continued, "the report was brought to your moshav by a supply truck a while ago. There were two copies. One was received by you and the other by someone named Ari."

"ARI!"

"I put a copy in your mailbox, Moshe," I lied. "Knowing how often you check it, the report could probably still be there."

"Hopefully, in the near future," the lieutenant continued, "we will be issuing green identity cards to those individuals who are known security risks. Employment of them will be at your own discretion."

As the meeting progressed we learned that many businesses and collective farms were looking into alternate labor supplies. Politics aside, the economics of the Intifada were quickly becoming the main consideration. With so many strike days called since the Intifada began, maximum productivity in all sectors of the economy had begun to lag. Hardest hit were farming and construction. Recently there was even talk of importing labor from as far away as the Far East.

For a moshav like ours, it meant everyone working a lot harder. The religious farming communities experienced particular difficulty because of their not working on the Sabbath. Our thinking of buying the French branch tying machine was an attempt to lessen reliance on Palestinian labor. Implementation of machine over man was not begun because of the Intifada, but its development in Israel reached a heightened frenzy since it began.

Successfully, we maneuvered most of Jaffa Road en route to King George Street in the heart of Jerusalem. I guess the only way to describe the streets at that moment was to say they were flooded by a raging sea of people. Walking was impossible. All one could do was just roll with the ebbing of the tide. Chaim and Aviva had all of their children together forming a human chain.

"Doesn't the music fill your soul, Vickie?" Aviva asked.

"Living in Tel Aviv, I guess I've lost touch with what Israel is all about," Vickie answered.

"Can we each have a shekel?" begged the kids.

"For what?" Chaim asked.

"Cans of shaving cream; what else did you think?" they responded in unison.

"Okay," I said as I handed Yitzchak, Chaim's oldest son himself home from reserve duty, a ten shekel note.

"There is still one thing I can't get used to," Vickie said to Aviva.

"What's that?"

"After two thousand years of exile, our people finally regain a country of their own . . ."

"So?" I interrupted.

"Yet, the only way we've found to celebrate our return is by squirting shaving cream and bonking each other with those silly plastic hammers."

"I think you're being a little unfair," I argued as booming sounds of Israeli music being played by bands everywhere filled the city air.

"Vickie, stop always being so critical," Chaim said. "Tell me, what would be more appropriate?"

"Certainly not a barbeque," Vickie said.

"And just how do you think they celebrate Independence Day in the United States? Parades, barbeques and fireworks," I answered.

"Ari, that's precisely what I mean," Vickie continued, "you of all people should see how void of any element of our heritage this gathering is."

"What about the music," Aviva said, "you can't get more Israeli than the song about golden Jerusalem that's playing now."

"You don't understand," Vickie sighed.

As we swam our way up King George Street, I began to see an element of what Vickie was trying to say. I looked at the hundreds of teenagers laughing, singing, squirting shaving cream everywhere and on everyone. Maybe Vickie was right. If you stopped and asked anyone of them what the day meant, would they say anymore than a giant street party?

What of the past history of our country? Wasn't that what the night was all about? At least I had the stories of my Dad from which to draw from. Wondering if the other kids in the street had the same, I wished for five minutes just to stand before them and say what it was all supposed to mean. I'd tell them about Yitzchak and my friend Yigal in whose names we should be celebrating.

Suddenly, I realized if they were both alive they would tell me, "Let them have their fun, Ari, dance and sing till their hearts content. Forget the times of grief and pain. Tonight's the time to be happy. That's why we died, for the freedom to be happy when and where we choose."

"Let's stay here for awhile," Aviva said standing in front of a large stage the city had erected at the corner of King George and Ben Yehuda streets.

A dance troupe was finishing their colorful performance as we settled in. Next up was a local band consisting of a guitar, accordion and base player, their repertoire comprised of "old Israeli favorites."

The crowd instantly began clapping and singing as the group completed song after song. In fact, a few people started to dance together and in that innocent activity Vickie would find her answer.

"Look, Ari," Vickie shouted, "I think those people dancing are recent immigrants from Russia."

"You're right," Aviva said.

They danced, the crowd stepping back to give them more room. Quickly their circle began to grow larger and larger. At least twenty immigrants from Russia were joined by eight from Ethiopia. Their dance became so infectious that even veteran Israelis, like Chaim and I, began to dance with them. The louder the accordionist sang, the faster we danced.

Within the crowd were a group of Soviet immigrants who must have been in their seventies. Those men and women proudly displayed their medals and honors on their chests attesting to a lifetime of Communist rule. Now, at last they were in Israel. Several of the younger Russians tried to coax them into joining ranks, but they repeatedly refused.

Then all of a sudden, the dancing circle shifted until the group of septuagenarians was standing dead center. Stunned at first, they just stood in amazement. The oldest of them, a woman, grabbed her husband and started to waltz in the middle of the circle. Then the others began ever so slowly to dance. A soldier, a recent immigrant from an Arab country, began to dance with one of the older Russian women.

"I guess beneath the shaving cream and noise makers this is really what it's all about," Vickie said as tears cascaded from her cheeks.

"I guess so," I said as I caught the next drop that fell from her cheek on the tip of my index finger.

Out of the blue people began squirting shaving cream all over Vickie and me. Unbeknownst to me, Vickie had one of those silly plastic hammers in her hands. Bop! I got it right on the nose.

"I think that settles everything between us now," I said to her.

"Oh! How I wish it really could, Ari.

212

TWENTY-SIX

"Two o'clock, Ari, be there," Amos yelled as I walked to the office to check my mail box.

"Don't you worry," I answered. "This year no one is going to get a goal by me."

"You say that every year. Ha! Ha!" Amos laughed as he went down the steps from the office.

Independence Day in Israel was the only official holiday the entire country enjoyed. For the more religious, most of the other holidays were spent in prayer with Shabbat like restrictions. Yet, on Independence Day everyone was off and the whole country literally closed down. Parks, beaches and forests were overflowing with families and groups. Everywhere the air was filled with the smoke and aroma of sizzling meat on hot coals.

Mevo Ayalon had a tradition started the first year of our community, everyone celebrating together. Communally cooked food was served around noon followed by our annual soccer match. Toward evening, everyone gathered in the social hall to hear a talk by a "notable." Usually it was someone who had a story to tell about the times around the country's founding years. Although mainly intended for our children's education, even the adults enjoyed the speeches; my Dad spoke our very first year.

This year Avigdor, our dairy advisor from the Ministry of Agriculture, was coming. Avigdor emigrated from Russia after a three year sojourn reaching Palestine precisely on May 15, 1948. As he debarked from his ship, simultaneously he was kissed by a beautiful Sabra, a native born Israeli girl, and handed a rifle by a Palmach soldier. All in all he had spent ten full years of his four decades here on active army duty defending our country.

Since no one ever wrote me, I only checked my mail once a week. I was surprised when I opened the little door to the box. Inside was an official notice of another month of reserve duty. Because the army year began and ended on April first, I've been called for back to back months of reserve duty. Luckily I worked in agriculture. Moshe, on behalf of the moshav, could request a postponement until after the grape harvest. Our army was pretty good about helping in the smooth running of the country's economy.

Receiving the call up gave me an idea. I decided to have my reserve duty assignments changed from the Golan Heights to the Hebron area. From the time I mustered out of active duty I've always done my reserve time in the north. I never minded being in that area of the country, the change of scenery and climate always refreshing. The Gaza a few months ago was a different climate altogether.

Chaim's been luckier. Having more than six children put him in the class of men who had to return home each night; rarely got called except for a day here or there. Being an officer, it seemed I was always in uniform; a another bone of contention between Vickie and me. Until Gaza I always looked forward to being uniform.

Transferring to Hebron would at least give me a chance to see Aisha. Even if she did come back to the vineyard, harvest time wasn't far away. Unless a miracle occurred, she'd have to return home. If I was in uniform, however, at least I could go to Deir El-Salam and search her out. There would be no telling what would happen then. In Deir El-Salam I was sure something would give one way or the other.

"What are you smiling about, Ari?"

"And good morning to you Aviva," I answered as I left the office.

"Don't you 'good morning' me, mister," Aviva said following me down the path.

"It was all my fault. I swear Chaim is innocent this time. He knew nothing about it," I said. "Now that I've confessed, would you please tell me what on earth I did wrong?"

"Cute, Ari, really cute. You know very well what you did."

"Good, Aviva, we're getting close."

"Ari, when are you going to stop leading Vickie on!" Aviva yelled.

"So, that's it," I laughed.

"It's not funny, Ari, you are playing with *her* emotions . . ."

"I'm playing with her emotions?"

"Are you trying to get back at her now? Is that it?"

"Aviva, has Vickie said anything at all to you about me?"

"No she hasn't, but she doesn't have to. I can see . . ."

"No, Aviva, you can't see because there is nothing to see."

"I don't care what you say, Ari, I know Vickie better than you think. She's hurt by your seeing someone else," authoritatively Aviva said. "I wish you both would stop acting like children and face up to the fact, before it's too late, that the divorce was a tragic mistake."

"Aviva, don't confuse the fact that we spent last night as old times with you and Chaim by thinking our divorce was a mistake."

"Ari, when two people love each other as much as you and Vickie do . . . well, you should be together, not apart," Aviva said with a mist in her eyes.

"Aviva, I could kiss you!" I screamed.

"You could what?"

"I'm just glad to hear you say that. I finally found someone who views love and life the same way as I do."

"I doubt that, Ari," Aviva puffed as she turned onto the path toward her house.

After my run in with Aviva, I decided to skip the festivities on the moshav and drive to the vineyard. I needed to be alone to clear my head. Stuffed inside my jeans pocket was Aisha's scarf and I tied it around my neck like a bandanna. I was backing the truck out when Chaim yelled.

"Good morning, Ari," he said, "that satisfies what I was asked to do."

"For the one thousand four hundred and fifty-third time in my life, Chaim, I have no idea what you are talking about."

"I don't know what you said to my poor wife, Ari, but you set her off in some mood."

"I'm sorry, Chaim, I didn't mean . . ."

"She burst through the door, looked me squarely in the eyes and said, 'he's your friend. You go talk to him.' My good morning fulfilled her request," Chaim laughed.

"It's just . . ."

"Ari, you don't have to explain. Where are you going?"

"I'm going to take a ride to the vineyard."

"Is she back?"

"No, I just want to be alone for a while."

"Are you going to be back for the soccer game?"

"Probably not."

"Good," Chaim said, "without you as goalie, we stand a chance of winning this year."

"Very funny, Chaim, very funny."

I drove straight for the clearing where I almost shot Aisha. Getting out of the truck, I decided to lie on the soft, warm sands and let the sun soak in. Its rays felt so good as each one penetrated my body filling me with a strangely relaxing warmth. My eyes stared at the cloudless sky while my thoughts drifted in the direction I wanted, toward Aisha.

"Anyone ever tell you that you make a lot of noise when you sleep?" Selah asked as he leaned over me.

"Yes, but you wouldn't believe who," I answered. "How did you get back today? I heard on the radio that the territories were sealed because of Independence Day."

"We left last night before the army closed everything," Selah said.

"Did you bring the other two boys we spoke about?"

"That's one of the reasons we came at night. I knew the army wouldn't let them leave the village."

"Just remember . . ."

"Don't say it, Ari, I know. They are at Abu Ali's now. I asked him to speak to them. There will be no trouble."

"Enough said then."

"Agreed."

"How's everything at home in your village?"

"My wife's never going to let Ali out of her sight that long again. She missed him terribly."

"Abu Ali told me your father got rid of his other wife."

"My mother always told me true love finds a way. I guess she's living proof of that, Ari."

"I'm glad to hear it Selah. It sort of renews my faith in the institution."

"It what, Ari?"

"Oh, nothing."

"You didn't ask me about my sister, Ari?" Selah perceptively asked.

"I assume she's okay. Isn't she?"

"Not really. She wanted to come back to the vineyard with me, but my Dad said no."

"He said no?" I asked as my heart fell from its place.

"It was really my mother. Can you believe it, Ari, she said she didn't trust you," Selah laughed.

"What's your sister going to do in Deir El-Salam?"

"According to her, she'll waste away. I can't understand what she fell in love with out here."

"Freedom," I muttered. "Maybe it was the freedom to be herself without someone always telling her what to do or making decisions for her."

"I didn't understand what you said, Ari."

"Selah, while you were home, how many times was your village under curfew?"

"Two."

"Out here there's no curfew, no Intifada and no politics, life in its pristine nature. Maybe what she saw was a chance to live an unmolested life. Wasn't that our fathers dream? Isn't it the dream of all men?"

"Maybe you are right, Ari," Selah said after a long pause of thought. "She told my Dad she wanted to run as far away from Deir El-Salam as she could."

"She did?"

"Next time I'm home, I'll speak to my father. Maybe what my sister needs most now, as you said, is to get away. Yes, she'll come back to the vineyard," Selah affirmed.

"Go now," I mumbled.

"What did you say, Ari, I didn't hear you."

"I said it's almost two. I have to get back to the moshav. We're having a soccer game this afternoon."

Driving, I barely exceeded forty kilometers per hour, happy just to think Aisha returning soon. Abu Ali's prediction would come true after all. Taking a long detour, I drove to the coast. Among the thousands of bodies cooking in the sun, I managed to find a patch of sand by the water. On it I wrote question upon question about Aisha and me. When I finished, I waited, I guess, for a hand from heaven to write the answers. Instead, the tide rolled in and washed the questions away while I felt like crying.

"Ari!" Chaim yelled as he saw me trying to sneak into my house, "guess what?"

"I give up Chaim," I answered as I took a cold beer from his hand.

"We voted you 'most valuable player' of the soccer game."

"But, I wasn't even there."

"We know. With Moshe playing goalie this year instead of you, we won 5-0."

"Cute, Chaim," I said, "Moshe?"

"Come with me, Ari," Chaim said pulling on my arm, "Avigdor's just starting to speak."

As I sat, listening to Avigdor, I couldn't help but think of my Dad. I needed to take a few days off and go to see him before it was too late. The more Avigdor talked, the more I saw my Dad telling me his stories.

Toward the end of his talk, Avigdor removed his shirt and shoes, his body a road map of Israel's collective wars. In the Six Day War his right shoulder was loaded with shrapnel. Mine fragments entered his foot during the Independence War. Yom Kippur War burned his back from a phosphorous grenade and the Lebanon War put a bullet in his left arm.

"I was always lucky," he said, "time was plenty enough to heal my wounds. Unfortunately, the wounds of many others will never heal."

When he finished, we all rose to sing HaTikva, our unofficial national anthem. Written in 1878 by Naphtali Herz Imber and adapted to music from an old Moldavian folk song by Samuel Cohen, it has inspired our people for over one hundred years. As we sang together its words said it all.

> *"Our hope is not yet lost*
> *the hope of two thousand years*
> *to be a free people in our land*
> *the land of Zion and Jerusalem."*

But the words stuck in my throat as I sang. Yes, we had finally returned to our homeland that so happened to be a shared homeland as well. And as the panels in Jerusalem reminded me, others have lived here not just the Jewish people through time immemorial. What to do with the indigenous Palestinian population will for eternity be the obstacle for peace in the land. The British never had to deal with such problems in taking over the world.

They simply killed off locals by importing blankets laden with smallpox, colonial germ warfare.

This land has a long and tumultuous history as a crossroads for religion, culture, commerce, and politics; among the earliest to see human habitation, agricultural communities and civilization; yet, perpetually bereft of peace. Salah ad-Din was correct when he warned the crusaders against shedding blood, indulging in it and making a habit of it, for blood never sleeps.

TWENTY-SEVEN

"Ever since Selah brought those two kids back, I've been uneasy," Chaim said as we sat under a carob tree eating lunch.

"You worry too much, Chaim."

"Ari, I'm willing to go along with most of your whims and hair brain schemes, but this time I think you've gone a little too far."

"What are you afraid of? A couple of kids?"

"Ari, listen to you now," Chaim said, "Remember when they left the vineyard? You were the one who said 'good riddance' and was relieved the Intifada would be over for us."

"They're just a couple of young kids who followed the wrong crowd," I defended.

"You don't even know what they did," Chaim pleaded.

"Selah said it was nothing major."

"Selah said. A very unbiased source, Ari, at least give their identity numbers to Moshe and let him run a check on them."

"No! Trust me on this Chaim," I begged, "they won't cause any trouble."

"Just suppose something does happen here. Who would you instinctively blame? Don't you still think they were the ones who cut the water lines?"

"What if it was them," I argued, "anyone, even a Palestinian, deserves a second chance, Chaim."

"You feel so damn sure nothing will happen that you are you willing to risk your life on it?"

"My life?"

"Yes, your life. That's how dangerous things are now. Don't forget, Ari, we work out here in the middle of nowhere . . ."

"Enough, Chaim, okay? Drop it."

"I hope you know what you're doing."

221

"Let's go to Ramle and buy some grass and weed killer. We're getting behind on spraying under the trees and between the rows," I said.

"You're right," agreed Chaim, "the grass is starting to grow tall and when it dies, it becomes highly combustible."

Chaim yelled as we drove down Herzl, Ramle's main street, "Ari, look at the park next to the vegetable market!"

"Look at what?"

"There, a group of our cousins surrounded by police. I wonder what happened." Chaim asked as he parked a block away from the agriculture supply company.

"What's all the commotion by the market?" I asked as we entered the store.

"That depends on who you ask," answered the clerk sitting on a chair with his feet propped up in the front store window.

"I'm asking you," Chaim said as he closed the door behind him.

"Ought to run them all back over the Green Line," the clerk said.

"Are they from the territories?" I asked.

"Never mind where they are from," Chaim said, "what did they do?"

"Either one of them tried to knife someone or the police discovered a makeshift bomb. That seems to be the pattern these days," the clerk continued, "if they'd send them all back to Jordan that will be . . . ."

". . . six liters of pre-emergent herbicide and ten liters of contact killer," I interrupted.

"It's the screwed up times in which we live," Chaim said as we passed the large cement factory on our way out of town.

"What about the times, Chaim?"

"Back in the store I realized all of us, especially myself, have an underlying prejudice against our cousins."

"You think we Israelis are the only ones who feel prejudice? It's the same with the French, English, Germans, Americans, even among our Palestinian cousins themselves," I said, "it's a natural feeling."

"So, how does someone combat prejudice if it means going against a person's nature?"

"Chaim, I honestly think I know how. I'll tell you, but you must swear never and I mean never let Vickie's father ever get an inkling of what I'm about to say."

"Why worry about him now, Ari?"

"That's one 'I told you so son' I could never live down. No; not from him. Another thing never let my Dad find out I ever saw the merit in anything my father-in-law said."

"Agreed," Chaim laughed.

"Vickie's father once told me that prejudice comes from never getting to know the other person."

"It's that simple?"

"No, Chaim, on the contrary, it's that difficult. We worked with Selah for many years and as you pointed out, we never even knew he had a family. Now I know as much about him as I do anyone else."

"That's only because you are in love with his sister," Chaim argued.

"Does it matter the reason? Because I feel closeness with him I harbor a trust, the process that eliminates prejudice. If we took the time to get to know our cousins better, I feel the times would be different."

"But what about our cousins, Ari? It can't be a one way street," Chaim countered.

"Precisely," I agreed, "they are as much at fault as we are. Aisha said to me once, after getting to know you and me, she couldn't believe the lifetime of lies and misconceptions she'd heard about Israelis."

"Ari, it can't be as simple as you are trying to make it out to be. All we need to do is have a couple of afternoon teas with a few Palestinian academics and there will be peace?"

"You asked me how to combat personal prejudice not a solution to global peace, Chaim."

"I just want to stop vacillating within myself on how I feel toward our cousins."

"One on one, Chaim, that's the way. You get to know one of them and in turn they get to know one of us. That will help you and it will be the most difficult first step to us living peacefully together. No overnight miracles or quick solutions will ever work."

"We're still doomed," Chaim said.

"Doomed?"

"Even if, let's say, we do get to know and understand each other better, then we still have the nations of the world to contend with," Chaim explained.

"For the first time I think I know what you are going to say, Chaim."

"You do?"

"Unfortunately, neither we nor our cousins are Western cultured or Christian. Right?"

"You got it. How can the world expect us to understand each other when they themselves don't understand either of us?"

"There can be only one thing to do," I said.

"Let's buy a beer," we shouted in unison.

By any measure, the rest of the week was most productive. Except for the upper part of the vineyard near Abu Ali, we had finished applying grass killer everywhere. Next week I was scheduled to begin another round of spraying. And Chaim, well, he spent an unusual amount of time drinking coffee and eating with Selah and the others. Everything seemed to be falling in place in our little corner of the world. Life was as it should have been.

Rainbows

To my delight, Selah was returning to Deir El-Salam on Friday night, everyone else leaving on Thursday, except the two kids who would have trouble with road blocks. Chaim of all people suggested they stay and look after things while Selah was gone.

Since most of the pre-harvest work was completed, we didn't need to work on Saturday. It was a good feeling to leave the vineyard on Friday afternoon and not come back until Sunday morning. To a certain extent I felt an appreciation for the Orthodox of our people who meticulously kept the Shabbat.

When I ran the vineyard, I worked seven days a week from January to October. Chaim, having a larger family, never put that much time in. Although I'd never admit it to him, he'd always gotten better results than I ever did. Maybe I'm getting older, but I see now being a workaholic isn't what it's cracked up to be.

"I forgot to tell Selah to water areas four, six and seven before he leaves," I said early Friday afternoon as Chaim and I approached Beit El-Safa enroute home.

"I'll do it tomorrow," Chaim volunteered, "my younger kids have been complaining I haven't taken them to the vineyard yet this season."

"You don't have to Chaim, I'll do it," I said as we entered Beit El-Safa. The screeching of our tires resounded as Chaim slammed on the breaks.

"Are you crazy?" I screamed, "Let's get out of here before we get pelted with rocks."

"I left my gun in the shed," he said as he turned the truck one hundred and eighty degrees in the middle of the road; spinning black smoke everywhere.

"Where are you going now?" I asked as I hung on for dear life.

"To get my gun!" Chaim yelled as we sped back in the direction of the vineyard.

To save time, Chaim took a detour through the fields of the neighboring kibbutz, the winding dirt trail passing at one point below Abu Ali's encampment. I talked Chaim into stopping off there on the way back for a cup of tea.

Approaching the pine trees just before area six, we saw a large cloud of smoke rising overhead. Where there is smoke there is fire. To our worst fears a few trees of French Colombard Chardonnay were already ablaze.

"Drive to the shed," I yelled, "and I'll get the tractor and sprayer."

"We'll get both tractors," Chaim said, "The other still has the cultivator attached. If we can't contain it, I'll make a firebreak by ripping up a couple of rows of trees."

"Call Moshe on the radio," I said, "so he can contact the Jewish National Fund. The trees in the forest have already caught fire too. We'll never be able to extinguish them by ourselves."

Chaim was the first to return to the fire with the old tractor. I had to wait the precious time it took to fill the five hundred liter tank of the sprayer. Attached to the sprayer were two hoses with hand nozzles. Hopefully they would be enough.

"You think it was the two kids?" Chaim asked as he walked behind me spraying the flame while I drove the tractor.

"Come on Chaim . . . ."

"Everyone else is gone except for them and Selah," he said.

"Selah!" I yelled.

"He didn't do it!"

"No, you idiot. Over there in the brush," I said jumping down from the tractor. "Selah's on the ground!"

We both ran to him lying motionless by the edge of the grass. Chaim rolled him over and we saw blood mixed with sand covering the back of his head. Luckily he was still breathing.

"Selah . . . Selah . . . !" Chaim kept screaming as his eyes gradually opened.

"Chaim there's a fire," Selah said slurring each word.

"We've got to get him to a hospital, Chaim."

"What about the fire?" Chaim asked, "we can't just leave it to burn out of control."

"Selah needs emergency care urgently," I demanded.

"Ari," Selah said struggling to sit up, "I'll be okay. Put the fire out first."

"Who hit you?" Chaim asked.

Before he could answer, a border police jeep, seeing the smoke, drove up. Chaim ran to ask if they had a first aid kit. It was Selah's lucky day, one of them having been a medic in the army. Chaim and the three other policemen resumed fighting the fire.

"He took some hit," the medic-policeman said. "To play it safe, he should have a full head x-ray."

"I could see smoke from the shed. Running up here, I saw a fire in the last two rows when I spied a white van out of the corner of my right eye. Before I knew, it someone grabbed me from behind."

"Did you get a good look at him?"

"No, but I don't think he was a Palestinian."

"Sure you'd say that," mumbled the medic/policeman.

"We'll never control it by ourselves!" Chaim yelled, "We need more help."

Getting up to help the others, I heard the faint noise of people coming through the trees. Suddenly, I saw about ten Palestinians running as fast as they could in our direction. Reflexively, the border policemen drew their weapons.

"Stop, don't shoot!" I screamed running into their line of fire.

"Get out of the way," one of the Border Police yelled.

"No, Stop! They came to help," I continued shouting.

I had recognized the Palestinians; two of them being the kids who worked for us and the rest were from Abu Ali. Selah had sent the two to get help when he first saw the smoke; boy were they a welcome sight in the end.

Together we worked to arrest the blaze, slowly making headway when suddenly the sprayer ran out of water. The late afternoon winds began to pick up causing the fire to spread faster.

227

"Honk! Honk!"

Resounding through the trees was the unmistakable sound of Abu Ali's tractor towing his water wagon. Two thousand liters of water would in minutes be helping to put out the fire. Chaim turned to me and said to remind him to give Abu Ali a credit for the water. We both laughed.

Attached to the valve of his wagon was a two inch diameter, fifty meter hose. It worked beautifully and in less than twenty minutes we had extinguished the fire among the grape trees.

By the time we turned our attention to the forest, the Jewish National Fund had arrived with their pumper truck. Chaim took our tractor with the cultivator attached into the forest to cut a firebreak. Luck was again on our side; except for about ten trees the forest was spared major harm.

Chaim and I took Selah to Ramle for an x-ray. The attending emergency room physician said he had a severe concussion which was normal given the trauma of the wound. He was very lucky. Someone had used a blunt instrument like a pipe. All things considered, we were in and out of the hospital fairly fast.

I wished I could say the same for our visit to the police station. We waited for an hour only to find out the officer who needed to take our report was out on a call. When Chaim asked the desk officer when he would return, we were told to be patient and wait. We promptly left.

Selah wanted to go to Abu Ali's encampment. Some short day, already past seven in the evening when we arrived. Graciously, we refused a third cup of coffee. Abu Ali wouldn't hear of our thanks and praises we heaped upon him, humbly saying that's what neighbors were for.

I told Selah I would return in the morning to drive him to Deir El-Salam. Persuasively, he said it might be a little dangerous for me to travel to that area. Abu Ali, always being the wiser, said he would take him. I agreed.

"Someday," I said as we walked down the path toward our homes.

"Some week," Chaim added. "I see what you mean now, Ari, about getting to know each other a little better."

"Do you mean anything specific?"

"Selah bled red blood, the same as you and me."

"Did you expect it to be green?"

"Until this week that's the color I probably would have expected it to be," Chaim admitted, "thanks, Ari."

"For what?"

"Just thanks, Ari, leave it at that," Chaim said as he closed the door to his house behind him.

TWENTY-EIGHT

Funny, how life deals its deck of cards. Because I had begun night spraying, Chaim was forced to work with the two kids alone. After the fire I don't think he worried anymore about them. Together they worked hard repairing the melted plastic water pipes and broken wires which held the vines.

Assessing the total damage was difficult. Our advisor from the Ministry of Agriculture said the true effects of the fire wouldn't be known until next season. What he was really worried about was insect infestation possibly destroying the roots. If real damage was done to the upper part of the tree, at least we'd be able to graft new cuttings to the rootstock. But the rootstock becoming infested would make the tree worthless. Like all things in life, it appeared only time would tell the true story.

Without either Selah or Aisha in the vineyard the night spraying grew very long. For the first time in my life I dreaded going to the vineyard. Toward the middle of the week I'd had enough. About midnight, I drove the tractor to Abu Ali's. Good old Rothschild saw to it that everyone was up and waiting by the time I arrived. One of Abu Ali's wives was already making a fire when I drew nearer to the tent.

"Come in . . . come in . . . please," Abu Ali said. "Excuse me if I don't rise to greet you."

"Abu Ali please forgive my intrusion into your night's peace. It's just that I . . ."

"Ari," Abu Ali interrupted, "first sit down and have a cup of coffee. The night has much time remaining to discuss whatever your heart desires."

"Okay," I said as I nestled among a group of gaily embroidered pillows and rugs.

To my amazement, Rothschild entered the tent and stretched out next to me. In all the years I visited Abu Ali, I never heard the dog not bark. I guessed he was exhausted like everyone else. Or maybe even he too had gotten to know me better? As I reached for my second cup of coffee, Rothschild lifted his head and growled at me. So much for my theory.

"Now, let's hear what's so important?" Abu Ali asked.

"Aisha, Abu Ali, its Aisha."

"That even my dog knew, Ari, what about her?"

"Maybe it's just that I'm too impatient, but I can't settle myself while she's not here. When you took Selah home, did you see her? Do you know how long it will be before she returns? Does her mother really suspect something between us or is she merely guessing? Do you think . . . ?"

"Questions aren't as important to you as the answers. Why do you spend so much time on them?"

"That's why I came to you, Abu Ali, I couldn't think of anyone else who could help me."

"Let me talk then. Maybe it's because the nights are getting cooler now. No, it's because of the season of the year, I think. At night, each night, I've been thinking of my first wife. For most people, returning spirits haunt a man's soul, but it has the opposite effect on me."

"No, thank you," I said turning down my fourth cup of coffee.

"Ari, people have a misconception about growing old. They think just because we reach sixty, seventy even eighty years of age we become wiser. Maybe we're a little more cautious, but definitely not wiser. If anything we become more foolish."

"Foolish, Abu Ali?"

"Ari, what makes a man wise? He lets his mind rule his heart. And when does he become the fool? Well, when his heart rules his mind."

"Which is the better?"

"Neither the fool nor the wise man would answer that, Ari. Both would rather leave it up to life itself to decide."

"And Aisha?"

"While in Deir El-Salam I had an opportunity to talk to her parents at length. It appears that all parents, Palestinian and Israeli, most times have difficulty understanding what's best for their children. In the end it was agreed for Aisha to return with Selah."

"Praised Be Allah!" I yelled.

"With him, but not to the vineyard," Abu Ali continued.

"To where?"

"She will stay with me," Abu Ali smiled.

"As a wife?"

"Does an old man need a fast horse to ride?" laughed Abu Ali. "Without her mother in the vineyard, it wouldn't be proper for her to stay in the shed alone."

"If she stays here, will I be able to see her?"

"A wise man would say no. The fool, on the other hand, would say yes."

"Which are you, Abu Ali? Wise man or fool?"

"I'm tired, Ari, only the stars in the heavens don't need to sleep at night. Go, continue what you were doing and let the sun bring another day," Abu Ali said as he rolled over toward the fire.

Walking down the trail to the tractor, I heard something behind me in the brush. Turning, I saw it was Rothschild. We both stood in place and stared at each other until he broke eye contact and lazily walked away. As I drove the tractor back to the vineyard, I saw a shooting star. Little did I know at the same moment Aisha was watching my star sail across her sky.

"Ari, it's simply amazing," Chaim said as we swapped the truck in the parking lot by the office.

"Yea, that I'm not already asleep," I said not wanting to prolong my being awake one minute.

"No, those two kids. You know why they got in trouble with the army? They are only sixteen and seventeen. All of their lives have been spent under Israeli occupation . . ."

"Israeli occupation, Chaim?"

"You know what I mean. They were born after the Six Day War. All they've ever heard is how bad we are and how great it was when they were free and independent under Jordanian rule."

"I'm sure there is a point here somewhere, Chaim."

"And who told them about the old times? It was their friends who are twenty years old," Chaim said, "no wonder they got into trouble. They listen to stories from other kids who were no older than babies before the war."

"Did you enlighten them as to the truth?"

"That naive I'm not, Ari, but I did say before drawing any conclusions, they should talk to the older people of their village in order to find out what life under Jordanian rule was really like."

"And they agreed?"

"One of them said he would. He knew a really old man," Chaim laughed, "who had to be at least forty. They would talk to him."

"At least forty?" I laughed aloud.

"Why are you two hysterical so early in the morning?" Moshe asked as he approached our truck.

"Moshe, how old are you?" Chaim asked.

"I'll be forty-five in August. Why?"

Chaim burst out with uncontrollable laughter calling Moshe an old man. I was laughing too hard to even speak.

"I think you two should stop eating so many fermented grapes during the day. Your brains have become affected," Moshe huffed as he walked to the office.

There were no headlines in the daily papers stating significant progress toward peace between Palestinians and Israelis was made at Mevo Ayalon. No matter. Chaim's understanding of why those two kids felt as they did was an extremely important step on the road to a lasting peace even if it didn't make a banner headline.

For two days I had watched the sun bring a new day like Abu Ali said, but not Aisha. Then, one morning while I was leaving the vineyard after all night of spraying, I saw Selah and Aisha walking up the dirt road. Looking at my watch, I realized I was already late getting back to the moshav. Chaim would be upset enough by waiting, but I decided he'd have to wait a little longer.

"Selah," I said as I stopped the truck, "how's your head?"

"By the time I left this morning I'd become a martyred hero of the Intifada," Selah laughed.

"A what?"

"Someone doesn't come back to my village bandaged unless he's been in a fight, these days usually with the police or army. Try as I did to say it was an accident in the vineyard, people believed what they heard in the streets," Selah continued, "we actually got cheers as we left."

"Homage to the hero," I laughed.

"Did they find out who set the fires, Ari?"

"I've been spraying nights so I really haven't talked to Chaim much, but he said they were thieves out here dividing their loot or struggling with each other for some reason. You just happened to be in the wrong place at the wrong time, Selah." I saw the question written on his face. "They were Israeli; the Border Police found them in the area again the next day. The fire was started by a fallen cigarette."

"Oh, Chaim, I'm sorry, Ari, will be waiting for you to return with the truck. You'd better go," Selah insisted.

"I have time to give you a ride to the shed," I said glancing each chance I could at Aisha.

"We were walking to Abu Ali's not the shed."

"Abu Ali?" I pretended to ask.

"My sister will be staying there. Without my mother here, the shed will be no place for her when the others return today."

"I'll take you to Abu Ali's then." I insisted.

"You don't have to," Selah protested.

"It's okay. I can go back by way of the kibbutz fields."

As we drove to Abu Ali's, Selah sat up front and Aisha was in the back seat with all they had brought. My eyes were glued to the rearview mirror, our eyes touching through its reflection. I don't know how many times I almost ran off the road because I kept looking at Aisha; each time Selah would ask if I was too tired to drive.

Once at Abu Ali's, Aisha was hurriedly swept into one of the tents. Rothschild came up to me without so much as a whimper. In my lifetime I'd jumped from planes, been in two wars, etc. Yet, I should have received a bravery medal for what I did next. I bent down and gave Rothschild a pat on his head amazed I still had all of my fingers intact.

"Come tonight and eat with us before you spray," Selah said to me as I closed the door to the truck.

"By the shed?"

"No, here at Abu Ali's. My mother sent us enough food to feed an army."

"Okay," I quickly said.

"You must have really acquired a taste for our food."

"Why's that?"

"Because the last time I invited you to eat with us, it took a half hour of persuasion," Selah laughed.

"It's the desert at the end of the meal." Abu Ali smiled from ear to ear.

Supper was quite the meal I'd expected. Abu Ali, playing the wise old fool all evening, saw to it I had plenty to eat, constantly telling Aisha to bring me more bread, coffee or fruit ad infinitum. Aisha, of course, didn't mind being told to play the gracious hostess. Nor did I mind being treated like a king.

Around eight o'clock, I realized if I didn't leave then there would be no spraying done. Selah said he would ride back with me to the shed. Walking to the truck, he told me he could see on Aisha's face it was right for her to leave Deir El-Salam.

"If you'd only seen how unhappy she was in Deir El-Salam, Ari."

"Selah, I truly hope things work out for the best with her."

Abu Ali told me not to be a stranger in his tent as he shut Selah's door. We drove away while I watched Aisha's image lit by the camp's fires grow smaller and smaller until it vanished completely into the darkness.

Hour after hour I sprayed the vineyard; night time was no longer a dreaded item to whisk away. Aisha had returned and that was all that mattered to me. Riding atop the tractor in my space suit, I thought of how on earth we could possibly meet. Now that she was living with Abu Ali too many people could see us together. Her being there created more potential problems, but nothing I was sure we couldn't overcome.

About two in the morning, I decided to take a break. Seemingly I had returned to the good graces of Aviva because all week she'd packed a thermos of hot coffee and cookies for me. I'm sure she'd mentioned our conversation to Vickie. Vickie, I trusted, set her straight.

"Some fire. Sorry I missed it."

"Aisha," I said spilling coffee inside my rain suit as I stumbled to get up.

Aisha stood there more beautiful than ever. By her side on a thin rope was Rothschild. He wasn't barking, growling or anything, just a hollow stare.

"Abu Ali gave him to me for protection," Aisha said as we together sat on the ground. "Up front I reached an agreement with Abu Ali while he was talking to my parents at our home."

"Agreement?"

"I pulled him aside on our porch and told him if I came back to his tent he couldn't prevent me from seeing you."

"What was his response?"

"He said, 'child, worry about tomorrow only after it has become yesterday,'" Aisha answered.

"That sounds exactly like Abu Ali," I laughed.

"Ari, I missed you terribly. I've made my mind up. I don't know how or when, but one day we'll eternally be together."

"I hope so, Aisha, those are also my prayers."

"Thank you for taking care of my brother," she said, "he's lucky to have had you there."

"Selah's lucky, but I don't think I was much help. He became a big hero in your village because of his wound?"

"Oh! That's my brother's doing. Nassir invented a story for his own good, not Selah's."

"What kind of story?"

"Nassir told everyone that on his way back to the village an army patrol stopped Selah. He was standing next to the jeep while they were checking his identity number against a computer printout. In the back of the jeep were three other Palestinians. Selah grabbed the printout away from one of the soldiers. While they were struggling, the driver hit him with the butt of his rifle."

"Some story," I said, "please continue."

"Then the other three jumped from the jeep, etc. In the end my brother was credited with rescuing the three," Aisha finished.

"But it's all a lie, Aisha."

"I know, Ari, my brother told everyone he could the truth. Nassir continued telling people in the village that Selah was afraid an informer would turn him. That's why he kept denying it to people."

"I'd like to meet your brother Nassir some day, Aisha."

"I pray you don't," Aisha cried, "He's an evil person."

"How's your mother feel now that she's the only one in your father's eye?" I asked trying to change the subject.

"All she did was cause trouble for me," Aisha complained. "Now that her faith in marriage has returned, constantly she talked about my settling down with someone."

"I agree with your mother."

"You do?" Aisha sheepishly said with a surprised look on her face.

"I meant you should settle down with me, Aisha."

"I'd like that most of all, Ari."

"So would I."

We sat only for a half hour when all of a sudden, Rothschild stood up. Adamant, Rothschild kept tugging on the string tied to Aisha's right hand.

I walked with Aisha part of the way. She insisted I finish spraying so I could get some rest. I had to finish everything this week so I could work days next week. Then my nights would be free for Aisha. As we parted, Aisha turned to me one last time.

"Ari, I love you," Aisha said as a solitary tear hung in her left eye.

"I know," I said, "and I love you too.

TWENTY-NINE

"I have to admit, Ari, all week you've been a lot happier. Aisha's coming back has been the best thing for me," Chaim said as we drove to the vineyard early Friday morning.

"For you?"

"Yeah, for me. You haven't noticed, but all week I've been giving you extra work and not once did you complain. You're still the old workaholic that I've known for many years."

"No, Chaim, I'm not the same. I just wanted to finish everything as fast as possible to sneak off and meet Aisha. That you didn't know," I laughed.

Unless there were any serious problems such as another fire we were scheduled to begin harvest at the end of the month. Chaim and I came in earlier each day to sample the sugar level of the grapes by using a special refractometer. Up and down a number of rows we walked randomly picking grapes and placing them into a large green bucket. After we had completed a specific area, we would stick our foot in the bucket to mash the grapes, take a few drops of juice and place it on the refractometer to read the sugar level.

Of course, our actions were primitive compared to how they did it in France. Once, while at the Israel Wine Institute, we saw a film on wine making in the South of France. Before us on the screen were beautiful girls barefoot descending into a large vat of grapes; as a violinist played, the girls started to dance and sing, juice pouring from the holes in the bottom of the vat. A far cry from our boots, but then we weren't drinking our juice either.

The whole testing process took both of us a couple of hours to complete. We checked the odd number areas one day and even the next just to break up the monotony. Making the harvest at exactly the right moment was extremely important financially, the winery paying a bonus for higher sugar levels. Depending on the level achieved, the price per ton could be more than fifty percent higher. Endlessly we walked row after row sampling grapes.

"Vineyard . . . vineyard . . . this . . . is . . . Moshe . . . do . . . you . . . hear . . . me . . . over . . ."

For several minutes the truck's radio chattered away. Since it was only Moshe, I figured I'd let Chaim answer it when he walked up from the bottom of area two, wanting to finish collecting grapes so I could eat breakfast with Selah and the others. Not that the food was special, but Aisha usually walked down from Abu Ali's at that time. Looking at my watch, I noticed we had finished early. Selah wouldn't eat for at least another hour.

"C-O-M-E . . . T-O . . . T-H-E . . . T-R-U-C-K . . . ," Chaim repeatedly yelled to me.

"I'm coming . . . I'm coming," I screamed as I lazily walked in the direction of the truck.

"Call Moshe immediately," was all Chaim would say.

"Moshe . . . Moshe . . . This is Ari, over."

"Ari, go to the nearest public telephone and call Vickie, over."

"Did she say what was wrong? Over."

"She didn't say, over."

We raced out of the vineyard so fast that the truck literally flew over all the bumps in the road. The nearest phone was just off the main road by a small grocery store. Chaim kept trying to assure me that everything was okay, but I knew Vickie would never call me like that unless it was something serious.

Vickie said sounding as if she had been crying.

"Vickie, what's the matter?"

"Ari . . . I don't know how to tell you," Vickie said as she burst into tears.

"It's my Dad, isn't it Vickie?"

"Yes," after a long pause of only hearing her cry on the other end, she continued, "your mother called me. You had already gone to work. She went in at seven to wake him for breakfast . . ." Vickie was unable to finish her sentence.

"Vickie," I said trying to keep my composure.

"Ari, I want to drive to the kibbutz with you, please?"

"I'll have to get Chaim to drive me back to the moshav. Maybe I should stay a couple of hours and help him. We have a lot to do today in the vineyard and for a week I won't be here."

"My, Ari, some things never change. You always did worry about the wrong things at the wrong time," Vickie said as she regained control. "I'll pick you up at the old train station in Ramle. It's not that far out of the way for me to the moshav. Besides, I want to see you, Ari."

"Okay, Vickie, I'll be there soon."

"Ari," Vickie said as she started to cry again, "I'm sorry."

"Don't be, Vickie, he lived a good life," I said as I hung up the phone.

"Chaim," I called as I got into the truck.

"I know, Ari, Moshe told me. Vickie wanted to tell you herself."

"Vickie is going to pick me up in Ramle."

"Do you want me to drive you to Ramle now?"

"No, take me to Abu Ali's. I have to tell Aisha."

"I'll tell her for you, Ari," Chaim offered, "there will be too many people around to see you two together."

"Thanks anyway, but I need to tell her myself."

We reached Abu Ali's quicker than I wanted. I didn't know what to say to Aisha or what I expected her to do. Chaim was right. It was going to be highly problematic being with Aisha there and Abu Ali was nowhere in sight to help.

I had no other recourse except walk right up to Aisha and start talking to her. We went into Abu Ali's big tent alone. Outside stood two guards, Chaim and Rothschild, to make sure we wouldn't be disturbed.

"What is wrong, Ari? Why have you come here like this?"

"Aisha, I have to go away from the vineyard for a few days."

"To the army?"

"No, Aisha, I have to go to my parent's home."

"Is something wrong, Ari? Please tell me."

"It's my Dad . . . he died this morning."

"Oh!" screamed Aisha as she fell against my chest and burst into tears.

At first I wanted to tell her to stop crying, but I didn't. I needed to feel her tightly against me. Responding to her emotions, I gave her a light hug with my arms. When I did, she embraced me even harder.

"Ari, why do you not cry?"

"Maybe it hasn't hit me yet, Aisha," I said. "I really don't know why."

"Ari, I hate the times in which we live," Aisha cried.

"Why?"

"I so want to be with you, but I know I can't. Ari you need someone with you who loves you and can care for you. It can't be me and that is why I'm upset. You'll be all alone."

Ironic how things always happen. Aisha was right that I needed someone to be with me who I knew loved me. How could I tell sweet Aisha not to worry? How did I dare tell her I'd be with Vickie?

Chaim came into the tent with Rothschild in the lead. He was right, we had to go. All I could think about during the drive to Ramle was that it wasn't fair Aisha couldn't fit into my world or I hers. Vickie was correct when she said we'd have to leave Israel to be together. What did it matter where we lived as long as we were with each other? How could I have had those thoughts on the day my Dad died? Or was it precisely because he was no longer here I could?

Standing up, I looked deeply into Vickie's eyes. We just stood there, each afraid to make the first move or was it really we feared to make the wrong move?

"Don't stand there and be a jerk," Chaim whispered to me.

"You are right, Chaim," I said as I walked toward Vickie. I leaned over and gave her a kiss on the right cheek. Our bodies naturally embraced as Vickie began to cry on my shoulder.

Vickie and I didn't talk much the way up to the kibbutz. Her father called on Vickie's car phone and offered his condolences. Although he had reservations later in the day to fly to Oslo on business, he was postponing his trip. I told him I would understand if he had to go, but he insisted on cancelling. He and I never saw eye to eye, but he was always good about things like this.

All Vickie wanted to do was keep my mind distracted from my Dad. Yet, no matter how hard she tried each, conversation drifted back to him. My Dad always thought our divorce was a terrible mistake. Neither of us would listen to his arguments for staying together. As we drove among the hills up north, I knew he was satisfied to look down and see us like we were.

As we entered the kibbutz, I told Vickie to stop the car wanting to walk to my parent's house alone. Vickie understood and let me out while she went ahead to be with my mother.

"Don't take too long, Ari," Vickie said, "your mother needs you."

Walking each step across the kibbutz, I felt as if I was reviewing my Dad's life. As I sat under a large pine tree opposite the central dining hall, I could see most of the kibbutz. Despite the national economic upheaval, Shaar HaGalil was still very successful. That in itself was the best summation of my Dad's life.

Living in Europe before the war, he never asked for any of the horror he endured. All he had dreamed of was a place and an opportunity to live a full life. That my Dad did and most of his life, achieved his dream.

In the final analysis, the value of a man's time on earth is judged by what he leaves behind. My Dad, like so many others, gave their lives so our people could have this little corner of earth to call our own forever. What higher value can the worth of a man's life be?

"Ari," my mother called as she got up from her chair as I walked through the kitchen door.

"*Mama.*"

Chaim's mother was sitting next to her sister, my mother, in the small kitchen of my parent's kibbutz home. Vickie was busy straightening up as a steady stream of people came in. Aviva phoned to say they were on the way.

Luckily I was occupied with helping make the final arrangements for the funeral. We would begin graveside at four o'clock to enable the people to return home before the Sabbath. My Dad, when last in the hospital, gave my mother a list of six people he wanted as pallbearers. Each one was in their own way a representative of a different period of his life.

First was Chaim's father. They had lived their lives together as close as two individuals could possibly do. Next was Raphael, the member of the religious platoon that July day who pulled our fathers to safety during the Battle of Latrun.

Third was Baruch. Although he walked with a cane, he said he would be able to manage. Baruch, the first manager of the kibbutz, greeted our fathers upon their arrival at Shaar HaGalil. It was also he and my Dad who bought the original ten dairy cows from a Palestinian in the village nearby.

Fourth was Yosef. Years ago my Dad was talked into heading the Association of Kibbutzim, he was his vice president during those years. Fifth was Avner, the young head of the kibbutz dairy. My Dad took a liking to him when he was just a kid; Avner spending all his free time with him in the dairy. Since I really preferred to work in the cotton fields, Avner was the son to carry on the family business so to speak.

And lastly, he wanted Vickie's father to be a pallbearer. It was an understatement to say they never agreed on any issue, but he always had the utmost respect for him. "A man of honor," my Dad would always say. Besides, he told my mother, he wanted to lie flat in his grave. Everyone else held right wing views. Vickie's father's leftist positions, he laughed, would level his rest through eternity.

My watch alarm chimed four o'clock exactly when the rabbi began the funeral procession to the gravesite. At his command, the pallbearers started their march. As was the custom of our people, they stopped seven times while the crowd followed behind stopping as he did. Like all customs of our people, I have no idea why we stopped seven times. Because it was our tradition, we did it nonetheless.

While the rabbi spoke, my mind wandered toward the faces of the crowd. Young and old, they had come to pay their final respects to their friend and associate. I was touched that most of my moshav was there. All in all, the crowd numbered in the hundreds. I wanted to walk up to each one individually and thank them for thinking enough of my Dad to come.

Unlike most places in the world, in Israel our custom was not to bury in a coffin. Some people assumed it was because we don't have enough wood in the country. The real reason, however, was our people's belief in the words from dust to dust; speaking about the cycle of life.

Bodies were ritually prepared in linen shrouds and lowered by rope into the grave below by the pallbearers. I kept looking into the empty pit that would soon be my Dad's eternal resting place while my mother squeezed my hand. I shed no tears.

Chaim's father gave the eulogy for my Dad. In a very brief way he summarized his life. "So many died," he said, "that it was up to those of us who survived to live our lives to the fullest. Before us is a man whose life was the epitome of what a man can and should accomplish."

Our sages of old instituted a practice centuries ago. When all was said, the relatives and friends rose and shoveled earth to fill the grave. Chaim's father and I helped my mother walk to the shovel. Painstakingly and with tears flowing, she lifted the first shovel full of dirt and cast it into the grave on her husband below. I was next, followed in turn by each of the pallbearers, Aviva and Vickie.

Psychologically, nothing confronts a person with the finality of their loved one being truly gone like the sound of the dirt striking his shrouded body. My mother insisted that the hole be completely filled in her presence.

Last to be done was my recital of the *Kaddish*, our memorial prayer. As I stumbled saying of each word of the prayer, I was struck by the fact no mention was made of death or mourning. Why then was that particular prayer said by those mourned?

Saying each of the remaining words, I realized that at the time of a death, the living needed to be given hope. The *Kaddish* prayer spoke of the one who gives life bringing a better time for us during our lifetime. It will be a time of eternal life not of death. I concluded the prayer with the words of the last line:

"He who makes peace above; May He make peace upon us and all Israel."

Amen, I thought to myself.

THIRTY

"Can I sit down or do you want to be alone?" Vickie asked as she approached my tree of refuge.

"No, please sit, Vickie, I'd like that."

"The doctor wanted to give your mother a sedative, but she refused."

"She should have taken it."

"Don't worry; we put it in the glass of milk she drank an hour ago. Chaim's mother took care of it. I don't think a sedative would hurt you either."

"No, I need to pull my thoughts together so I can get back to work tomorrow. Vickie, I need to return to a normal life as soon as possible."

"Ari, things never will be normal again. Forget about work. Your Dad just died."

"I don't need you to tell me that, Vickie," I said in a very loud voice.

"I'm sorry, Ari, I never meant to upset you," Vickie said fighting back the tears.

"No, I'm the one who should be sorry. I owe you a lot."

"Ari, we don't owe each other anything. No, not between us are debts to be paid and repaid."

"Please forgive me, Vickie, but I really don't want to talk now. Tell my mother I am going for a drive and not to worry."

"Ari, you shouldn't go by yourself. Chaim can . . ."

"I need to be alone," I insisted.

"Take my car then, it has telephone in case you need anything."

Driving through the night, I couldn't help but sense the peacefulness of the evening. My Dad had picked a good day to depart from this world, leaving undisturbed while the entire country enjoyed the Sabbath rest. I drove not knowing where to stop and turn around, however, the further away from the kibbutz, the more relaxed I became.

"*Safed.*"

The sign read ten kilometers. Why not? I decided to go to Safed. There must have been a reason I headed to that of all cities, my curiosity unable to rest until I found out why. Rising one thousand meters above the Jordan Valley, Safed looked down on the Upper Galilean Mountains in one direction and the Sea of Galilee in the other.

Safed has long been associated as the seat of Jewish mysticism. Being one of Judaism's four holy cities, rabbis of old flocked to spend in Safed their remaining time on earth. In Safed, the laws of our people were codified and the first Hebrew book ever printed was there in 1598.

During our Independence Years, the city's bitterly contested limits were held strategically important by all sides. Our capture of the city itself revealed the true mystical nature of the area. By a sheer miracle, a highly outmanned band of one hundred and twenty Palmach soldiers drove out an entire Palestinian population of over ten thousand.

Being the Sabbath night, everything was closed as if the town itself had died. I parked in the center of the business district and walked around the restored Old City. Approaching, I felt the air filled with gaiety in honor of the Sabbath. The town may have died, but the Old City was very much alive.

I stood at the edge of the Old City overlooking the cemetery below, my thoughts naturally of my Dad. For what must have been hours, I just stared at the valley, time moving ever so slowly.

Gazing in the direction of the Sea of Galilee, I saw an unusual sight. All over the hills settlements dotted the countryside. Yet, late that night each appeared to be a ship on an ocean sailing through a sea of darkness. I kept marveling at the beauty of their images.

"You should see the valley after it rains," a cracked voice from the dark said.

Startled, I slowly turned around. Coming out of the night was the bent frame of an old man in a long black coat walking toward me. From his face grew a long, jagged, white beard. But his eyes, sunken beneath the cracks of his face, radiated such a warmth I felt they could almost create life itself.

"What's so special about the rain?" I asked as he leaned against the wall next to me.

"Not the rain itself," he said, "but what comes after the rain."

"And what comes after the rain?" I asked playing along with the old man's game.

"A rainbow, though not just any rainbow, it's always the largest one around. You can see it rise out of the water below and arch over the mountains. No one really knows where the other end reaches."

"I do," I said. "I've seen the other end. Hey! Don't I know you?"

"We've never met, I'm sure," the old man said.

"I remember. Not long ago I was in Jerusalem by the Western Wall. Didn't I see you putting a slip of paper in one of the cracks?"

"Son, what you saw only you know," he responded.

"I swear . . . maybe it was someone else."

"Why do you look so troubled? It's the Sabbath."

"My Dad died this morning," I said as he looked deeply into my eyes.

"Blessed be the Judge of Truth," the old man said looking to the heavens.

"Tell me, if you can, why is it wherever I go a rainbow is my life?"

"First, you must understand what a rainbow represents," he said as we sat on the wall together.

"It's oil particles refracted by the sun after a rain . . ."

"No! No!" he interrupted, "don't answer with what your mind or heart tells you. Truth comes from one's soul alone."

"When I look at the rainbow, I see beauty. You'll never know what beautiful things I've seen there."

"Good," the old man smiled. "A rainbow is a promise from the artist of all beauty that the world will always be at peace."

"How can you say that," I asked, "when there is nothing but hatred surrounding us."

"A rainbow is a symbol of peace, each color distinctly bright unto itself. Yet, together they coexist to make a bow of many colors. It's a unity, if you like, that is a wonder of nature."

"Why can't people live together as the rainbow does?"

"We can if we learn its lesson well. Harmony comes by each of us appreciating what we were given in life, not by wanting what the other has. It matters not whether you are talking about one person or a whole nation of people," the old man spoke with such conviction as he continued, "we must learn to live together as the colors of the rainbow. If they mixed with one another, what would the image be then?"

"I don't see it totally that way," I said. "We are all only people on this earth. What does it matter if we mix? What would you say if I told you I was in love with a Palestinian girl? How could you say love is wrong?"

"I know you are not in love with who you think. Be careful. Our sages of old have said gazing at the rainbow is one of the three actions that can make a man's eyes grow dim. Don't let the colors totally obstruct your clear vision of what life really is," the old man said as he rose.

"You have to say what you are saying," I challenged, "because you are Orthodox. Life is all written out for you."

"The same author wrote your life too, my son. Tell me did you also put a scrap of paper in the cracks of the wall that day?"

"No, I don't feel any obligation to do those things anymore, not since I was a child."

"Obligation! Is your mother still alive?" asked the old man knowing the answer before I gave it.

"Yes."

"That's where your obligation is now, my son. Go home to your mother. She needs you now as much as you need her."

"I need to get back to a normal life. I'm going to work tomorrow," I said.

"Our sages of old have proscribed a seven day mourning period. Adhere to what they have said in this regard. Then you will understand their wisdom about life itself," the old man said as he silhouetted in the darkness.

"Wait a moment," I yelled, "I don't even know your name."

"Once I was called Reb Yitzchak. Shabbat shalom," he said as he blended into the night.

So much time had passed since I left the kibbutz. During the ride back, the car telephone kept ringing and ringing. I knew it was Vickie trying to see if I was okay. I let it ring. Vickie was standing in the door as I drove up.

"The doctor gave her a double dose of sedative," Vickie said as we entered the house, "but she insisted on waiting up until you came back."

As I walked into the living room, I saw my mother seated on the couch next to my Dad's empty chair. Chaim and Aviva were asleep on the other end.

"Come, Ari," my mother said as she stood, "let's go to sleep. Tomorrow's sun will bring us another day."

Finally I cried!

THIRTY-ONE

In anticipation of the harvest, Chaim sent Selah home to bring extra workers. Always it was the Emerald Riesling to ripen first and that year was no exception. I was already busy ordering two trucks for tomorrow to haul the grapes to the winery. All we needed was Selah to return and we'd be set. "Bingo," yelled Chaim as he held his refractometer toward the sun.

Harvest time was always exciting. Chaim and I were like conductors practicing a symphony an entire year. Hard work, rehearsals, changes in the score all were the labors that went into a single, ephemeral performance. When the curtain went up at the symphony hall, the climax was reached; so too with harvest time. Was our year the best it could have been? The first truck delivered to the winery would be our curtain call.

"Confirmed," Moshe said over the radio as he relayed the wineries approval of two trucks. Moshe, always being the eternal moshav manager, wanted to know why we didn't order four trucks like we had in past years. How could I explain to him Chaim had a feeling we'd be lucky to get two finished?

While we sat under some carob tree eating lunch, Ephraim came to deliver the crates we would use for the harvest. Our workers endlessly cut grapes from the trees and threw them into the large, wooden crates. Chaim's job was to see they were placed along the rows and move them to the edge of an area once filled.

Trucks from the winery had three, large, steel vats hinged on their backs, taking approximately twelve crates with an average net weight of two tons to fill each one. My job was to stand while balancing atop the vats and direct Chaim's or Selah's dumping the grapes from the crates into the vats, specifically looking for rocks and vines.

The winery charged a stiff penalty if too many vines and limbs were attached to the grape clusters. Rocks, on the other hand, would break their machinery. Because of the Intifada we worried about our cousins tossing a few rocks in for good measure. Selah was warned if we received a fine it was his problem not ours. We hoped he would be able to control his people. I would watch, nonetheless, just in case.

"Hey Chaim, don't your workers come from near Hebron?" Ephraim asked as he joined us under the carob tree.

"Why do you ask?"

"I heard on the radio during the drive up here that some Intifada cell leader was shot and the villages nearby are under curfew until they apprehended him."

Chaim and I just looked dumbfounded at each other scared to ask the next question.

"Did they say what village?" I asked.

"Yeah," Ephraim said, "it was called Deir El-Salam. I remembered it because it struck me funny. So much trouble coming from a village whose name in Arabic means City of Peace."

"I'll call Moshe," Chaim said as he got up to walk to the truck.

"No, Chaim," I interrupted, "Selah will make it out of his village. I'm sure he wouldn't let us down. Don't cancel the trucks."

"Why risk it?" Chaim asked.

"We have never had a sugar level this high. Tomorrow's already Tuesday. With four trucks every day the rest of the week we can finish the Riesling and cash in."

"Okay," Chaim relented, "the worst that can happen is we pay for the trucks going back empty."

I left Chaim to pace back and forth around the vineyard by himself; looking like a father impatiently waiting for his wife to give birth. Chaim was only like this during harvest time. The rest of the year he was generally laid back, but for me it was the opposite. I was hyper all year and subdued during harvest and that's why we made such a good team. We were masters at complementing each other's abilities and shortcomings.

I trekked toward Abu Ali's, halfway there meeting Aisha. My watched chimed exactly noon as we drew near.

"I thought you promised Abu Ali not to come to the vineyard while Selah was gone."

"I did, but I was sitting in a tree when I saw you walking up the hill."

"Aisha, why on earth were you sitting in a tree?"

"Ari, the world is so bright and full of life I wanted to see as much of it as I could today!"

"Well, let's see a little of it together then," I said as we walked back toward Abu Ali's. "I have nothing left to do today but wait."

"Wait for what?"

"Tomorrow we start the harvest," I gleefully said.

"Oh!" Aisha responded.

"Why did you stop smiling?"

"A cloud just passed in front of my sun."

Approximately a hundred meters east of Abu Ali's encampment was a small clearing on a hillside. Shepherds years ago built a small stone hut to shelter themselves from the elements. Aisha and I walked to that secluded spot before we spoke further.

"Aisha, I don't understand your sudden mood change. What did I say wrong?"

"Ari, it's the harvest."

"It will be a fun few weeks, I promise, ask Selah. At night although everyone is dead tired there is a special atmosphere . . ."

"And after the harvest, Ari?" Aisha said as tears formed in her eyes. "What then?"

"Oh, I guess I got caught up in the euphoria of finally reaching harvest time, Aisha, please forgive me. What will we do?"

"Abu Ali said I could stay with him as long as I wanted, but he knew my mother would insist I return with my brother."

"Selah only stays a week after the harvest," I said.

"Will we be together for these next few weeks and then never see each other again?" cried Aisha.

I tried to pull Aisha close to me in order to comfort her. Instead, she stood and ran to the edge of the small clearing. Deciding she needed some time alone, I sat on the ground throwing rocks at the stone house. About a quarter of an hour later Aisha walked over and sat down opposite me on her knees, her beautiful, tear laden, blue eyes looking into my very soul.

"Ari, I know we've talked about this before. I'm prepared to leave my past behind and make a future with you. Are you still willing to do the same for me?"

"Yes, Aisha," I said as a small lump formed in my throat, "in the weeks since my Dad died I decided I could."

"Where can we go?"

"It will have to be an English speaking country," I said. "I prefer if it wasn't the United States."

"I guess that leaves England," Aisha said.

"No, Aisha, I was thinking more of South Africa."

"Ari, the world is upside down in that country the same as it is here," Aisha argued.

"That's exactly why South Africa. We could get lost there better than any place else."

"As long as we are together, that's all that matters, Ari," Aisha said.

"Immediately after the harvest we'll get all the necessary travel documents together and just go." When I said those words Aisha's face signaled the clouds blowing away from her sun once again.

Selah showed up around three o'clock with enough workers to harvest. In the end, the army caught the wounded cell leader and called off the curfew. I had wished it had been Nassir. Tomorrow morning at four o'clock we would begin cutting grapes.

"You look green, Ari," Chaim said as we left the vineyard enroute to the winery to receive the shipping documents we would need for the harvest tomorrow, "are you okay?"

Barely hearing Chaim, I didn't reply, his words sounding as if they passed through an echo chamber before reaching my brain. No wonder I looked green, I felt like I had to . . .

"Pull over and stop immediately!" I screamed.

As soon as the truck slowed down enough on the road's shoulder, I leaped out and began violently vomiting. After I'd finished, my stomach kept convulsing with dry heaves. With all of my strength gone, I laid down on the road behind the truck feeling like I had died.

"Are you okay?" Chaim asked. "I've only seen you like this once before, Ari. Remember? During the Sinai Campaign we happened upon an Egyptian tank destroyed with all of its crew inside burned beyond recognition . . ."

"Chaim, do you want to make me throw up again?"

"No, I'm sorry. We'll go to the hospital in Rishon le Zion first," Chaim said as he helped me back into the truck.

"I'm okay. Go straight to the winery. I'll be alright."

"I don't know, a person doesn't usually get suddenly sick like that unless he's really ill, but in your case, mental illness could be enough," Chaim laughed trying to put me in better spirits.

We arrived at the winery office ten minutes before they closed. Chaim went inside while I just walked around for some badly needed fresh air. The winery had a small store selling not only their wines, but soda as well for some reason. Pondering their wares, I saw several bottles emblazoned with the picture of Baron Edmond de Rothschild.

"Those belong to our vintage collection," the old man behind the counter said as I picked up a Cabernet Sauvignon, "and they are extremely expensive."

"Will they get you drunk?"

"Sonny, those bottles are only for people who appreciate the tremendous effort it takes to produce a premium wine of its caliber. In the corner is what you are looking for," the old man sarcastically said.

"I'll have these," I said picking up the two oldest bottles of Rothschild they had.

"I hope you enjoy them," the old man added, "they cost more than I make here in a week."

When Chaim finally returned with the shipping documents, I was already finishing the first bottle. Picking up the empty, barely glancing at me, Chaim shut the truck door. He knew how expensive each bottle was, but more importantly, he sensed I was really upset about something serious.

Until that drive home, I never really appreciated how close Chaim and I were. Not once did he say anything to me the entire drive back to the moshav, patiently driving while I ingested the contents of the remaining bottle. It wasn't until we reached the door to my house did he say anything at all.

"I'll wake you at two-thirty," was all Chaim said as he watched me fall against the back door as I fumbled to open the lock.

"Ring . . . ring . . . . ring."

"Oh! Hello Vickie," I said slurring those few words.

"Are you okay, Ari?"

"Remember once during the Yom Kippur War I saved two men who were pinned down by machine gun fire?"

"Yes, Ari, but why on earth are you bringing it up?"

"And when we were at your parents . . ."

"You mean our fight," Vickie interrupted.

"You got it," I said as I hiccupped, "your father called me a hero for what I had done," *hiccup*, "and you laughed saying I was the biggest coward you'd ever met."

"Ari, what has this got to do with anything now?"

"Today I understood what heroism is all about. A person is neither born a hero nor a coward. Any given," *hiccup*, "set of circumstances can create both. For one specific pulse of time a person is either a hero or a coward . . ."

"Ari, you're rambling so. Drinking again?"

"And when the pulse ceases to beat, so does the heroism or cowardice. But in everyday life, it sometimes takes a hero to be a coward or a coward to be a hero."

"Ari, maybe I'd better call you back tomorrow."

"No, Vickie, I'm quite serious. Tell me, when a man says to a woman, 'I love you,' which is he being? A coward or a hero?"

"I guess a hero, Ari."

"And why not a coward?"

"I don't think a coward would have what it would take to tell someone he didn't love those words."

"You'd be surprised, Vickie, what a coward is capable of doing. He can even be heroic."

"Ari, would you mind telling me what this is all about? Did something happen to you today?"

"Why did you call, Vickie?"

"I just wanted to hear how you were doing. Aviva told me today you vomited for no reason. That's all. I still care about you, Ari."

"Well, I couldn't be lousier if I had woken up this morning and planned it that way." I said as I hung up the phone.

"Ring . . . ring . . . ring . . . ring . . ."

I laid on my bed listening to the telephone play its song. Vickie would grow tired of dialing after awhile I was sure. Yet, I was more impatient than she at the moment. For the life of me I couldn't figure out why I hadn't passed out yet.

I had done something I'd never in my life considered possible, lying to Aisha. Desperately I wanted to spend eternity with her, but I really didn't think I could leave Israel and all I had known. Being without Vickie most of all would be difficult. How on earth could I possibly leave my mother at this time? Was it pure cowardice my

261

telling Aisha I could? The thought of not being totally honest with her had made me sick to my stomach earlier in the day.

My Dad's death, I thought, had freed me to leave. Was it his ghost that was haunting me? Reb Yitzchak was right. What determines a man's true essence is already carved on his soul. Neither his mind nor his heart has power over it.

Nonetheless, I would leave Israel with Aisha and begin a new life somewhere else, Aisha never suspecting anything different than our being in love. It might have been cowardice not to tell her the truth, but it would be nothing less than heroic to see she got the life she dreamed of.

"*Splash!* Good morning," Chaim laughed holding an empty pail in his right hand.

"You could have at least tried to wake me first," I said drying my face with the corner of my soaked pillow.

"It's three o'clock. That's just what I've been trying to do for the past ten minutes."

"Funny," I said as I threw my wet pillow and hit Chaim squarely on the face.

THIRTY-TWO

By any standard, our year's work was a success, all four types of grapes reaching their maximum levels. Even Moshe was happy when Chaim told him how much of a bonus we should expect. Since luck was running with us, I told Chaim we could save a few extra shekels if he was game. To save money Chaim was always prepared.

We calculated our yield at approximately three tons per dunam; if we planned it right we might squeeze the transportation costs of at least one if not two trucks out of the picture. Accomplishing it would be a little risky, but worth the effort. If we overloaded every truck, at the end we would need one less. It worked, saving the transportation cost of two trucks. Moshe even came up to me and admitted I always looked out for the best interests of the moshav.

Aisha was very helpful to Selah and the others keeping cool water available for them to drink. All day she was up and down the rows with her blue, plastic water bottle giving them drink. As a result the workers didn't have to leave the rows to get water giving them had more stamina by always being able to quench their thirst. We never harvested as fast as we did that year. Even Selah was amazed at the productivity.

Standing high above each area on top of the truck's vats, I could see everyone at one time. Most of all I could watch Aisha at work. The more I looked at her, the more my heart began to rule my soul. Why was I not looking forward to spending the rest of my life with her? She truly was beauty in motion. All I had ever wanted in life was to feel someone loved me, Vickie providing that for so many years. Aisha would take over now.

Only one day remained until we completed the French Colombard. When it was done, our harvest would be finished for another year. Chaim calculated we saved an entire day's time over the previous years. To my surprise he even recognized the value of our little Gunga Din. Next year, he told Selah, he would hire someone just to provide water as she had done.

While Chaim and I were getting ready to leave the shed area, a white sedan with a license plate from the Hebron area drove up. Selah motioned to us he knew who it was. Chaim and I returned to what we were doing inside the shed. A few moments later we heard yelling. Immediately we ran outside to see what the problem was.

Selah was screaming at the passenger of the car. When he returned the screams, Selah and the others bodily tried to force him into the sedan, a fist fight erupting. Chaim wanted to break it up, but I said let them be.

With the help of a few of our workers, the man was thrown into the backseat. Selah leaned over to the driver and after a few words stepped cautiously away from the car. The driver started the car and proceeded to drive away in the direction of Abu Ali.

"If you don't want to tell us what that was all about, we'll understand," Chaim said to Selah.

"Thanks for not interfering," Selah said, "if you had it really would have made matters worse."

"Who was he?" I asked. "Was he a friend of yours?"

"He was no friend. Let's just say he was someone I thought I once knew."

"No trouble, please?" Chaim begged. "We only have one more day. Four trucks are coming earlier than usual tomorrow."

Parking the truck, Chaim invited me for a drink after supper to celebrate the harvest's end.

"Chaim, I'm surprised at you," I said, "we still have one day left and you want to celebrate tonight. You're usually too paranoid before it's actually over."

"Well, it's not really in honor of the harvest," Chaim admitted. "Aviva invited Vickie for supper tonight."

"Oh, that's it."

"I was supposed to ask you for supper, but today I saw you watching Aisha from the truck," Chaim continued. "Well, after that I didn't think it appropriate. A drink, on the other hand, I knew you'd never refuse."

"I'll come for supper, Chaim."

"Thanks, Ari."

Opening my mailbox, I was pleasantly surprised by its contents. Inside was an envelope from the army containing my reserve duty orders; in less than two months I had to report to beautiful downtown Hebron. I could see Aisha after the harvest like I hoped. Then I caught myself. She and I were leaving Israel for good together probably in the next few weeks and I'd never do reserve duty again. Crumbling the notice in my hand, I threw it to the ground as I left the office.

Supper was very romantic. Just Chaim, Aviva, Vickie, myself and four of their screaming children. As I tried to eat, I complemented Chaim on his patience with children.

"It's all in having them young," he said, "remember we had our first child right after we got married."

"I wouldn't know what it would be like not to have children around," Aviva added. Vickie sighed with a tear in her eye.

Vickie invited herself over to my house for coffee after supper. We sat and talked like old times for hours. I never really understood how a person gets himself into the situations he does. Sometimes I guess they're just unavoidable. Pawns, knights and bishops maneuver skillfully around the chessboard. Checkmate! That's how it was that night.

I awoke at two-thirty in the morning not any wiser and maybe a little more foolish than the night before. Stumbling in the dark, I almost fell over my shoes. The clock by the bed read quarter to three as I went into the kitchen to make coffee. Coming back into the bedroom, I placed my full cup of coffee on the night stand in front of the clock. Now the clock read three.

"You'd better get up now. I have to go soon. There's coffee by the clock," I said leaning over to hand Vickie her clothes.

"Call me tonight, please, Ari?" she said as I left the room.

One last day and all the grapes would be gone. Chaim was excited the whole drive to the vineyard. I thought of last night. As was our tradition, Chaim brought a bottle of wine he'd made from last year's crop. When the last truck pulled out of the vineyard, Chaim would pour the wine into crystal goblets he'd bought years ago for the occasion. Then we would make a toast to the next year's harvest.

"Selah, where's Aisha?" I asked midmorning. "Is she coming down today?"

At first he didn't answer, looking at me much the same way Rothschild had done. I was dying inside to know what was wrong, but I remained quiet until he spoke.

"She went back to my parent's last night," Selah finally answered.

"I hope everything is okay."

"It will be now," Selah said.

Dazed by what Selah had said, I climbed onto the truck and stood between the last two vats. What on earth went wrong? Selah must have found out about us. I couldn't confront him though. If I did and something else was the problem, well, I was stuck. My only salvation was Abu Ali, but he would have to wait until the very end of the day. All I could think about was Aisha while I bent down to remove a bunch of vines in the vat . . .

"Where am I?" I asked. "Oh, my head. Ouch! My arm."

"We're in the emergency room in Ramle," Chaim said.

"What are we doing here?"

"About two hours ago you were suppose to be standing on top of a truck looking for vines and rocks."

"If I wasn't standing on a truck, ouch, where was I?"

"Oh, you were standing on the truck, but you must have been on another planet. I kept yelling for you to move as Selah was raising a crate full of grapes to dump in the vat. You didn't even see the crate when it broadsided you off the truck."

"Selah knocked me off the truck?" I asked as my head continued to throb.

"Boy was he upset about it too."

"Where is he now?"

"He stayed to complete the last truck while I brought you here."

"What time is it, Chaim?"

"It's after five. Don't worry; I'm sure the truck made it to the winery before closing."

"We have to get back to the vineyard. I want to talk to Selah."

"Funny thing, Ari, he told me this morning as soon as we got to the vineyard that he had to go back to his village tonight. The others would stay till the end of the week, but he doubted whether he'd return."

"Yeah, funny thing," I kept mumbling.

Unfortunately nothing was broken. All I had was a severe concussion and a sprain of my left shoulder. The radiologist thought I was nuts when I was disappointed.

As the nurse was filling the syringe with pain killer, she saw no humor while I begged to drink the whole bottle. My head was wrapped with gauze and my left arm was in a sling. It only hurt when I laughed and I was in no laughing mood.

"Hey, Ari," Moshe said as Chaim helped me out of the truck, "you finally got the lobotomy you needed I see."

"Chaim, just do me one favor. Remind me when I'm healed to get Moshe back."

"Okay," Chaim laughed.

"One other thing; ask Aviva to call Vickie for me. I was supposed to call her tonight, but for some reason I don't think I'll be able to. Tell her I'll call tomorrow. I'd do it myself, but . . ."

"You're just too scared to."

"Maybe I am. Tomorrow I want you to drive me to Abu Ali's."

"Ari, I'm not going to look at the vineyard until the end of the week. I promised Aviva that we'd go to Eilat with the kids for a couple of days after the harvest was over," Chaim explained.

I lay down on my bed as the pain reliever started to take effect. Something was wrong, but I couldn't place it. Looking around the bedroom I realized what it was. Vickie, before she left, made the bed and straightened up the room. The last time it looked that orderly was when she lived with me.

"Ring . . . ring . . . ring"

"No, I wasn't trying to commit suicide after we spent last night together, Vickie."

"Ari, I just called . . ."

". . . to tell me that last night was a terrible mistake and I shouldn't read anymore into it than the moment itself . . ."

"Damn it, Ari, can't you ever shut up," Vickie screamed.

"I'm sorry."

"You should be. I called to tell you the opposite if you'd listen."

"You did?"

"After you left this morning, I just laid in bed for the longest time. For the first time, I realized a lot."

"Like what?"

"Well, it was my bed I was in, my wallpaper on the wall, and I had made the curtains on the windows."

"I'd love to talk with you, Vickie, but . . ."

"Ari, in all the time I'd been back to the house I never noticed you'd changed nothing. Why?"

"I never expected you to be gone as long as you have been, Vickie. I always wanted it to be just the way you left it when you returned."

"Ari, I want to come back to my house."

"Vickie, please don't say that to me now. No, please."

"Why? Ari, I love you."

"And I you, but it's not the right time for us."

"Because of Aisha?"

"She's only part of it. It's me Vickie. I need more time to sort out my life."

"And when you finish, Ari, will I be in your tomorrow?"

"A man I've grown to respect a lot recently said something I think you should take to heart."

"What was that?"

"Worry about tomorrow only after it becomes yesterday."

"Ari, I meant what I said. I want to try a life together again. You'll have the time you need."

"I love you, Vickie." Was I being heroic or a coward?

"I had hoped you still did," Vickie said as she hung up.

I rolled over to go to sleep, faintly smelling a familiar aroma. Vickie's perfume was scented on my pillow. I hugged the pillow as I passed out.

THIRTY-THREE

Three-thirty. How could it possibly be three-thirty *in the afternoon?* The nurse must have given me some sedative. Trying to sit up in bed, I couldn't, the room spinning round and round and . . . I lay back down and after about twenty minutes finally made a successful attempt at sitting up.

With a tremendous effort, I made it to the truck. Even though I felt horrible, I had to see Abu Ali. I was still left with a lot of unanswered questions. Hopefully Abu Ali held the answers I sought. As I approached the vineyard, the sun had already begun its slow fall beyond the horizon. At that precise moment before day gave way to night, a man could see all the beauty in heaven he would ever need.

Driving up to Abu Ali's, I got part of my answer before I opened the truck door. Rothschild stood there barking away at me, taking Abu Ali's whistle to silence him. Something inside of me said I'd be better off leaving with just Rothschild's answer. I didn't listen.

"Ari, I hope at least you feel better than you look," Abu Ali laughed as he walked to meet me halfway.

"Unfortunately, I don't."

"Come inside, we have just what you need."

"I'm afraid I need more than a cup of coffee. Another head would be nicer."

"No, I have a tea made with a few herbs and spices, you'll see," Abu Ali said as one of his wives brought me extra pillows on which to lie.

"Do you think I can have some of this tea to take with me? You were right," I said after only ten minutes had passed since the first cup.

"Tea is no problem; that I can give you. It's what else you want I'm afraid I'll have trouble providing," Abu Ali said as he motioned for a bag of tea to be prepared for me.

"Thank you. Now, all I need is a little peace of mind," I said slowly sipping my second cup of tea.

"About Aisha we must wait a few moments to talk."

"Tell me, you must have heard it was Selah who knocked me from the truck. Was it on purpose? I must know," I begged.

"Maybe we have to start at the end after all. Hopefully the picture won't be so blurred."

"Aisha then, Abu Ali, why did she leave so suddenly without even saying good-bye?"

"She left with her brother Nassir," Abu Ali said never removing his coffee cup from his lips.

"Nassir! When was he here?"

"You saw him, Ari. Selah told me you and Chaim were by the shed when they fought."

"So that's who that was," I said nodding my head. "What on earth was he doing here? He's a wanted man!"

"Well, it seems," Abu Ali began as he leaned back on his pillow bed, "the mother found poems Aisha had written while she was home."

"Poems?"

"Love poems, Ari, about Aisha and you."

"And my name was mentioned?"

"Very much so," Abu Ali answered, "her mother showed them to Nassir in hopes that he could talk some sense into Aisha. Unfortunately, Fatima never understood how crazy her son, Nassir, really is. He vowed to come to the vineyard in order to kill you."

"Kill me? You can't be serious, Abu Ali."

"Oh, I'm afraid so," Abu Ali rose as he walked to the tent opening and yelled something in Arabic to one of his sons.

"Did Selah know Nassir wanted to kill me when he was by the shed?" I asked as Abu Ali knelt to lie down again.

272

"Yes, Nassir had a pistol with him and if Selah hadn't thrown him back into the sedan, he might have had his way."

"Oh!" I said looking down at the ground.

"It was only luck that they had to bypass many road blocks reaching the vineyard later than they had anticipated. Nassir's plan was to drive by and shoot you while you were working."

"What happened to the gun?"

"One of the two kids you let come back took it away from him."

"And then Nassir came straight to your encampment to get Aisha."

"Ari, how could I prevent him from taking her back?" Abu Ali sighed.

"Did Aisha say anything at all to you about me before she left?"

"She wanted you to know that she loves you very much."

"That's all?"

"No, she will try to send you a letter."

"I don't read Arabic and she can only speak English."

"Aisha has a person who will help her. One of her teachers lived for a time in England. Aisha and she are very close. She'll write the letter, Ari."

"But won't that put her in danger if she tells the teacher about us?"

"I don't think so, Ari. The teacher was the one who helped Aisha express herself in prose," Abu Ali said offering me another cup of tea.

"Abu Ali, did Selah knock me off the truck intentionally?"

"Selah wouldn't talk to me about it before he left except to say you'd met with an accident. Do you think he did, Ari?"

"No, I don't. I believe no matter how mad he might have been, he wouldn't have done me harm."

"I agree, it's not Selah's nature," confirmed Abu Ali.

"So, what should I do now? Tell me what could I possibly do?"

"Aisha and you will settle your hearts when it's the proper time."

"Abu Ali, I have to be totally honest. I don't know any more if I can go through with running away with Aisha. I've realized over the past weeks how rooted I am in this country and with my people. It's exactly as you said it would be, remember? No matter how much pleasure Aisha could give me, I don't think it would be enough to ease my pain."

"Everything is healed in time, Ari. The question is how much time? Aisha is young and in love. The sweet child has a life worth of time ahead of her. You, on the other hand, have already lived much of yours," Abu Ali said as he momentarily paused. "I agree, it's not an easy situation you find yourself in."

"Is there nothing I can do?" I pleaded.

"Ari, I'm sure soon you will hear from Aisha. Until then all you can do is watch the sunrise and wait till the sun sets."

Leaving Abu Ali's I felt for the first time in my life I had no place to go. Two wonderful women wanted to spend their remaining days with me. Yet, driving aimlessly I had never been more alone in all my life.

All of a sudden I remembered something my mother always told me. "Ari," she would say, "home is a place you can always go. The door will never be locked."

Not even when Vickie and I separated did I run back home. That night I did just that. It was past midnight when I walked into the kitchen. My mother was sitting by the small table next to the refrigerator waiting for her water to boil.

"Come sit down," she said, "I'll get another cup, but first please indulge your poor old mother. What on earth has happened to you?"

"I'm sorry, Mom, I forgot about my bandages. I hope you didn't get nervous when I walked through the door?"

"Remember once when you were twelve," my mother said as she poured water into my cup while I added Abu Ali's tea, "Chaim and you were playing by the citrus packing plant."

"I remember."

"Although you had broken your arm you didn't tell me it hurt until the next morning out of fear I'd be upset. Since then I've always been thankful you've had a special knack for survival. Your Dad did also. I don't worry about you, Ari. Maybe I should, but I know deep inside of me everything works out for the best."

I wished I shared my mother's confidence in my ability to survive. Sipping tea with my mother, I felt ashamed I couldn't tell her what was bothering me. My mother, I was sure, sensed something must be troubling me a great deal to come home. She would never mention anything first. If I wanted to talk about it, she would wait for me to say the first word. We drank tea and I remained silent.

The next morning I bid my mother good-bye at nine o'clock. Before heading back to Mevo Ayalon, I decided to walk to my Dad's grave only a kilometer from the kibbutz near an orange grove. Before reaching my Dad's grave, I read the names on the other tombstones. Funny, I thought, how just the name of a person automatically evoked certain memories.

Finally I reached my Dad. Since the funeral, the dirt mound over the grave had settled considerably. My mother and I last night spoke of a marker. She said my Dad only wanted something simple. I agreed. Yet, standing there looking at his spirit below, I couldn't understand how a simple marker would be appropriate. A man's life like my Dad's should have a billboard.

"Dad, we never talked much while you were alive. Whose fault was that? I think we both are to blame. Now I need you more than ever to be here. Even though we cannot see each other face to face, I feel your presence. There's so much I'd like to say . . . so much I should say. I guess now you're in a world of true knowledge." I stopped for a moment while tears started to break loose from my eyes.

"You probably see everything from where you are anyway. Tell me then, Dad, how does it all end for me? Vickie? Aisha? Send me a clue, please. I know which you prefer. Don't worry I'd rather go back to Vickie, but what of Aisha? I'm responsible for her as well. You always taught me that honor and a good name live long after a person is gone. In your case I see now how true it is. What of me? If I don't stay with Aisha, will my honor remain?" Near the graveyard was the sound of tractors working in the orange grove. I paused briefly until they passed.

"I guess no matter what I do my end will be the same as yours. I can almost hear your voice, Dad, 'make the most of what you have.' Is that what you said? What does it mean Dad? Why did you have to leave me now? Why do I suddenly feel like a bird being thrown from the nest? I suppose that's life itself, isn't it Dad? Flap your wings or you hit the ground!"

Rising from the grave, I brushed the soil from the knees of my jeans and placed a small rock on his grave, another of our people's customs for which I have no explanation. Apparently my Dad had plenty of company during the past few weeks, mine not being the only rock.

After Chaim returned from Eilat, we spent the next few days readying the vineyard for the winter months. It was good to be there each day only with Chaim. Just like old times or did I mean times before Aisha? Daily I thought of her especially at sunrise. Still nothing appeared in my mailbox. In less than a month I'd be in Hebron. If I didn't hear from her by then at least I could try to find her in Deir El-Salam.

Vickie kept her word giving me all the time I needed to get my life in order. At times she too understood. Often I wished she'd come over one night and demand a reconciliation. I doubted if I ever would have the guts to ask her back into my life. What I feared most was it not working out a second time. I could never take losing Vickie again.

One day there it was as I opened my mailbox. Aisha's letter had been mailed from, of all places, Jerusalem. As I unfolded her letter, I could hear Aisha's voice rising from the words within.

Rainbows

Dearest Ari,

How have I spent these weeks away from you? I have missed you so. Abu Ali of all people came to my parent's house four days ago. He brought the rest of my things I left behind. I was worried when he told me you hadn't been to see him much after I left. I had no idea of the accident until he told me. My brother mentioned nothing, nor did I mention it to him after I heard. I pray to Allah that all is well.

Ari, you must believe I didn't want to go. My brother, Nassir, came. He said he was going to kill you if I didn't leave. Oh! How could I possibly deny how I feel for you? How could I lie about that?

Nassir's gun is under the wheel of the water wagon. My brother didn't know what to do with it. Ari, I'm in prison here. No, it's even worse than that. Nassir makes me go with him each day. I'm forced to throw rocks at settler's cars as they pass our village. I fear him if I don't.

I need you to rescue me, my love. I count the days until your reserve duty. Please try to come to Deir El-Salam. Don't worry, I will find you if you do. I see the faces of all the soldiers hoping one will be yours. All I can do is wait till you come.

> *Your love,*
> *Aisha*

Sitting in my kitchen, I read Aisha's letter over and over again, each time her image growing keener until I could almost see her next to me. In Deir El-Salam I would encounter destiny.

THIRTY-FOUR

Someone from behind the stairs yelled as I entered the military command headquarters in Hebron. It was Meir, my commanding officer in Gaza.

"I thought you were condemned to spend your remaining days in Gaza, Meir," I said handing my orders to the clerk seated at the building's entrance.

Meir, a career officer, during his years of service, he'd seen it all. As he told me in Gaza, he had fought on the soils of Egypt, Jordan, Lebanon, and Syria. Once during the Sinai Campaign near Sharm El-Sheikh, he almost had an opportunity to set foot in Saudi Arabia.

Unfortunately, his combat experience showed. We used to make a joke about Meir in Gaza, his not being as tough as he looked. Someone once saw him putting sugar into the bowl of nails he always ate for breakfast.

"Come, Ari," Meir said as he guided me to a large map on the wall, "Let's decide where in this armpit of the earth you should be exiled for the next month."

I sat quietly as Meir explained the situation in the area, listing village after village, I waited for him to reach the only one I wanted. Sure enough, at the end he came to it.

"Deir El-Salam," Meir called out.

"I'll go there."

"No, it's become a hotbed in the last few weeks."

"And my time in Gaza doesn't qualify me?" I argued.

"Ari, there is a basic difference between here and Gaza," Meir continued. "In Gaza they are mainly Islamic fundamentalists. West Bank Palestinians, especially around Hebron, are more political not having the refugee mentality like the Gazans."

"What difference does it make, Meir?"

"Being political, the Palestinians around here are more calculating. In Gaza, force was an effective weapon because all they wanted was to create violence. Here, on the other hand, the Palestinians want a state of their own. They play poker with us and we always run a close game. Many times they fold their cards only to win the hand in the international media."

"No, I have my reasons for wanting to be in Deir El-Salam."

"This is no place for personal vendettas. Get that out your mind," Meir adamantly said. "We are here to do a job the best way humanly possible. When an error occurs, it's an honest mistake."

"No, it's nothing like that I promise."

"Okay then. Be sure of it," Meir conceded, "let's go up to my office and talk further."

As Meir closed the door to his office, he told his beautiful blond secretary not to disturb us any more than she already had. Looking around the room, I was amazed not having been in a battle office since a field headquarters during a war. On each wall were maps of the entire command area including topographical and aerial. Behind Meir was a small arsenal of M-16's and Uzi's. Upon his desk sat four telephones plus a hand held radio. On the side of his desk was a sign reading "complaint department" with an arrow pointing down to a trash basket.

"Looks like you are ready for war," I said as I sat opposite Meir in front of his desk.

"Oh, make no mistake about it, Ari, we are at war. My boys out there on patrol have their guns locked and loaded ready to fire the same as if they were in Beirut. You put your life on the line every minute of the day here."

"So, it's pretty much the same as it was in Gaza."

"Ari, at first I thought so, but now I see the difference. While in Gaza none of us understood what the Intifada was all about. I was there when it started. Remember the trigger?"

"Wasn't it a traffic accident or something? Activists claimed it was revenge for the slain salesman, if I remember correctly."

"From that moment on we kept dealing with the Intifada as a riot situation. First we thought water cannons and rubber bullets would solve the problem, however, the Palestinians weren't intimidated. All it got us was an image in the media of acting like they did in South Africa."

"One of my father-in-law's favorite sayings."

"Now we realize it's a war to the finish. The concept of the Intifada is one of control," Meir explained.

"I know. Like in Gaza our opening stores after the Intifada leadership ordered them closed."

"I mean a different kind of control. We have to find measures that will keep order. You know what has happened recently?" Meir asked.

"I'm afraid I don't know what you are referring to."

"My men have complained that the army is no longer presenting a deterrent to the unrest. Palestinians in the streets laugh at them. Soldiers in the field are complaining about wanting to be soldiers not policemen."

"You said it was a war zone here," I reminded him.

"Ari, my men out there are what, eighteen, nineteen, maybe twenty or twenty-one. They never envisioned being engaged in a pitched battle against women and children when they were drafted in the army," Meir said as he struck his fist on the desk. "The war is against women and children. They are the soldiers fighting us."

"I've seen it almost every day. Whenever we got stoned driving through Beit El-Safa it was from kids," I said.

"Remember West Bank Palestinians are more political. Using women and children is a calculated battle plan. They thought they would win on two fronts. First, we'd receive bad press if we harmed them. Second, they probably felt our young soldiers wouldn't have the stomach to hurt women and children."

"But they have been successful on both fronts," I argued.

"To a point, Ari, we are becoming smarter," Meir said. "Two weeks ago near Hebron University a patrol was attacked by a rioting mob. I saw one particular soldier I knew was from a left wing kibbutz hitting a kid about sixteen."

"Boy, were his actions out of character."

"I thought so too. The next day I saw him here at headquarters and asked him about it. I think his answer speaks for itself. 'If someone throws a rock at me, then believe me, I have no problem beating him. I didn't feel that way when I first entered the army. After I got pelted in the face and arms a few times by rocks, I began to realize sometimes you have to compromise your conscience. There's a limit to how much of a bleeding heart you can be out here,' he said. Can you believe it?"

"Meir," I said, "beating Palestinians isn't going to end the Intifada."

"I said control, Ari. At first I thought throwing a troublemaker in prison for a while would at least keep him off the streets. After eighteen days he's released unless we have enough evidence to charge him," Meir continued. "If we break his arm he won't throw stones for a good two to three months."

"Meir, when a democracy like ours uses a policy of beatings and arm breakings we stand to lose more than control."

"You know, Ari, what really bothers me about that statement? Most people in Israel don't understand the war we are fighting. They don't see the physical and psychological casualties on our side. What they see even in our own media is the accidental shooting of a three year old child or a seven year old girl hospitalized because tear gas inhalation. Did they ever ask what proceeded all of those things?"

"Meir, I agree. If the kids were off the streets they would be safer, but the so called leadership of the uprising puts them at risk."

"It's only a half hour drive from here to Jerusalem and maximum an hour to Tel Aviv. Tonight, when you are walking around risking your life, think about the rest of the country sleeping safely in bed while you are in the war zone with live ammunition prepared to kill if need be in order to protect your life or the lives of your men."

Riding to Deir El-Salam in the back of the jeep, I couldn't help but think of my conversation with Meir. Despite all Meir said, he'd left out one very important fact. Measure any other army's performance under similar conditions and our defense forces pass with the highest of colors.

Yet, we have been unjustly branded as the worst army since Attila the Hun. All because of the fact we open ourselves to scrutiny from anyone who wishes to look. Our neighbors in the region surely cannot admit to that. Even the Western countries, I fear, aren't as cooperative as we were. My Dad always said, "There is a game played by free journalists' worldwide. The game is called Israel bashing. Rules are easy. There are none."

I was to command a group of forty soldiers in Deir El-Salam. Our residence was a girl's school house commandeered by the army. While the accommodations weren't the best, they sure beat the tents we had in Gaza.

We had three missions to accomplish. First, to keep order in the village and second, the road through Deir El-Salam was a major artery connecting the Jewish settlements in the area. Keeping the free flow of traffic maintained was of primary importance. Although construction was begun on a bypass road, it wasn't scheduled to open for at least half a year. And third, keep confrontation to a minimum.

To accomplish our missions we used three methods: jeep patrols, foot patrols and rooftop lookouts. Hopefully each one element would enhance the overall effectiveness of our mission.

Jeep patrols were primarily used to show a presence in a large area. Recently all jeeps were outfitted with bullet proof glass on all sides including the roof. Our cousins had gotten into the habit of throwing mini boulders from rooftops. Now a soldier was free to look out of the jeep without fear of being pelted with stones.

Foot patrols were designed to go where jeeps couldn't effectively maneuver. Most of the village streets were very narrow designed long ago to accommodate horse and wagon traffic. Communication was a primary function of a foot patrol. Since they were constantly among the population, their eyes observed more than any others could.

Finally, rooftop lookouts were placed strategically at intersections or overlooking trouble spots such as schools or mosques. Soldiers complained that the lookouts were the worst place to be. Either they froze in the winter or they baked during the summer. A rooftop lookout was easily seen from a distance. High above the sand bag placement shielding the soldiers flew a large blue and white Israeli flag. I guessed it was all part of the control Meir spoke about.

All of the training we had received in the army recently was geared to not killing people, exactly the opposite of what most people thought. Plastic and rubber bullets were invented for that reason, but the ever present danger around the next corner could change everything. It was always left up to the field commander to use his judgment within army rules of fire in sizing up a situation to determine the type and amount of force to use. Even turning and running away was preferable to the loss of human life.

As I said, we had three primary missions to accomplish, but myself, I had only one. I was in Deir El-Salam for twenty-eight more days to find Aisha at whatever the cost, her desperate plea more than I could bear. I knew I could never live with myself if I didn't help her. Wasn't it I who caused her misery, not Nassir?

Finally I sat on my bed in the principal's office of the school mentally and physically exhausted from the day. Maybe it was the moment that compelled me to do something I rarely if ever had done. Slowly I began a prayer asking for courage and strength to accomplish my mission. I pleaded for no harm to come as a result of my orders or involvement to any one Palestinian or Israeli.

"Crash . . . crash . . . .crash!"

My prayers were interrupted by the welcoming committee from the neighborhood. Sixteen windows on the west side of the school house were broken. They were, I think, the last sixteen left intact before that night.

My first week in Deir El-Salam was uneventful. The most serious occurrence was slogan painters. I don't think there was any wall at all in the whole city that didn't have some kind of Intifada slogan painted on it, each storefront having three or four rows. As fast as they went up, we painted over them. I stopped my jeep once in front of "Al-Bustan Restaurant and Sweet Shop." All four of us had a good laugh. Someone had painted in English, "Yankee Go Home."

Within the center of the village was its focal point, the mosque. Aisha told me once some sheik came years ago from Saudi Arabia and gave money to build it. Architecturally, it was rather beautiful. The building itself was two stories high with no right angles on the corners, sort of a hexagon in shape. Along the top below the roof were a mass of Arabic inscriptions. One of my men, born in Yemin, said they were passages from the Koran asking the prophet to guard and protect the mosque and all who entered to pray.

The main entrance was a beautiful ogee arch built from a mixture of pink, red, brown and white limestone. The roof housed a hexagon based dome in keeping with the symmetry of the structure. At its pinnacle stood a crescent, originally a Turkish emblem, but later adopted by Mohammedans as a symbol of political force. Showing age, the dome's blue green paint was flaking on all sides.

Most striking of all was the minaret from which the muezzin summoned the faithful to prayer. The first level consisted of layers of pink, aqua and white block. Next the middle level was emblazoned with various arabesque designs. And the third and final level just below the actual platform was built of the same geometric designs as the level below only in reverse order. Unto itself the mosque was a true building of serenity.

However, just the opposite was true. Most of the riots and disturbances had occurred in the square directly opposite the entrance usually midday on Friday after prayer services. We tried two different approaches to keep order. Either we showed no presence at all or we were there with excessive force, neither approach proving effective. I had decided I personally would take direct field command on Fridays around the mosque. If there was an error of judgment, I wanted my subordinates free of blame.

Then it happened. During my second week, I saw Aisha walking down the street. I was in a jeep with two other people. How could I lose what could be my only opportunity to see her?

"See that girl?"

"Which one?" the driver asked.

"In front of the store that says "Deir El-Salam Trading Company."

"What about her?" the soldier in the back asked.

"Arrest her!"

"Her?" they both asked.

"Yes . . . her!" I commanded.

We turned the jeep around and sped to the other side of the street. Simultaneously we three jumped from the jeep. The other two pointed their rifles at Aisha. Neither of them could understand the look of joy instead of fright on her face as she got into the back of the jeep as we headed to the school. Once inside Aisha and I walked into my office.

"Oh, Ari," Aisha said as tears rolled onto her cheeks.

"I've been here two weeks."

"I know. I saw you last week by the mosque," Aisha said.

"You must not go near there. It is very dangerous," I pleaded.

"Ari, I have no choice. Nassir forces me to be in the crowds threatening to tell everyone I'm in love with you. The people will tear me apart if they find out," Aisha said as she cried evermore.

"When I finish my reserve duty in a couple of weeks, we will leave together," I promised Aisha.

"Ari, please let me come stay with you now," Aisha begged.

"You can't. They would never allow it."

"Then take me somewhere else . . . anywhere but here. I fear two weeks could be too late."

"We'll have to wait. Remember how Abu Ali always says we rush too many things before their proper time. Two weeks isn't long when you consider we'll be together forever. If you feel in danger, then come here. I'll give you a note. Show it to any soldier and he will bring you to me."

Sitting down, I took pen and paper to write Aisha's note. In it I explained she was an important informer and should be regarded as an extremely valuable part of our security arrangements. I ordered any soldier, at whatever the cost, to immediately bring her to me at headquarters.

"Ari, I've missed you so."

"And I you," I said affixing my official seal to the letter. "Now keep this with you at all times and guard it well so no one finds it. I'll take you back where we picked you up."

"You'd better not. Most of the boys who worked for you in the vineyard live in my neighborhood."

"When will I see you again?"

"I'm afraid, Ari, we shouldn't. It would be too risky for me. Just look out your window at night and that will be enough."

"I don't understand, Aisha."

"Since I first saw you I steal away at night and watch the school hoping to get a glimpse of you," Aisha explained.

"I didn't know."

"Ari, this was my school. Most of my life's best memories are contained within her walls. It's only fitting for you to be here. Let's just part knowing the next time we are together we'll never have to part." Aisha cried as all of the blue in her eyes gave way to red.

I walked Aisha outside and ordered a jeep to take her back. Leaning over to the driver, I gave special instructions to make sure no harm came to her. They were also ordered to patrol the area where she would be left off for at least an hour to see there were no disturbances. At the same time Aisha left the compound, but who should appear.

"Meir, what brings you to beautiful downtown Deir El-Salam?" I asked as I opened the door of his jeep.

"Let's go inside. We've just received new orders," Meir said as his shadow stood tall as he got out of the jeep.

What had changed was how we dealt with people wearing masks, a recent phenomenon. Recently some masked men were caught with arms, once even returning fire at a patrol.

"Now was time to get tough," Meir said. "We are to regard anyone wearing a mask as extremely dangerous. We have orders, at our discretion within the rules of engagement, to shoot to kill anyone in a mask."

Later that night, unable to sleep, I went outside the school house to get a pail of water. I started to wash the windows in my office both inside and out. While I was washing, a young lieutenant passed by.

"Excuse me, Sir," he said standing in the doorway, "but you'll make yourself highly visible from the outside if you clean the windows."

"That's my intent, lieutenant."

Unsure if I was crazy or a fool he shook his head as he left my office. Myself, I turned the light out and stood in front of the cleaned window for almost an hour. Soon that would become my nightly ritual before turning in.

THIRTY-FIVE

For some unexplained reason, last night was the first full night's sleep I had gotten since coming to Deir El-Salam. In fact, it had been months since I awoke so well rested. I walked over to my desk and tore yesterday's date from the calendar. Friday! Four more days until I would be released from purgatory.

Monday was to be my day of reckoning, I thought to myself. If all went as planned, either Sunday or Monday Aisha would come to me. By Monday noon if she hadn't arrived, I would tear Deir El-Salam from its very foundations until I found her. I only could wait in earnest for that day to come. Since I saw her last, the image of fright on her face wouldn't leave my mind.

Not once had I seen her. Although I had the resources of the entire defense establishment at my command, I felt totally impotent to do anything for Aisha until next week. I began to worry I'd made a mistake by letting her return home. Was it a mistake? Had harm already come to her? I was foolish for not at least taking her away from her hell. Abu Ali's words, however, gave me presence of mind. I would have to wait and let time play the upper hand.

Downstairs we had the usual morning briefing, each of us noting we should expect trouble by the mosque. Last Friday passed by too uneventfully. One thing the Intifada had taught us, a quiet atmosphere was covered by an extremely thin layer of calm. And calm was usually a sign of trouble brewing.

During the past week we had our most serious incident yet. A foot patrol near the market came under attack by a mob. In addition to the usual bombardment of bottles, stones etc, someone from the crowd started lobbing Molotov cocktails. They were specially made containing not only gasoline, but rubber cement or some other kind of glue. One private was burned badly because the flaming glue stuck to his clothing as they caught fire.

The next day supply brought special fire suits. They looked like regular uniforms except the material was designed to burn quickly and not injure the person wearing it. I only wished we'd had them issued last week. Luckily the soldier would completely recover. Meir was right. We were at war.

All hope, I guess, wasn't lost by our presence. I noticed the younger kids, Ali's age, relating to us. Sometimes they would even take gum or candy from us. Once, a little girl gave a soldier a flower. Later he told me he felt like a G.I. in one of those old World War II movies handing out chocolate bars while invading Italy.

Older kids, however, had hate spelled in every language possible on their faces. They were our enemy in the street. After the past few weeks I saw firsthand what Meir had told me. No one wanted to battle against women and children, but none of us wanted to get seriously hurt either. After all that has always been a soldier's lot. Like the line of the Kipling poem read "to do or die."

Soon the air was filled with the call to prayer by the muezzin standing high on the minaret. On that particular Friday it seemed as if all of Deir El-Salam had become religious. Nonetheless, I decided to minimize our presence. I radioed Meir to ask his advice. He agreed. If I thought things were potentially volatile, then a show of superiority might just be the catalyst to provoke trouble.

They were a strange lot going in the mosque. Some were old men regally dressed in long white or grey robes. Many wore a special head cover Aisha once told me symbolized their travelling to Mecca for the Haj. Most, however, were dressed in jeans and work clothes. It was obvious Deir El-Salam contained few men of leisure, the majority toiling daily in order to eke out their meager existence.

"What should we do, sir?" asked the radio man from the rooftop lookout across the street.

"Wait! What else can we do?"

"I have a feeling that this Friday will pass like last week," my driver said.

"Are your 'feelings' usually right?"

"Almost always they are wrong!" he laughed.

Now the square opposite the mosque was all but deserted. Everyone was somewhere, but none were to be seen. Prayers filled the air around the mosque. Without their sound there would have been no life at all. Only a deathly silence prevailed. I thought of my Dad.

How could I have ever made him understand while he was alive my feelings for Aisha? I chuckled a little. Confusion! I remembered how that one word ruled my very being for so long. Yet, now sitting outside the mosque, I for the first time understood in which direction my life would take and why. Hopefully from my Dad's current vantage point he saw clearly enough to understand what I was about to do.

"Some old guys really giving it to them from the pulpit in the mosque where the imam stands to deliver sermons," one of the men reported after he'd walked in front of the mosque.

"They're starting to come out, Ari," the radioman from the rooftop said as his words broke the silence in the air.

"Just act normal and keep your eyes open," I said. "Call up the other jeep and tell them to stay out of sight."

No problems occurred as a group of men began to emerge from the mosque. Suddenly someone on top of the minaret started screaming.

"Look sir, he's waving a Palestinian flag up there."

At that precise moment I recalled from memory the only description which aptly described those initial seconds. During the Sinai Campaign, Chaim pointed out a strange phenomenon once during the height of a tank battle. He called attention to the fact you could see a shell hit its target, explode and destroy it well before the sound reached your ears. No matter how the destruction in front of us looked, without the sound registering it was as if it wasn't real.

What we heard in front of the mosque was very real. From the crowd a Molotov Cocktail was thrown dead center into the rooftop lookout post, the exploding gasoline catching the canvas roof on fire. As the Israeli flag burned above, the crowd changed into the frenzy of a mob.

"Call the jeep up now!" I yelled. "Radio the school for every available man to come. Get me Meir on the line."

First we threw teargas, but many carried onions to counteract its effect. Rubber bullets were a last resort, at close range being lethal. We had live ammunition in case we were at risk of life.

"Look by the right side of the mosque," my driver screamed," about ten of them wearing black masks."

Seeing no other option, we began shooting rubber bullets only into the air. It had its effect, some of the crowd running from fear. Yet, the group of masked men disappeared as the second jeep arrived. Before the four men got out of the jeep, two Molotov Cocktails were thrown with one hitting it. The group of masked men had scored their second victory.

"Give chase," I ordered as the masked men ran through the narrow street across from the mosque.

Five of us, with our lives in our throats, ran as fast as we could through a maze of streets which were really only paths between houses after them. It was difficult watching ahead and above at the same time. Narrowly a small boulder thrown from a rooftop missed the sergeant directly behind me. We had lost sight of the masked men. I gave the order to stop. In the heat of the pursuit, we hadn't paid any attention to where we were. Slowly we walked ahead prepared for the worst.

The street we were on made a right angle turn ahead out of view. I took the lead with the others spread about a meter apart, dashing into the turn expecting trouble. Nothing! Further up it appeared the street opened into a courtyard.

There they were at the opposite end of the courtyard standing in the entrance to the street's continuation. All of the masked men were grouped together. We held each other in checkmate. I could hear, in the silence that prevailed, the seconds tick away from someone's watch behind me.

"Bang!"

One of the masked men had drawn a pistol and shot at us while we fell to the ground in shock. The rules of engagement had quickly altered; now it was our lives or theirs. We attacked across the courtyard in pursuit of the ten. I saw three of them trying to scale a wall between two buildings. Obviously, the other seven had been more successful in their flight. In vain, however, the remaining three grasped at the wall.

Without warning one of them let go of the wall and jumped to the ground. Beginning to stand erect, he grabbed one of the masked men trying to scale the wall, wrenching him off and holding in front like a human shield. In disbelief we saw him raise his pistol and try to shoot. Before he could pull the trigger, we opened fire, their lifeless bodies sinking to the earth below. The third one turned from the wall threw up his hands high in the air shaking for dear life.

For a brief time we stood stunned at what had just occurred. All we wanted to do was keep order. Yet, two people lay dead in front of us. Meir had spoken of control. We had done everything by the book. Oh! What went wrong?

Cautiously we approached. The sergeant headed for the scared kid still shaking his hands high above his head and took his mask off. Mercifully I'd never seen him before. I was certainly relieved about that. The sergeant turned him around and secured his hands with nylon ties.

I approached the masked man who had drawn the pistol; pushing it from his hand with the point of my M-16 while another removed his mask. Rolling his body over, I recognized Nassir.

"Hey, the other's a girl!"someone yelled!

EPILOGUE

The sun is not ashamed to show its face when the day darkens from grief? What right does it have to shine in a world gone dim? I ran to see the other body, my men never understanding what happened next. I fell on her blood, soaked essence and cried bitterly, hugging her lifeless form, whispering one solitary word . . . "Aisha!"

An hour later routine shackled my emotions. We followed the standard operating procedures, the rules of engagement to the letter; Meir told me not be concerned. Disbelief and shock for a short time would save me, but it would not last. My men later confided to Meir my actions; holding Aisha's lifeless body until they finally pulled her from me. I told Meir about the rainbows and the now tarnished worthless pot of gold at its end. He slowly shook his head and said, "That was one helluva story, my friend."

Later the next morning, Selah and his parents came to claim Nasser and Aisha. They could not look at me or me at them; neither would any of us ever receive closure. Aisha's family refused an autopsy. I was glad of that; searching the only cemetery in Deir El-Salam for freshly dug graves, but found none.

I was cleared of wrong doing by a military board of inquiry, laughing when the presiding officer pronounced I was guiltless. My laughter turned to tears. Privately, they suggested I be assigned in the future to noncombat reserve duty. I chose instead to resign my commission and leave the army for good.

Chaim hired an Israeli Arab from Ramle named Rashid to be the new foreman. He knew more Hebrew than he did Arabic. It was funny because he could read Israeli daily papers better than Chaim. All in all, the match would work very well, but he was no Selah by any means. I never returned to working with Chaim in the vineyard. In a bit of poetic justice, Moshe was finishing his tenure as the moshav manager so he was assigned to replace me.

Vickie and I after two months agreed to give ourselves one more try. I said we should live in Jerusalem and she insisted she wanted to live on the moshav again. I said no and resigned my membership from the moshav finally moving into *our* cottage in Yemin Moshe. Of all things, I took a job working for Vickie's father. I discovered that the trip he cancelled to Oslo to attend my father's funeral was for the purposes of starting a dialogue between the Palestinians and the Israelis at the highest government level. Now he and I were doing it together.

All my life, I have valued truth and honesty; at times brutally. Vickie too always epitomized those values. Yet, we both struggled, trying to decide if we should tell my mother and her parents about Aisha and the rainbows. No one on the moshav had any idea except Chaim and Aviva who swore we didn't have to ask for their silence. Vickie being Vickie asked anyway. Then one night as we crawled into bed together she put her arm around my chest and said, "I guess the best stories in life are the untold ones, Ari." I turned out the light.

"You know, Ari, I'm going to miss it here without you," Chaim said fighting back the tears. Chaim and I rarely spoke about Aisha directly; he referring to her only as my "pot of gold." If I brought her up, he'd listen. For that matter, we never talked much about any of the changes until his telling me earlier he would miss me while Vickie and I were packing my things. Now for the first time in our lives we'd be apart. I think after all that had happened we both could handle it.

One night while we were walking in Jerusalem's Old City, Vickie suggested I go in the morning to the vineyard to see Abu Ali. Since I returned from Hebron, I never went back to the vineyard; not once. Now it was late fall and the vineyard would be resting until spring by itself. She was right; it was a trip I needed to make.

The encampment was different, but I couldn't put my finger on it. "Abu Ali, where is Rothschild?" I asked. "I'll tell you over coffee," he replied extending his hand in mine. Rothschild had died two weeks earlier from old age, he explained, as he too was going to do soon. Doctors found stage four cancer teeming through Abu Ali's body. I didn't know what to say.

"Here, these are for you to hold," Abu Ali said handing me several pieces of paper with burned edges. "After we lay to rest Nasser and Aisha next to where Ibrahim is buried, we went back to their home. Fatima wailing ran to the fire, casting theses scraps to burn with the devil as she said. They are the love poems that Aisha wrote to you. I took them from the fire thinking of my Jewish wife. "Prophet Muhammad, peace be upon him, used to go walking with Aisha, may Allah be pleased with her, at night while talking with each other," I told them. "They were the perfect love story. These words too were written in love; they are holy to me."

"May I keep them?"

Abu Ali laughed. "No, soon enough I will give them back to Aisha myself."

Going back to see Abu Ali gave me freedom to fully love Vickie. As we parted, knowing we would never see each other again, Abu Ali put his arm around my shoulders. "You know the marriage of our Prophet Muhammad and Aisha was only possible after the death of Khadeejah the prophet's first wife and the mother of his children. I vowed never to marry again after my Moroccan wife left. Only after I heard she died did I seek another."

I nodded, understanding his intent. Then he shared the name of his first wife, Chaya, and spoke to me of the meaning of Aisha's name. "Her name means 'she who lives' and Chaya's name means 'living' let that be the comfort we share."

For a long time I tried to assess what had gone wrong. Looking back with 20-20 hindsight, I realized we erred not. Aisha and I were swept away by the tide of man's inhumanity to man. Both Abu Ali and Reb Yitzckak had spoken of preserving the distinction among peoples. Were their comments racial or just a reflection of the natural order of man? I no longer try to make judgments. Life's too short, I now know, for judgments of any kind.

Vickie and I? Well, in the spring while Chaim, Moshe and Rashid were starting to spray the vineyard, we spent time in Eilat. Her family owns a timesharing in one of the five star hotels. We didn't have to start anew like we both thought; we simply picked up our love where we left it waiting.

One day the strangest thing happened. At the pool, I dove into the water and as I swam beneath, I could swear Aisha was there. I thought of that day in the vineyard and the sun soaking my body as sweat poured down my face; walking to the water wagon to get a drink before going to the pump house; bending over to splash its coolness all over my face. I hurriedly swam toward the surface wondering if when I opened my eyes this time I again would see rainbows. Leaping into the air like a whale rising from the depths I opened my eyes. No rainbows! All I saw was Vickie sitting, reading a novel, her being the true colors of my world.

www.ingramcontent.com/pod-product-compliance
Lightning Source LLC
Chambersburg PA
CBHW070655180626
46817CB00006B/2378